AND THE TREES STARE BACK

GIGI GRIFFIS

HOLIDAY HOUSE　NEW YORK

For content warnings and other resources, please visit gigigriffis.com.

Copyright © 2025 by Gigi Griffis
All Rights Reserved
HOLIDAY HOUSE is registered in the U.S. Patent and Trademark Office.
Printed and bound in March 2025 at Sheridan, Chelsea, MI, USA.
www.holidayhouse.com
First Edition
1 3 5 7 9 10 8 6 4 2

Library of Congress Cataloging-in-Publication Data is available.

ISBN: 978-0-8234-5912-4 (hardcover)

EU Authorized Representative: HackettFlynn Ltd, 36 Cloch Choirneal,
Balrothery, Co. Dublin, K32 C942, Ireland. EU@walkerpublishinggroup.com

This one's for younger me.
It gets better.

I
FIRE

If I had a feather for every time an adult told me not to go into the bog, I could build a pair of wings and fly away. If I had a feather for every time I disobeyed them, I could build a pair for everyone I've ever loved.

I've been sneaking past the tree line since I was five. The first time, only a few steps. A thrill. Would the trees swallow me up? Would the still pools pull me down into their depths?

They didn't. Instead, the sun filtered through the branches, scattered across the ground like gold. The moss felt soft between my fingers, smelled earthy when I pressed my nose to it. And I fell in love with the place that no one in our village dared go unless they wanted to disappear.

Because disappear they did. Men, women, children. A few times a year, someone in the village would wander too far past the boundary, stumble drunk into the trees, attempt to trap a rabbit and slip too far in. Most never came back. Some turned up dead. *Suicide*, they whispered. *Cursed*, they said aloud.

The forest has teeth, you see. Teeth and claws and mysteries. Mysteries wrapped in bark and buried under dirt and sunk into deep pools so blue it's like they invented the word. Mysteries that called to me, even at five.

Now, I'm eleven. I can name the trees and stuff myself full of bright orange sea buckthorn berries and take twenty steps past the tree line before a thrill races down my spine, cold and ominous, and I stop before I go too far in.

Today is my sister Anna's fifth birthday and the first time I'm bringing her with me to this place I secretly love. My forbidden hideout. I want to show her the plant that eats bugs: tempts them in with dewdrops, sticks them to its leaves, and digests them from the outside in.

They're usually much farther into the bog. Here at the edge of the village, what we call the bog is really still just forest. But the bog plants sneak toward the tree line as I sneak toward the bog, and there's one bug-eating monster plant I found twenty steps in, just close enough that you can still see the edge of the trees, still dart out if the wind kicks up and ravens start calling throaty warnings.

I lead Anna to the edge of the trees and look back, grinning.

"Vik," she whispers, her eyes sparkling with mischief to match my own, "will you read the cards for me?"

"Yes, of course!" I pull the oracle deck from my skirt pocket, thumb the familiar edges of the worn cards.

The one thing I love more than the bog is my cards. They're hand drawn, the most beautiful thing I own, a gift from my mama. When I was five, she pressed the deck into my palms and closed her hands warm and firm over mine, and I knew this gift was sacred. It was her prayer, her protective spell over my life.

I carry them with me everywhere so they'll never get lost.

I glance at Anna, one step behind me, blue eyes wide, wispy white-blond hair curling up around her ears, cheeks pink in the morning cold. She's the exact opposite of me: her all golds and blues and pinks, me all shades of brown—brown eyes, brown hair, brown freckles against white skin.

She bites her lip, looking at the cards, waiting for her fortune. What will come to her now that she's five?

At the edge of the trees, the ground is spongy, like a trampoline, like the springboards gymnasts use to vault through the air in the Olympics. I drop to the mossy forest floor, pull Anna down beside me, and we both cross our legs, facing each other.

"All right," I say, leaning forward, fanning the cards in front of her. "Pick a card."

A nervous giggle bubbles from her chest, and she picks one straight from the middle, flips it over on the ground.

Fire. My favorite card. I laugh out loud. Of course she'd pick my favorite. It's her birthday, and we're in my favorite place.

The Fire card is a huge tree burning from the inside out, its inky branches reaching so high they escape off the edges of the card. A girl has leapt off the highest branches and is plummeting toward the ground, arms outstretched as if, at the last second, she'll simply fly away. Escape the Soviet soldiers. Escape the endless parade of rules. Escape to places where Christmas isn't illegal and where kids wear new-bought clothes instead of hand-me-downs.

The Fire card means great change, Mama says, but I always think it looks like freedom. Like how I'd feel if I could fly away. No more soldiers threatening us when we break a rule. No more being told I'll never go to Finland without special papers. I could see the whole world if I could fly away. I'd have a pair of jeans, and I'd go on adventures like the people in the banned American movies we used to watch on my cousin's VCR until my uncle caught us and confiscated the tapes and my cousin said it was my idea.

I start to stand, to take Anna farther in and show her the sundew assassin plant.

"Vik! You have to explain it!"

"You know what Fire means. I've told you before."

"I like it when you tell me." She looks eager and I feel warm, protective.

Anna isn't like other little sisters. She doesn't annoy me on purpose or throw tantrums or tell my secrets to Mama. She's more than a sister; she's my friend. Small, silly sometimes, but my friend. I love that she wants me to explain things even if I explained them before. I love that she thinks I'm brave and interesting, not weird like the kids at school seem to think. None of them would dare step a toe past the tree line, but Anna's trust in me is bigger than her fear of this place.

I swell with the pride of it. Her trust in me.

I smile, drop back down, and poke her gently in the tummy. "The Fire card means your life is going to change. It means you can fly—fly away!"

She grins so hard her nose wrinkles and her lip rises, showing the familiar gap between her front teeth. I pull her to her feet. "Come on—the assassin plant is just here! Maybe you got Fire because the assassin plant will change your life!"

I lean over to retrieve the Fire card, but she takes it first.

"Can I hold it awhile?" she asks, and it's her birthday, so I say yes. I remember what it was like to turn five, to have someone share their most precious thing. I remember the awe of Mama handing me the cards—hand-drawn, thumb-smudged, beautiful whorls of ink depicting the mysteries of the forest. It's the biggest, the most adult, the most important I've ever felt, and I hope Anna feels that now.

She tucks Fire in the front of her hand-me-down plaid dress, pats it reverently.

There's a patch of lilacs just before the trees, and I gasp. "Anna, look!"

I drop beside them, counting petals. Five-petaled lilacs are lucky. If you eat them, your wishes come true. Anna giggles as I touch each bloom, one at a time, and then—triumphant—I yell, "Ah-ha!"

I pluck the five-petaled flower and hold it out. It's Anna's birthday; she gets the wish.

"Eat it and make a secret wish!" I tell her.

She pops it into her mouth and swallows as I take her hand once again and lead her deeper in—past the tree that looks like a wizard if you squint just right, over the fallen log where the bugs live, behind the slate-gray stone where the lizards sun themselves. Then I kneel again, letting go of Anna to point at the tiny red plant sprouting sticky teardrop-shaped leaves adorned with poison like dew. It's well hidden against a background of rust-colored moss.

"They can only eat a few bugs in their lifetime," I say with authority, examining the plant from several angles. "Liis's mama told me. She says they use the sticky dewdrops to lure bugs in and trap them. The bugs think it's something good to eat, but it's really poison that digests them!"

I stare down at the plant for a long time, willing a bug to wander in as we watch. "Did you know there's more than one type of bug-eating plant in here? I hope someday I get to see them all. I visit this one a lot because I want to see it trap a bug. But so far I'm always unlucky..."

I'm so entranced, so lost in the gorgeous danger of the flytrap, that I don't know how long it is before I look up. Before I notice that Anna isn't there.

When I do, my stomach turns and the back of my mouth goes sour. Where Anna should be standing just beside me, behind me, there's nothing but trees and moss and springy earth—and a handful of cranberries, red as drops of blood against the rich, brown dirt.

"Anna?" I call, my voice soft, uncertain, as I scan the trees around me.

There's no answer. No sign of white-blond hair against the gnarled brown bark and rich-green leaves. No giggle from behind a rock. No scent of the rough soap Mama used on her hair this morning.

"Anna?" I call again, louder.

And now I'm walking, going farther into the bog than I ever have before, where the trees grow thicker and the light is dim. She must have just wandered off. Followed a bug or a bird deeper in. Too deep.

My stomach writhes like there are snakes inside, alive and angry and ready to strike. I told her before we came that she couldn't wander off—that it wasn't dangerous like they said, but it *was* dangerous if we got separated—and Anna's never disobeyed me before. She's the good one. The angel baby, Mama calls her. *I'm* the one who wanders off. I'm the one who breaks the rules. I'm the one with enough feathers to build a flying machine.

I keep calling, even as my throat tightens and my voice comes out as a squeak. I still can't see her, can't hear her. I couldn't have been talking for more than a few minutes. She couldn't have made it so far in that she wouldn't hear me calling and come back.

And yet, she's not here. She's not anywhere.

Anna is gone.

II
KNIVES

The seagulls are screaming, but my mouth is too dry to join them. I've never been afraid of them before, but now I am. Their screams are omens. They're telling me that I was warned. Warned and warned, and I never listened.

The forest—so bright a moment ago—feels dark. An open mouth waiting to swallow me whole. The dewdrops on the fly-trap aren't dewdrops; they're poison. The trees aren't my friends; they're sentries, soldiers. The bog isn't my secret home; it's Soviet territory.

But maybe I'm wrong. I cling to the thought, try to swallow. *Maybe Anna got scared and went home. Maybe she didn't go farther in at all.* I need to go home and find out.

When I get to the house, it's quiet. Mama is sitting cross-legged in a sunny spot on the couch, mending a pair of work pants, humming a patriotic song to herself. Anna isn't there.

My face goes cold, my hands too. And I run to the bedrooms, check under the bed, in the cupboard. She *has* to be here. She *has* to be hiding.

"Viktoria, what are you doing?" Alarm flashes through Mama's voice as she appears in the doorway. "What's wrong?"

I'm sobbing. I didn't even notice before. I stand and stare at Mama, knowing that saying it out loud will change everything. *Anna's gone. Anna's gone into the forest.* What will her face look like when I tell her? What will she do? I think I might be sick.

I want to run to Mama and throw my arms around her, but I'm stuck to the floor. Like I'm one of the trees, part of the forest, rooted to the earth.

"Vik?" Her voice is higher now, pitchy, and I know I have to tell her.

The story comes pouring out between sobs, and I watch as Mama's eyebrows live a hundred lives—bunched together in concern, flying upward in surprise, covered by her hands as she pushes them into her forehead. She makes me tell it twice. Balls her fists at her sides. Starts to shake.

"Stay here," she says, finally. Her voice is someone else's. Hard. Deep. Calm in the same way the assassin plant is—the way that'll dissolve you if you come too close.

She spins and strides from the room. I hear the front door fly open and smack closed, and I come unrooted. I can't stay here. I'm suddenly terrified of being alone. I have to help. Whatever she's doing, I have to help.

I rush to follow her, but I stay far back. I need to help, but I don't want her to yell at me for leaving the house.

She tears past the neighbors' houses and onto the path to my best friend Liis's house, which is the last house in town, the house closest to the bog itself. It's painted deep green, and the roof is covered in moss. The trees edge closer to the back of the house each year, like someday the bog will claim it for its own.

The kids at school call it the witch's house, though Liis's mom isn't really a witch. Witches aren't allowed here—or real. If we speak of them, we speak of them in whispers, like forest spirits, trees that stand up and move in the night, bog trails that rearrange themselves. No, they are not witches. But Liis's mom keeps preserved vipers in jars on her shelves and herbs hanging from the kitchen ceiling, and she's the one we go to for remedies, and she's where we take a bird that's hurt its wing.

The tightness in my chest loosens a little. If anyone will know what to do, it's Liis's mom, Riina, the only adult who has ever told me to call her by her first name. Or Liis herself. Liis who taught me about assassin plants and which berries you can eat and the bog plants that give you headaches to tell you to leave them alone. Liis who nurses baby squirrels back to health in her spare time and then sets them free. Liis who is the bravest girl in our class. Brave in the way Anna thinks I am.

Mama flings the door open without knocking and disappears inside, but I stop at the front step. If I go inside, she'll be mad I left the house after she told me to stay. I decide to go around the windows and try to listen instead.

It's not hard to find her. Mama's voice is too loud. It's coming from the kitchen window at the back left of the house, wild and strange, the sound of a cornered animal. I press myself against the rough wood of the house beside the window and listen.

"Slow down, Maarja. What do you mean Anna's gone?" Riina's voice is steady, no-nonsense. I picture her in my mind's eye: tight black curls wild around her face, the skin between her eyebrows creased with concern, brown eyes narrowed as she listens to Mama.

Something brushes my arm and I jump, then turn. Liis is pressed along the house beside me, listening, wide-eyed. She's a miniature version of her mother. Eyes so dark they're almost black, dark, untamed curls, skin white with a constellation of freckles. The only difference is that Liis was born with a left arm that ends just above the elbow, soft and rounded with no hand, and her mama has two conventional arms and two hands. Without that difference, Liis could be a clone.

The lightest flutter of relief—silk soft as a butterfly wing— cools my skin at her closeness. Liis is the only other person who has gone beyond the trees with me. She'll help. Her mama will help. Liis will brave the bog with me. We'll look for Anna together.

"What happened?" she whispers.

"I took Anna to see the assassin plant. When I turned around, she was gone."

Liis's mouth makes an O, and her dark eyes widen even more.

Mama is talking again, and I wave at Liis to let me listen.

"How could Vik do this? She took Anna into the bog! I've told her a thousand times not to go near the trees. She never listens! She killed her sister!"

Every part of me turns to ice. Liis is nudging my arm, but I can't look at her. Instead, I stare straight ahead as my eyes burn and fill with tears.

She said I killed my sister.

It can't be true. But maybe it is. Maybe she's dead. I tense at the thought, ball my fists as if I could fight it. My head starts to pound.

"Maarja, she's eleven." Riina's voice is low. "She's always been your rebel child. She didn't know anything would happen." There's a pause before she goes on. "And maybe nothing has happened. We'll go look for her right now." Her voice grows stronger as she continues. "The whole village will help. We'll get a search party…"

The thought is comforting but wrong. There are something like eight hundred people who live in and around our village, but not a single one is going to go marching into the bog.

The bog. *My* bog. My friend. Really an enemy all along.

Inside, there's a rustling noise, the sound of footsteps fast across the floor, then the front door swings open and shut. Riina has her arms around my mama as they walk steadily away from the house, toward the village. They don't look back.

I force myself to face Liis, and she wraps herself around me in a hug, her warm body blazing against my freezing one.

"They'll find her," she says. "Don't worry. They'll find her."

But I push her away.

"I have to find her myself." I choke the words out past my

sandpaper throat. "I know where she went in. They didn't even ask."

"I'll come with you."

"No." My stomach swoops like I'm falling, and the word rushes out of my mouth with a force I didn't expect.

My mother's words flash through my head again.

She killed her sister.

Just minutes ago, I wanted Liis to go with me. But now I know: Liis *can't* come with me. I'm dangerous. I know suddenly—with a certainty I've never felt before—that if I take Liis into the bog, she'll go away too.

"Don't be foolish. I'm going to get my jacket."

She turns and heads into the house, and as soon as she's out of sight, I run. When we were eight, Liis and I made a pact: always share our secrets, never tell each other's, and never leave each other behind. Now—for the first time—I break it.

I leave her behind.

She's *not* coming with me. I'm not going to kill anyone else.

I run so fast I can barely breathe, skirting the tree line until I come to my favorite spot. The place with the assassin plant. The place where I last saw Anna.

It's quiet. Still no white curls flashing against the dark wood. Just the bloodred berries two steps from the bloodred assassin plant—in the exact spot where Anna disappeared.

Anna. I start screaming her name again, and I march straight into the heart of the forest, my heart beating in time with my footsteps—fast and painful. This time I'm going to keep going until I find her. Ten steps in, twenty steps in, a thousand steps in. It doesn't matter. I can't go back without her now.

I scream and march for hours, I think, and I'm so very lost now. The trees lose their familiar shapes. The bog opens up before me, trees thinning. Pools of water spread out ahead—dark blue, maybe as deep as a puddle, maybe as deep as the sea. I have a headache, and I think about the flowers that don't want me here. I loved them when Liis told me about them, but now I think they must hate me as much as the rest of this place.

I touch the oracle cards in my pocket and think desperately that if the bog will give my sister back, I'll give it my cards. My one precious thing. Of course, it doesn't answer. Or, if it does, it only laughs. You can't trade your most precious possession to get your sister back in real life; that story is for fairy tales. Anna picked Fire, but she should have picked the Knives—a card with three daggers aimed at the heart, my heart, ready to tear it into pieces.

It's getting dark, and I'm so tired my eyelids barely stay open, even as I stumble around another blue-blue pool. I don't know which way is home, and I couldn't go there if I wanted to. Not without Anna. Not when it's my fault she's gone.

She killed her sister.

I can't go back unless I prove her wrong.

Out of the corner of my eye, there's a flicker of strange light. Flame or spark, lightning bug or lantern eyes.

Soovana. The spirit of the bog. My heart leaps into my throat, a frog desperate for a fly, a bird startled into flight. Hope and fear tangled up together.

His is my favorite of the old stories—the trickster who lures unwary travelers deeper into the bog with his lantern eyes. Reclusive, mercurial. Usually peaceful, as connected to the bog as the trees, the foxes, the assassin plants. When he breathes, the bog breathes. When his pulse flutters, so does its. But make him angry and he will flicker those glowing eyes, draw you from the sturdy, reliable forest floor into sinkholes or bog pools or endless mirror paths.

"Soovana?" I whisper his name.

Could he have taken Anna?

"Please," I say, because I have no other words.

There is no answer. No second flicker in the dark. No clearing of an otherworldly throat. Only a howl in the distance.

Wolves.

Maybe they got her. Maybe they'll get me too. My silent tears turn to sobs, the kind that shake you to your core, the kind that bend you in half. I'm tired. So very tired. And now afraid of the wolves.

Not just the wolves. Mist rises, wispy and white, in the distance. A branch cracks, and when I turn, the stunted trees of the true bog seem closer than they were before. They say Soovana can turn into mist. They say the trees feel what he feels. They are his eyes and ears, his heartbeat. His will.

I open my mouth to say his name again, but the only thing that comes out is a shaky breath. Even that is swallowed by another howl.

There's a hollow at the base of a tree to my right, and I move toward it. I'm not even sure why. It just looks safe, small. Like somewhere I can tuck myself away until this is over. Like somewhere I can live if I never go home.

I fold myself into the small space and cry until I fall asleep. And I don't even know how long I'm there, because the next thing I remember—vague, like a dream—is my uncle pulling me from the tree and carrying me home, where I can hear Mama breaking down in the next room, and all I can think is *Dangerous, dangerous, dangerous.*

I'm dangerous.

And I'll never pretend I'm safe again.

III
STORM

Mama's breathing is slow and even, her chest rising and falling as I count. *In, one-two-three, out, one-two-three.* My heart slows with each breath. She's alive. She's here. She's real. Sometimes I'm so sure I'll lose her. Like Anna, she'll slip away from me when I'm not looking. Like Da, who was forced to serve in the Soviet army and never came back. I'll blink, and she'll be gone forever.

I feel that way often, and when the feeling gets too big, I check. Count her breaths, feel them against the back of my hand, wait for my pulse to stop racing. I'm glad she's a deep sleeper. I can't imagine what she'd think if she knew how often I came in to check her breathing.

The checking happens on other days too, but it always happens on the anniversary of Anna's disappearance. Her birthday. The worst day. The day I'm sure I'm a single heartbeat away from losing everything.

I stop in Mama's doorway, turning to watch the slow rise and fall of her chest one more time before I go. *In, one-two-three, out, one-two-three.* Something releases inside me, and I slip from the room, then from the house, closing the door gently. The click of the latch is a mere whisper, and the garland hung on the door—there to protect us from evil, as if evil hasn't already taken what we loved—shivers in a gentle breeze.

It's five thirty in the morning, and the light is pink. It's only sunrise, but it looks like the world is on fire. An omen for Anna's birthday. A reminder of the card she chose.

A warning not to walk past the trees.

But the sunrise doesn't need to warn me. I haven't gone back in since that day. Since I went looking for Anna and sobbed myself to sleep in that tree. Since Uncle Silver rescued me and no one rescued the sister I lost. Since I left Liis behind and never found my way back to her.

Since everything changed.

I still come to the edge, but only ever the edge now. The place we went in. Where we dropped to the dirt and read the cards. Fire—sudden change—tucked into Anna's dress and vanished with her.

Returning is a ritual. I read the cards for her again. Like I can rewrite history. Like if I choose the right one, she'll walk back out and everything will be okay.

I stop at the tree line, close my eyes, and breathe the wet, earthy scent of the forest. The smell of darkness, decay—rotting, half-devoured fallen trees disintegrating into the earth, leaves already abandoning their branches to die quiet deaths upon the forest floor. A shiver whispers through me, and I wonder if it's me or the bog itself. There used to be thunder here, the adults say, but not from the sky. From the trees, the boulders, the earth. As if the forest itself were clearing its throat. Announcing something to come.

Something ominous. Or beautiful. Or both.

I pull the deck from my pocket and lower myself to the ground, staring into the forest as my fingers caress the edges of the cards, feather soft in the way of all well-loved things. *Soovana, are you out there? Are you real? Did you take her?* Or is there another spirit playing with our lives? Perhaps Hiid, the angry, holy hero spirit of the forests. Kivialune, protector of caves and canyons, who turns himself into a rock if he hears you coming. Or Metsavana, who can transform into trees and whisper to you through their leaves. Nobody talks about them like they're real, but Estonia used to believe in them. Maybe our great-great-grandparents knew something we've forgotten.

Maybe the cards might call out to them.

I shuffle the cards in my lap—over and over until it feels right. Until it feels like they must be out of order. Until I couldn't possibly pick the same card I picked last year. The same card I've picked every year since she disappeared.

I breathe deep, closing my eyes and running a finger along their tops. Another shiver, another breath. Then I stop, pull a card, and flip it over on the ground. My stomach tightens like a fist. The trees glare at me.

It's the card I dread every year.

Storm.

In my deck, the Storm card is a young, dark-haired woman surrounded by trees, her face turned away as she reaches toward the lightning-streaked sky. She's half a step away from giving herself to the storm, embracing the danger.

This time the card is upright — not upside down like the years before. Normally the inky woman faces the forest. Today she faces me.

When reading cards, upright and upside down are opposites. Fire upright is sudden change, chaos. Upside down it's the fear of change. The Knives upright is heartbreak. Upside down it's optimism. And Storm — upright it means change, transformation. Upside down, resistance.

I stare at the card with my eyes burning. What is it trying to tell me? That in past years I was resisting something, and now I'm supposed to transform? I can only think it means for me to give up on Anna, and I suddenly hate these cards. They never brought Anna back before, so why did I think I needed to do a reading today? I'm such a fool. A dangerous, worthless, helpless fool.

I snatch up the card and brush off the dirt before returning the deck to my pocket. I hate myself for coming here. I always do, but today it's worse. On the day Anna would have turned ten. Five years. *Five years.* Five years means she's probably gone forever. It means something terrible happened — something more than losing her way. The cards are probably right. I should give up. Transform.

As if I could.

I wrap my arms around my rib cage as if I can hold myself together. It's mid-August, but the mornings are cool, and sitting on the damp earth has chilled me. I stare into the forest for a few more seconds, then turn for home. I'll be back long before Mama is up, tuck myself back into bed, maybe even sleep for a few more fitful minutes.

She'd go mad if she knew I snuck out to read the cards along the tree line. When I proposed it that first year, she sobbed so hard I thought she was choking, asked me if I was trying to destroy her. So I go in secret, with the sunrise. Because I can't *not* go. And I can't disappoint Mama. And I have no other choices.

Minutes later, I slip through the front door—and my stomach drops with an unpleasant swoop. Mama is on the living room couch, white as a ghost, her knees tucked to her chest like she's a child. I've never seen her look so small.

Next to her, lips pursed, hands clasped on his sharp knees, is Uncle Silver—a more masculine version of his sister, my mama, with his white-blond hair and mustache, fair skin, and sharp angles. They're twins, and the resemblance is uncanny, though their personalities are about as far apart as you can get. Where Mama is quiet, Silver is confident. Where Mama loves music, Silver thinks it's a waste of time. He's a prominent scientist, a party member, an important man in Communist Estonia. She's a factory worker who used to sing to herself while she made shoes.

I know him being in my living room can't mean anything good, and I stand still, like a deer frozen to avoid a predator.

"Your mother woke up and you were gone." Uncle Silver's voice is calm and disapproving, an unpleasantly familiar tone.

She must have called him. Like most of the people here, we don't have a phone. Just the pay phone outside the grocery. But Uncle Silver is an important person, so he has one at home.

Mama stares at me with that haunted look she gets sometimes, and the guilt of it skitters through me like spiders fleeing when you lift a rock they've been hiding under. I scared her. She thought I'd gone—like Anna, like Da. When she gets like this, it's like she's floating away from me. Still here in the room, but somehow not. Her body anchored. Her eyes empty.

She wasn't like this before Anna disappeared. Or maybe she was and I never noticed. But now she is. I check her breathing and she floats away, both of us changed by a girl who was here and then not here. I suppose our sanity went with her into the trees.

Uncle Silver goes on: "Maarja, you can see she's safe. Why don't you get some more sleep? You look awful."

I frown at him. She does look awful, but what does it help to say a thing like that out loud? Still, she doesn't look offended. She just rises, silent, stares at me a moment longer, and then slides into her bedroom like a ghost.

"Now, Viktoria,"—he clears his throat and pats the couch beside him—"you can't keep doing this to your mother. You know how she gets. It's six in the morning. Where did you even go?"

I sit and turn toward him. I can't think of a good excuse, and anyway, Uncle Silver is the one person I know who isn't afraid of the forest. Truth is as good an answer as any.

"I went to the edge of the bog—not inside, just to the edge."

I don't add that the thought of not going to the bog on the anniversary of Anna's disappearance makes me feel shaky and sick. That there's a certainty deep in my bones that one year she'll come back, and if I'm not there, she'll think I don't care, and she'll go back into the bog, and I'll never know she was here, right here, just five minutes from our door.

"Your mother told you not to go there anymore." Uncle Silver strokes his mustache.

"I'm sorry I scared her—and that she woke you. I promise I didn't go in. I just…thought maybe Anna…" I trail off.

Uncle Silver sighs. "Anna is gone, Viktoria. We've talked about this. It's been five years. You and your mother have to find a way to live without thinking she's coming back."

My stomach turns at the thought. Give up on Anna? Give up on hope? I know Uncle Silver means well. I know he's only trying to help. But he doesn't understand how impossible what he's asking for is. Doesn't understand that if I let go of Anna, I let go of myself too.

He stands, paces the room. "There are other things you need to focus on. You're sixteen. In a couple of years, you'll be going to university. Making decisions about your life. We live in a world where capitalism is causing more crises and catastrophic wars every year. A world where America could drop a nuclear bomb on us any day now—like Stalin predicted."

His voice rises, and I try to pretend I'm still listening, but I've heard this speech too many times before; it has lost its urgency, its horror. The gist is always the same: Uncle Silver works for the government and loves it, and everyone else should too. We should *stop* thinking about Finnish television and Nike sneakers and—heaven forbid—traveling to Italy one day and *start* thinking about taking our role as USSR nationalists seriously. We should devote ourselves to the state, for the state devotes itself to us. If we don't, America will bomb the life out of us and then burn the world down.

He's not wrong about the bombs. We do nuclear drills in school every week when we're not on summer vacation. He's probably not wrong about any of it. But it's hard to care about something so far away when there's so much to care about here and now.

When I start paying attention again, he's asking me a question. "So, can I count on you to focus? To stop wallowing in the past? If you want to protect your poor mother's nerves, you're going to have to."

My answering nod is a complete lie. Today everyone wants me to move on. The oracle cards. My uncle. Probably my mother when she comes back from wherever she goes inside herself. But I can't. I'll never be able to. Even trying sounds exhausting.

My fingers itch for the comfort of my oracle deck, the soothing rhythm of shuffling, flipping, and I suddenly wish I'd stayed at the edge of the bog. Pulled another card. Stared longer into the trees. Done the opposite of what everyone wants from me. Showed Anna that not only will I never give up on her, *but I will double down.*

"May I go to bed now?" I ask.

Uncle Silver nods. "Think about what I've said. What matters is moving forward. You're smart, Viktoria. You could do important things."

Even as the words make me want to scream, part of me wonders if he's right. If the cards are right. If someday I'll follow his footsteps into party privilege, probably far from the village.

If someday I'll be forced to let Anna go.

The thought is an unbearable barb under my skin. A scream trapped in my throat. A knot in my stomach that won't untangle. I close my door behind me and ball my fists at my sides, leaning back against it. My heart pulls tight, stretching toward the bog like I'm attached to it by a thousand tiny threads. Attached to Anna, somewhere inside it.

I wait until Uncle Silver leaves, closing the front door with his characteristic smack. Then I give in to the idea taking shape in my mind.

I'm going back to the bog. Doubling down when asked to give up. Telling Anna—even if she never comes back—that I will never, *ever* stop.

I will pull another card. I will call her name into the darkness. I will ask Soovana, Metsavana, the trees, the pools, the creeping things, the moon, the sun, the thunder, the rain to give her back.

Give her back.

Give her back.

IV
ASPEN GROVE, INVERTED

I steal toward the bog like a thief in the night, pressing the Aspen Grove card between my fingers. Maybe drawing it was my subconscious trying to comfort me because it's a card I used to love: two girls in long skirts surrounded by aspen trees, each reaching out to touch a different trunk. It means community and homecoming and connection. Because even though they're touching trees on opposite sides of the card, aspens share the same root, so both girls are actually touching the same tree. When we were little, Liis and I played in the aspen grove and posed like the girls in the art. It made us feel strong. Connected even when we couldn't reach each other.

I wonder if she can still feel that connection; I do, even though we rarely talk now.

"Where are you going?" My cousin Margit—her dark blond hair in a braid, her skin pink from the sun—catches me at the edge of my yard, her voice loud in the quiet of the early morning.

Something like panic pinches in my chest. So much for secretly disobeying Uncle Silver. Margit is no secret keeper, no safe space. She's a miniature version of her da, but with more energy and nothing better to do than try to make me more enthusiastic about government service—especially during the summer holidays when we're both out of school.

I guess that's no surprise, with both her parents being government officials. You can tell she thinks they're superior, like party membership is the reason she's one of the only people in town who has two parents, even if her mama is always away on some mysterious assignment or another. Most of the rest of us lost one of ours to the army draft, the bog, or vodka. The triple threats of Soviet life.

"Where are you going?" she demands again.

"Nowhere." I try to sidestep her.

She holds up a hand to stop me. "Da said you were missing."

Irritation tightens around me like a pair of wrong-sized hand-me-down shoes. I just want to be alone. To go back to the bog. To be there if Anna comes back. Why can't everyone just let me hold on to her?

I try to pass Margit again.

"Go ahead then. I'll just follow you." She lets her hand drop.

I stop, turn to face her. "I just went out early, and Mama got scared." I put on my best no-big-deal expression.

She raises a skeptical eyebrow.

"You know how she is." I feel guilty for throwing Mama under the bus. But it's the only way I can think to end the conversation. There's no way Margit would understand my real reasons. The way I *have to* go and read the cards, like I'm tethering Anna to myself across the bog, like that tether is the one thing keeping her from being gone for good.

"Now, will you leave me alone?"

"Not a chance."

I purse my lips, ball my fists, and start back toward my front door without saying a word. She's always smug but not normally this persistent, and I hate that she's being like this today, of all days. I open the front door wide and motion for her to enter first. As soon as she's through the door, I shut it behind her and wedge the old shovel on our porch under the handle. It won't hold long, but it'll give me a few seconds. Long enough to get away.

Because if Margit follows me, it's all ruined. I need quiet and focus. And Margit is the opposite of silence, the enemy of focus.

"Hey, what—" Her muffled, indignant shout beats through the door as I turn and sprint around the neighbor's house and out of sight, not slowing until I'm sure she hasn't followed. Hopefully she'll decide it's too much trouble to even try.

I let out a long, slow breath and follow the subtle curves of the well-worn footpaths between the houses. *I'm coming back, Anna*, my heart hums. *I didn't give up, even though they asked me to.*

The village is arranged in a spiral, with houses all along the outer edges and a small collection of shops in the center. In between, low brush and thin trees grow in patches on ground that's sturdier than the springy forest floor leading into the bog. Just outside town to the northeast is the shoe factory where most people work. To the southwest, the asylum, where Uncle Silver works and the rest of us avoid, stands against the trees, there to remind us all that dissent is illness. The thin dirt path I'm on leads around the outside of the spiral, along the edge of the bog.

Up ahead, I can still see the imprint of my shoes in the dirt from less than an hour ago. The place I stood, then sat, to draw a card. To tell the bog—to tell Anna—that I am still here. Still waiting. I have not given up; I will not give up.

I stop in those same footprints, stare into the morning forest. The trees whisper in a shivering wind. Something unseen scrapes audibly across rock or bark, and I feel eyes upon me. Creature or spirit or the very trees themselves. Watching.

Waiting.

What if I stepped across the boundary?

I haven't done it since Uncle Silver carried me out, haven't pressed a toe over the tree line. Would it change something if I did? I've offered the bog my cards, and it ignored me. But would it take the deal if I offered more? Traded myself for Anna. Would the spirits of forest, cave, bog, or trees give her back?

My heart races with the thought, the reckless impossibility of it, but my fear roots me to the ground.

I can't move, but I find my voice. The barest whisper. "Would you take me instead of her?"

The forest goes quiet, staring. Watching. And then—

"Vik."

In the silence, my name is the crack of first thunder. I jump, unrooted, and stumble forward, falling across the line that I never cross. My hands crash into moss—the forest floor. My palms

32

sting with the impact, my knees throbbing where they met the packed wet dirt. And I freeze.

Across the border, between the trees. My heart beats loud in my ears. My muscles bunch like snakes about to strike.

Then a hand is on my shoulder, helping me up and back. It unfreezes me, and I stumble backward a few steps, breathing unevenly.

I crossed the tree line. I crossed the border.

I turn, panting, dazed with the electric fear of what I've just done, and I see her. The hand on my shoulder, the word crashing through the quiet—it was Liis. All wild hair and sharp cheekbones and courage to step beyond the tree line.

The only person, really, who it could have been here.

Beside her is a bucket full of bright red berries that she must have been collecting. A few feet behind her, a small, one-eyed fox—Kaos—noses at the dirt, after some invisible bug or mouse or tasty root. Liis must have rescued her a couple of years ago because one day Liis was coming to school solo and the next this little menace was ever at her heels.

"Kaos is a terrible name for a fox," Margit said back then.

"If you could see the hole she ate in the couch, you'd think it was the perfect name," Liis retorted.

"Why would you keep something that eats your couch?" Margit was scandalized, and Liis and I exchanged a moment of silent laughter. One of only a few moments where it felt like nothing had happened, that we were as we had always been.

"Liis."

It's too many heartbeats before I say her name now. Too long staring at my former best friend as if she's a ghost. We haven't talked much since Anna went into the forest. I never knew what to say, and after a while, I could tell she was mad at me—for my moods, for never having the words anymore, for something I couldn't put my finger on.

I still love everything about Liis—from her habit of keeping rescued animals in the house to her terrible dad jokes about her little arm. If a kid acted weird around her in school, she'd make jokes like, "If I raise this arm, does that mean I only have half a question?" and I'd chime in: "Should you offer to give the teacher a hand?" Grinning, she'd return, "I would, but I already gave mine away," to break the tension.

I even miss how we'd get in trouble together. Like when we were nine and tried to sneak onto the asylum grounds. Like the bog, the danger of that place wasn't as real to us as our curiosity. I've never seen Uncle Silver so livid as when a security guard caught us and escorted us home. "There are *dangerous* people here, Viktoria! You could have been hurt!"

We took our lectures from Mama, then Riina, and I got a third lecture from Uncle Silver when Liis wasn't around, but we snickered about it later. Turned it into an adventure story where we'd barely escaped the claws of death.

"What are you doing out here, Vik? You haven't come this far since…" She cocks her head and brushes some dirt from my left palm.

"I miss you."

I blurt the words even though they don't answer her question, have nothing to do with her question actually. My cheeks immediately go hot with the admission, and I wish I could shove it back down my throat. What is wrong with me?

Her eyebrows arch in surprise, her mouth making a tiny O.

Love battles it out with the shame in my chest. I simultaneously want to talk to Liis—to make a joke, to fall over laughing like we used to, to tell her *everything*—and to run away from her as fast and far as I can. Because I ran away without her five years ago and I've never found my way back. The longer you go without talking, the harder it is to find the words. The more shame chokes apologies before they get past your throat. Shame that you left. Shame that you stayed away. Shame that you were never worthy of that love in the first place. And I know how much it must have hurt when I ignored her because I didn't know what else to do.

"I miss you too." She reaches out with her right arm and squeezes my shoulder. My throat closes, and tears leap to my eyes. Nobody touches me much anymore, and my body electrifies with the gesture, all my emotions rising to the surface.

She still misses me. After all these years. All the times I ignored her invitations. The times she asked a question or made a joke and I couldn't respond. The times I walked the other way when I saw her coming because I was so scared of what letting her close would do to her. What it could do to her still. No matter how much I want her to still love me, I am still dangerous.

Nothing has changed.

After a pause, she speaks again, her voice an unbearably kind whisper. "Vik?"

I let out a strangled laugh. Then I attempt an unconcerned shrug, but it probably comes out as wrong as everything else I do. "Yeah, I'm—"

The word *fine* lodges in my throat. Because it's a lie. Because I can't tell Liis the truth. And because I'm suddenly charged with the shock of what I see out of the corner of my eye.

The only thing that could steal my attention from Liis in this moment.

Liis sucks in a sharp breath. At the edge of my vision, Kaos flattens her ears against her head and issues a low, gurgling growl. And behind Liis, Margit's voice tells me that she's found us and she sees what I see. "What the hell…"

I whip my body around to face the trees, and everything melts away—Margit's curses, Kaos's low growls, the way Liis's eyebrows bunch like caterpillars about to embark on a journey—as I stand, frozen, staring. One heartbeat. Two. Three. Then something releases inside me, and I run into the bog, the second time today that I've crossed that invisible line. My feet pound into the dirt with power that echoes through my body, breath held in my chest hard and burning like a fire.

There, just a few feet inside the trees—white curls against brown bark, green moss, orange berries—is the only thing I've wanted to see for five long years. The only thing that could change my life. The only thing that could redeem me.

It's my sister.

Anna is back.

V
THE LYNX, INVERTED

I drag Anna from the forest, throw my arms around her, and fall to my knees, sobbing into her neck until my throat feels like it'll tear into shreds. Her heart beats against my chest, fast and fragile as a bird's, and her curls tickle my cheek. She's real. Warm. *Here.* The bog gave her back. It finally gave her back.

I pull back just enough to look at her. That face—the slightly upturned nose, the round, flushed cheeks, the white-blond ringlets—it's Anna exactly as I remember her. Exactly herself. Exactly—

My heart stops, sputters, restarts.

Something's not right.

I stare at Anna's face, the wild relief of a moment ago turning sour in my gut. It takes me so long to understand what is wrong. It's a splinter in my mind, an invisible pebble in my shoe, a room where something is just barely out of place.

I don't realize what it is until I turn to the girls, who have gone quiet behind me. Liis's mouth is open. Margit is frozen, her hands balled into fists.

It's Liis who speaks first, her voice just above a whisper as she puts words to the wrongness that my mind is tripping over. "Vik, why does she look the same?"

The same.

She looks *the same*. Five years have passed, and Anna looks the same. We all look older, but Anna looks the same.

It's like being pushed into cold water. A sudden shock and my temperature plummets. My hands go numb; my teeth chatter.

I turn back to Anna, my heart a tight, twisted thing as I take her in. Her dress is dirty. Her left shoe is missing. And her face...

It's Anna. It's definitely Anna. But it's Anna as if she'd been stopped in time the day I lost her. Five years have passed, and she should be ten, but instead she's five. Or even younger. As if the bog preserved her just as she was and then spit her back out into the world.

She's staring at the girls behind me, eyes wide and mouth pressed closed. She tries to shy away, but there's no way I'm letting go of her shoulders. If she runs back into the bog, I know I'll never see her again. If I lose her twice, there will be no third chance. I know it in my skin and bones and teeth.

"Anna?" I whisper. "What happened, Anna?"

She doesn't answer, only takes my hand and starts to pull me back toward the trees.

My whole body breaks out in goose bumps, terror turning the summer warmth on my skin to winter in an instant. All cracking ice and dead green things buried under snowdrifts and hot breath turning into ghosts when it leaves your throat.

I cannot follow Anna into the woods, cross that invisible line again. And I certainly can't let her go without me.

I clutch at her hand, pulling her back into my arms forcefully, though she still leans hard toward the shadow trunks of thin and twisted trees. "No, Anna, no."

She finds my gaze and opens her mouth as if to speak, but no sound comes out. Instead, behind us, a gasp.

"It's witchcraft," an unfamiliar voice says, and I whip my head around to see two women have stopped on the path beside Liis and Margit.

"There's no such thing." Margit finds her voice and scowls at the women.

"Lenin save us," the other woman says, ignoring her and pressing a hand to her chest.

Liis throws me a worried look.

The alarm on their faces sends another shiver through me, my own fear rising up to meet theirs. They're afraid of Anna, but *I'm afraid of them*. Afraid of what people do when they're scared of witchcraft. Afraid of what they'll report to the Soviet soldiers.

I have to get Anna out of here. Away from the bog she's straining toward. Away from the women whispering their greatest fear into the air between us. Somewhere safe even when nowhere is safe.

I wrap my arms around her waist and lift her to my chest. Her body is tense and unwieldy, but I don't care how uncomfortable this is. I'd carry her home twenty times over just to keep her with me.

Liis rushes forward. "Can I help?"

I start to shake my head, so used to saying no. But this is an emergency. Yes, she can help.

I nod. "Run toward the factory. Tell Mama. She'll be on her way there by now. Tell her to come home."

Liis summons Kaos with a shrill whistle, and then the two are running as fast as they can toward the shoe factory. Kaos thinks it's a game and nips at Liis's ankles, but she doesn't slow down. I take off in the other direction, leaving Margit standing stone-still on the path beside the two women. I hear one of them say something about ghosts before I'm out of earshot, and I shudder.

Can't they see she's flesh and blood? Warm and real and growing heavier in my arms.

But is she? Something inside me snags on the question. Her breath is a tickle on my neck, her body solid in my arms. But she's Anna *as she was*, not Anna as she should be. And what does that mean? What does that make her? The girl still five years old when she should be ten. The girl who tried to pull me back into the bog.

She still hasn't spoken, but the tension seems to drain from her as soon as we're out of sight of the two women.

I was afraid of them too, I want to tell her. But maybe that would make her own fear worse, so instead I say, "I love you, Anna."

She tucks her face into my neck and whispers something almost too soft to hear, something that makes my heart expand in my chest, relief bloom warm across my skin. Something that sounds a lot like my name.

⁓

At home, I settle Anna at the kitchen table, give her water, bread. She shoves the whole slice in her mouth like she's starving. Then she reaches into her pockets and spills handfuls of cranberries onto the table alongside the plate. Like an offering.

My heart seizes at the sight of those bloodred berries. The same kind left behind when Anna disappeared that day. The same they say grow from Soovana's head and beard. The ones we sometimes offered him as children. Sacred ritual. Blood rite.

I open my mouth to ask about them, but I don't get the words past my throat before Mama bursts through the door already crying. She falls on her knees beside Anna's chair and wraps her hands around Anna's tiny ones.

"What happened, *kullake*, my sweetheart, my angel? What happened?"

Anna bites her lip and studies Mama's face but doesn't speak. She looks over Mama's head at me as if asking what she should do.

I lean across Mama and wrap my finger around one of Anna's curls, just like I used to do.

"What happened? Where were you?" I whisper, an echo of my mother without the sobs, because my tears have dried up, lodged inside me as a ball of worry.

Before she can answer, our front door slaps open, and Liis and Kaos rush into the kitchen followed by her mama—cheeks flushed with rushing or worry or some combination of both.

Riina throws herself on the floor beside Mama and wraps an arm around her shoulders, but Mama doesn't respond. Five years ago, she would have hugged Riina back, but Liis and I aren't the only ones who've grown stiff and distant.

Liis. She comes to stand beside me. I want her to hug me like Riina is hugging Mama, but instead we just stand there—the inches between us as good as a hundred miles. Kaos reads the room as only a fox can and decides licking Anna's elbow is the best course of action. It doesn't diffuse the tension.

"Anna, *kullake*, you can tell us anything." Mama's voice is pleading.

"Maarja," Riina murmurs, "perhaps she's in shock. She may not be able to tell us anything right now. Here,"—she stands and moves around the kitchen like she belongs here, even though it's been years since she visited us—"I'll make her some tea. Soup too. We could all use some soup."

"Riina, why is she…" Mama trails off, but I know what she wants to ask. The same question burrowing into my bones.

Why is she five?

Riina is looking at Mama from behind Anna, shaking her head a little. I know what that means too. *I have no idea.* And *Don't upset her.* And maybe *We'll talk later.*

Mama nods, and I push one of our chairs to her. "Mama, sit."

"Signe," Anna whispers.

It's the second word she's said—an Estonian girl's name—and we all snap our heads toward her and hold our breath. She's staring at Liis, and Liis glances over at me, then asks, "Is Signe someone who helped you? Someone who took you?"

Anna looks uncertain again, and I reach into my pocket and run my fingers along the oracle cards for comfort. If I read them right now, what would they tell me? Would I flip the the Lynx upside down for silence and withdrawal? Midnight for good luck?

Because this *is* good luck...isn't it? I always thought if Anna came back, I'd burst from the joy of it, the jubilation. We'd dance through the lilac patches, and hug until we couldn't breathe, and laugh and never stop laughing.

Instead, I feel sick. Scared. I don't understand why she isn't talking. I don't understand why she didn't grow up. I *really* don't understand why she started to pull me back toward the bog. And not understanding makes it feel like this isn't over. Like I could lose her all over again in an instant.

I thumb the cards more insistently in my pocket and think of Mama's breaths this morning. *In, one-two-three, out, one-two-three.* I force myself to follow the rhythm, to keep the panic from swallowing me like the bog.

Anna doesn't answer Liis's question. Instead, she turns her attention to me, her eyes searching my face for something. I try to manage a comforting smile, but I'm not sure I pull it off. I could very well be grimacing at her. My face feels so disconnected from the rest of me that I can't tell.

But I must look okay, because for the second time today, she says my name.

"Vik." She says it tentatively, like she's testing the word.

Relief and something darker tangle inside me. Relief to hear my name in my little sister's mouth again after all this time. Relief knowing she's here. *Finally here.* And yet—a dark uncertainty because *is she here?* Is she Anna? This frozen-in-time child who looks so much like my sister but is still impossibly five years old.

"Yes, Anna?" I breathe.

And then she answers: "карты."

My body goes cold all over again, and I struggle to swallow. Anna is back, but everything about her is wrong. She's five years old when she should be ten. She won't tell us what happened. And the word she just said isn't Estonian.

It's Russian.

Anna—my Anna—doesn't speak Russian.

VI
BEAR

The room goes quiet, the only sound Kaos, who has decided to dig at one of the floorboards. Everyone ignores her. Who cares about floorboards right now?

I pull the cards from my pocket and hold them out to Anna. "You want me to do a reading?"

At the edge of my vision, Riina starts blinking fast, as if to stave off tears. Kaos thwacks at the floorboard and chitters; Liis makes a hushing sound in her direction. But Anna just stares.

She doesn't understand me. The thought makes me uneasy, like a puckered seam. Unseen, wrong, rubbing at me 'til I bleed. How is it possible to forget your own language?

I repeat myself in Russian. Everyone learns it in school starting at seven. Because not knowing Russian as an adult wouldn't work—not when it's the official language, the only way to communicate in hospitals and government offices and the factories where most people work. I'm fluent, as most teenagers are. But before seven, most Estonian kids speak Estonian. Anna only knew a few basic Russian phrases when she left.

You want me to do a reading?

This time Anna's eyes spark with recognition in a way they

haven't before, and she nods. Is this why she wasn't answering the questions, then? Not shock but a lack of understanding? And how is that possible—for her to leave as an Estonian chatterbox and come back not understanding the simplest phrases? My stomach balls into a fist at the questions.

"You want me to do a reading." I repeat myself because I can't form any other words. And I realize as I say it that Anna magically forgetting her first language isn't the only thing pinching under my skin. It's the fact that I'm speaking Russian *here*—in my house. Russian is for everywhere else. Home is Estonian. Always has been.

My body contracts with the truth of it, the way these Russian words break the invisible barrier between *out there* and *in here*. It's like by answering her in Russian, I've exposed us. Taken the personal—the things that were just ours—and rendered them understandable by so many other ears.

Mama stares at me, her face reflecting my own unease. Kaos gives up on the floorboards and curls up on Liis's feet. Riina has soup on the stove now, and the room smells like herbs.

I sit across the table from Anna and shuffle the cards, spread them out face down. I don't know what else to say, so I do what she asked me to. "Pick a card," I say in Russian. "Choose it with your left hand because left is where the heart is."

First, she looks up at Liis and offers the longest sentence she has so far. "What happened to your arm?" This time, it's mostly in Russian, but she's used the Estonian word for arm. And that's even stranger in a way I can't quite put my finger on.

Liis instinctively turns away to shield her small arm. Normally, she'd say something sarcastic. Like when we went on a school trip to Tallinn and people kept asking about her arm and she changed her answer every time, her face deadpan while I snorted with laughter beside her. "Shark attack." "Aliens." "Caught spying on the Americans." This time, it's too weird, and Liis says nothing. I didn't know the unsettled feeling in my stomach could go deeper, but it does now.

"She's always been like that." My voice is strained. "Nothing happened. She's just Liis."

Anna shifts in her seat and furrows her brow at Liis but doesn't offer any additional explanation, and I'm not sure what to ask her.

"You don't remember?" I try. But Anna shuts her mouth and shakes her head, then reaches across the table and points to a card on my far right.

I flip it for her.

It's the Bear—the power card. In my deck, the art is somehow both a bear and a man. Strong, tall, and unyielding. He's facing forward, standing at full height on his back legs, teeth protruding from a strong jaw. In the corner, a cat shies away from the ominous figure.

Liis slips from the room, and I open my mouth to tell Anna she's drawn the power card. Before I can speak, our door flies open again, and this time Uncle Silver and Margit come barreling through. Margit must have gone for him after we found Anna.

Everyone turns toward them. Kaos jumps up and flattens

herself into a corner with her mouth open, ready for an attack. Anna makes a strangled, surprised noise. I snatch up my cards and stuff them in my pocket.

Uncle Silver knows about the cards, of course. Everyone knows about them. But I'm never quite sure whether the Soviets would consider them religious. Ban them like Christmas. Ever since he caught us with that American movie and took it away, I've been protective of the cards. Because Uncle Silver would never understand loving something like my deck. He's not one for skirting the rules. He wouldn't think twice about confiscating them if he thought they might be a gateway drug to religion. Yes, he saved my life. He pulled me out of the forest. He risked himself to get me. And I love him. But he doesn't understand.

I turn back to Anna, but she's no longer paying attention to me. Her white face has gone even paler, and her knuckles stretch tight as she grasps the back of the chair. As if she thinks Margit and Silver have come to take her away. I have the sudden terrible thought that maybe a man took her and now she's afraid of them. Or if Soovana did take her, maybe she's been away from people so long that our presence is simply overwhelming.

"It's okay," I tell her, reaching across the table with my palm open. "It's Uncle Silver." She doesn't take my offered hand.

"Dear Lenin, so it is true." Uncle Silver swallows hard and shakes his head. *"Fakk."*

I've never heard him swear before, and I almost laugh out loud at the ridiculousness of stoical, serious Uncle Silver saying the f-word. I'm glad I don't, though. Now is most definitely *not* the time for laughing. Still, nerves jangle in my chest, ready to burst into a guffaw at the most inappropriate moment.

"Maarja, what happened?" he asks, his glance darting between Mama, Anna, and Riina behind her at the stove.

My own gaze follows. Do any of us have answers? What answer could there possibly be? There is nothing in the world that freezes people in time. Except perhaps the thing we aren't supposed to believe in here: *magic*. Spirit time that ticks by differently than ours.

"We don't know, Silver," Mama whispers. Her eyes are steady and present, not like this morning, but her voice is still distant. "She hasn't been able to tell us anything."

She switches back to Russian, reaches out to push Anna's curls tenderly back with a thumb. "Baby, what happened?"

Uncle Silver's voice is stern when he turns his attention on Anna too, taking a cue from Mama and speaking Russian. "Yes, Anna, what happened? Did someone take you?"

Anna doesn't answer, only grows paler. If I hadn't held her, warm and alive, in my arms just minutes ago, I would think her a ghost.

"She's in shock," he announces after a long silence, and Riina nods in the background. "We should let her rest. Eat something. Don't question her too much."

He pauses, kneels to be eye to eye with Anna. It's a tender gesture, but his voice is still stern. He never can help coming across as if he's giving a lecture. "Anna, don't worry. I'll be watching out for you." He pauses, pats her on the knee. "You understand?"

After another long pause, she nods—just the barest amount—and there's something comforting in it. At least she knows that she is safe now. That we are watching out for her. That if fear is the thing keeping her from telling us the truth, she can start to let it go.

I t's just Mama, Anna, Margit, and me in the house now. Uncle Silver is back at work. Riina and Liis left after Riina declared that we needed space. She was right; with Liis in the room, it's hard to focus on anything except her. Except how I messed things up. Except how much I wish things were different—wish *I* were different.

Without her here, I can focus. I've already asked Anna two more times what happened, but she hasn't said a word since everyone left.

When she does finally open her mouth, it's to ask for the toilet.

"Of course, Anna. You don't have to ask."

She slips off the chair and takes my hand. "Where is it?"

The question is another gut punch. Another reminder that something is wrong. Anna doesn't remember our house? For me, losing Anna froze my memory in time. I still remember how the couch used to be a foot to the left, the rug was light blue instead of dark (Mama dyed it when it started looking depressingly dingy). I can trace every way this room has changed in five years. But

Anna is the opposite. If every second of that day is burned into my mind, it's like it's abandoned hers entirely. Liis's small arm. The house layout. What else has she forgotten? What else have we lost?

Why are there pieces of her missing, and where did they go?

My stomach turns over yet again. From the look on Mama's face, she feels the same. But this time I don't express my surprise. I just squeeze Anna's tiny, warm hand in mine and lead her where she needs to go.

Before I leave her alone in the bathroom, I check that the window is locked. I don't know if I'm locking the bog out or Anna in. Would she try to pull me back there again if I let in the breeze? Is it calling to her even now? The hair on the back of my neck stands at attention.

I wait outside the door, my back pressed to the wall, straining to hear. She's too little to reach the window, but my unreasonable heart is terrified that somehow she'll unlock it and disappear again anyway. That any moment my eyes aren't on her is a moment the bog might snatch her back.

I barely breathe until she emerges, and even then fear sticks in my throat like a barb. *She doesn't remember our house. She doesn't remember her language.* What exists in this world that could have done this?

Witchcraft. I hear the women on the path so clearly in my mind. *Soovana*, I hear my own voice call across the years.

When we get back to the kitchen, Mama has spread out

Anna's collection of washed yogurt cups—the ones she used to play tea party with—on the table. Next to them: a sawdust-filled teddy bear, Anna's favorite dress, a bright pink hair ribbon. Mama's been keeping them safe all these years, her way of staying tethered to Anna across the unknown distance. Now she lays these things Anna loved out on the table just like I laid out the cards. As if they'll tell us the future, the past, and the truth. A mother's divination.

I sit on a hard wooden chair beside Anna. Margit sits across the table, looking uncomfortable. And Mama runs slender fingers over each object, watching Anna's face.

"Remember our tea parties, *kullake*?" Mama whispers, stroking Anna's hair. "Remember the dollhouse we made from old cardboard boxes?"

Anna only seems to grow smaller with the question, her eyebrows pinching in distress.

"Don't worry, baby." Mama taps her thumb gently on Anna's cheek, and my own cheek burns with the absence of that touch.

I lift the photos Mama's also brought out. We don't have many, but there's Da holding Anna as a newborn with me handing her the teddy bear Mama has on the table. Anna's first gift. A welcome-to-the-world present. The next photo is all of us, posed for a formal portrait, which Uncle Silver commissioned and paid for. Then there's one of just me and Anna. I'm holding her, but I'm too little to do it properly and her pudgy legs slip halfway off my lap.

I show Anna the first photo as Mama hands her the bear. "See, Anna, it was your first toy."

Mama's knuckles clutch white around the bear as Anna—who should remember, who should be happy, who is back, finally, finally, *finally* back—instead bursts into inconsolable sobs. They shudder through her like winter waves, rocking her whole body.

Is she crying because she remembers or because she doesn't? Is she crying because of what she's lost or what she's found?

I open my arms instinctively, and she jumps off the chair, pushes past Mama, and throws herself into them, tears warm and wet against my shirt. And then I'm crying too. Because I don't know any of the answers for her. And I don't know any of the answers for me. I can't name these twisted, knotty emotions impossibly tangled in my chest.

Am I crying because she's back?

Or am I crying because she's not quite back, not quite herself, *not quite Anna*?

VII
MOON, INVERTED

For the rest of the day, we don't let Anna out of our sight. Like if we do, she'll vanish again, slip through our clutching fingers. Mama braids and rebraids Anna's wispy hair, plies her with soups, sings her lullabies I haven't heard on her lips for years. She used to sing all the time before Da left for the war in Afghanistan, a little less after, and almost never since Anna's been gone. She used to bake too. And laugh. And braid my hair like she's braiding Anna's.

Throughout the afternoon, villagers come by the house to gawk at Anna, but after the first handful, we stop answering the door. Still, the knocks come. Sometimes tentative. Sometimes strong. They're here to tell us congratulations. They're here to see for themselves. They're here to whisper she's a witch. They're here to confirm the bog has done something evil again. They're here to tell us the stories of their own loved ones lost—disappeared forever or, worse, found dead—as if Anna's return has broken a dam on their own emotions.

Karl. Kristel. Eliise. We learn a thousand things we didn't know about those the bog has taken. Karl was learning to play the piano. Kristel loved honey so much her mama called her *Little*

Bear. Karl's grandpa followed him into the forest the next day, leaving only a note behind. Just one sentence: *My heart's already in there; might as well take the rest of me.*

Every story comes with an unspoken question, heavy and barbed: Why Anna? Why not the people they loved?

Karl's grandpa is the last story I can bear to hear. The one that makes me stop answering the door.

To buy herself the day away from work, I discover that Mama has traded a pair of shoes—stolen from the factory—for a doctor's note excusing her from her job. That's how things are done here. If you want something, you can wait for it to come into the stores (which it never will), you can pay for it (which most of us can't afford), you can know someone who'll do you a favor, or you can steal and trade. Shoe factory workers trade shoes. Sausage factory workers trade sausage. Everyone trades homemade vodka ever since the dry law came into effect and you can't find it in stores anymore.

When day sharpens into night, I leave my bed and climb into Anna's because I am certain that I won't sleep unless I can feel her breathing. *In, one-two-three, out, one-two-three.* Before we sleep, I start telling her stories. Like I used to.

Folktales, you might call them. About the fingernail hat that makes its wearer invisible. About the forests that pick up and move in the night because the villagers weren't grateful enough to have them. About women turned into rocks and fir trees to save them from their pursuers. Even about Soovana.

"His is the pulse of the bog, the heartbeat of the trees, the life of the mosses," I whisper in my best myth-retelling voice, trying to recreate our younger years. "But he's a trickster too, his eyes like lanterns as he leads fools into the deep."

I have to stop just a few sentences into that story. I always loved Soovana before. I used to tell Anna this very tale. But now talking about getting lost in the bog makes my heart beat funny and my body go too alert. His name feels like a prayer. Like inviting trouble. Like saying his name out loud will call to him, tell him where to find the girl he lost.

I ask her if that's what she saw in the bog: Flickering lights? A lantern shimmering through the trees? She only presses her lips together and refuses to answer.

So my stories fade into nervous silence, her own silence a slammed door that leaves me and my questions out in the cold. I try to focus on the feeling of Anna curled against my belly. The butterfly-delicate flutter of her breath. The familiar rhythm: *in, one-two-three, out, one-two-three.* I pace my breaths with it. Let myself drift on the perfect consistency of it. Drift, and drift, and drift...

I jerk awake. It feels like I only closed my eyes for a second, but it must have been longer. The room is a deeper shade of dark, the candle burned completely down, and the warm press of Anna's spine against my stomach...gone.

Anna is *gone.*

I untangle myself from the blanket, pulse spiking. *Please let her just be getting a glass of water. Please, please.*

"Anna." I whisper her name through the thick dark, slipping barefoot into the living room.

Empty. The room is empty. The house is dark.

And the front door is cracked open—just enough to see a tiny figure crossing the lawn in the moonlight.

I tear after her, not bothering with shoes. Or a jacket. Or a flashlight. Not bothering with anything but the all-consuming need to get her before I blink and she's gone. Before the nightmare sucks us in deeper, steals her away yet again.

"Anna," I whisper desperately through the night as I reach her just before the path she's on curves toward the forest—out of sight of our front door. If I'd woken ten seconds later, I would have missed her.

"Vik." She turns to face me under the neighbor's shade tree.

Standing there, her eyes are too deep in shadow to see, and I have the horrible thought that she is not her. Anna is not Anna. That something else is looking out from those shadows.

They say if you don't burn the bodies of the dead, their spirits wander forever. I always imagined spirits would look insubstantial. Shapes shifting in the mist, blown away by a breeze. They'd be a whisper you couldn't quite hear, a chill you couldn't quite place. But what if the spirits look just like themselves? What if they are mirror images of the people they used to be, with fading memories, fading humanity?

What if Anna died in the bog? What if this is not Anna?

The questions are hot guilt and cold terror. I shouldn't ask them. I need to ask them.

"Vik, come." She reaches out and takes my hand, hers warm in mine. There's a comfort in it, especially when she pulls me beyond the shade of the tree, and I can see her eyes again. Alive and afraid and determined.

"Come where, Anna? It's the middle of the night." I try to lead her back toward the house.

She digs in her heels. "Come. I'll show you."

"Show me what?"

"I can't tell you."

"Why can't you tell me?"

"Because he's listening."

He's listening.

I'm suddenly too aware of every noise around me: cricket song and skittery breeze through piney branches, the gurgle of frogs insistent in the dark, the distant hoot of the owl who will devour them.

He's listening.

"Who, Anna?"

She only releases a shivery breath and pulls me forward yet again. Toward whoever is listening? I strain my eyes in the dark, looking for any silhouette out of place. Him. Whatever creature, kidnapper, bog spirit made her believe that he can see and hear her.

Who is making me believe it too.

My body slows with the fear of what's at the end of this walk. And yet I can't quite stop us. Can't keep my heart from reaching longingly toward the answers. If Anna pulls aside the veil, conjures the spirit that took her, shows me the truth—will the knowledge destroy us? Or will knowing what happened put things right? Return Anna's native tongue, her memories, her *self*.

The remaining resistance bleeds out of me, and I let her lead me along the path, in and out of shadowed moonlight. My feet press into cold dirt, sharp brush. The air tastes of autumn to come, a hint of ice. The wind carries the soft nickers of horses from a neighbor's pasture up ahead, harmonizing with the frogs and owls and shivery breeze.

In a cluster of trees along a neighbor's yard, two white orbs hover high in the trees, watching. My heart seizes until the yellow eyes in their centers blink in unison, and faces come into focus. Not ghosts, not spirits. Not kidnapper, not forest god.

Owls.

They whisper *kuu* into the wind. The Estonian word for moon. Like they are calling to him. Asking him to stay in the sky instead of sneaking off to woo fair maidens, like in the tales.

I think of my Moon card—one of the most cryptic cards in my deck. It shows a lightly shaded moon with three shadowy figures in the foreground. I've always thought they're a woman, a girl, and a wolf—but the third could be a fox or a dog. The edges seem intentionally indistinct, the artist trying to show a world where nothing is as it seems.

Upright, the meaning is illusion and fear. Wading through darkness to search for the light, through fog to seek out clarity. Upside down, it is courage. Bright light chasing the shadows away.

Courage, perhaps, like what I am doing now. Letting this strange, distorted version of my sister lead me down a midnight path.

Please let there be answers at its end.

No sooner do I think it than we reach that end. I am mid-step when the first boom vibrates through the air, followed by a second, a third. Sharp and unexpected. Like trees falling in the forest, only we are still in the village—with no one and nothing around.

I startle at the sound and wrench my ankle. Anna jolts into the air. And we both whip our heads toward the source of the noise.

Not thunder or storm or falling tree, not gunfire or American bomb.

My mind can't comprehend it at first. The shine of a pair of eyes through the night.

Taller than a man, unblinking.

Soovana?

No.

It's a horse. Just a horse. One of the neighbor's mares, standing in a fenced field. Nothing supernatural. Just a horse and a noise and—

Time slows. The horse is there, and *then she is not*. Her eyes lock on mine, and then she disappears. There and then gone. A gentle wicker on the wind and then a startled, inhuman noise as she falls.

Falls.

Straight down into the sinkhole that has opened like a mouth in the earth.

I start toward the fence, then stop myself, press a fist to my mouth. I cannot pull the horse from her fate. But if I go too close, will the earth swallow us too? And—the world grows icier with the thought—*Was this what Anna wanted to show me? Did she know this would happen?*

Did she *make it* happen?

My stomach twists, my skin tight and hot and alien over my bones as I turn to stare at her pale, worried face. No, she didn't. She couldn't. She is scared. She is as scared as I am.

Isn't she?

As I turn back toward the fence, I am made of indecision. Knock on the door and tell the neighbors what they've lost? Expose Anna's presence here when everyone already thinks she's a witch? Run and run and run as far from this place as fast as we can? Scream into the night and demand that whoever is listening reveal himself?

The last idea is too terrifying to linger on. Disturb his peace and Soovana's wrath can be terrible. Is that what happened? Anna and I disturbed his peace, and now—so many years of paying for it later—do I dare disturb him again, even for answers?

The air splits with another crack, and before I can decide what to do, the decision is made for me. The house's lights flicker on, a figure racing by windows toward the front door. They will find their horse. They will find the sinkhole. And I know, from the tips of my toes to the marrow in my bones, that they cannot find us here.

I grab Anna and we run.

VIII
RAIN

I don't sleep. I don't wake Mama. I don't breathe a word of the events of last night.

I'm afraid if I do, it will be too much for her. The blankness behind her eyes will overtake her once and for all. Our fragile mama will finally shatter into too many pieces to ever put back together. I will lose her like we lost Da, like we lost Anna.

And I will lose Anna again too.

Because if I tell Mama, *that makes it real*. Real that a horse disappeared into a sinkhole. Real that Anna led me to that place at that moment, hinted at answers and only handed me more questions. I will see those questions—those thousand horrible, unanswerable questions—in Mama's face. In the widening of an eye, the downward twitch of the corner of her mouth. And that will make it all true: Anna isn't Anna, and she didn't come back, and I killed my sister.

When I hear Mama stirring in the other room, I slip quietly to the edge of the hall and watch as she gathers her things. The stolen shoes bought us one day, but she has to go back to work now. There's only so much you can miss, even with a doctor's note, unless you want to be seen as work-shy. Unless you want to attract attention. Her face is pale as she stops at the front door, hand shaking on the knob. I know she doesn't want to leave Anna, but what can she do? We can't afford for her to lose her job.

"Don't let her out of your sight," she whispers, and I nod.

I should probably comfort Mama with more than a nod, but I never know how to. I never know how to talk to her at all, ever since I heard what she said to Riina. Ever since I learned how dangerous I am to love. Now, the feeling sinks deeper. Because I have secrets and I cannot tell them. Cannot tell her about the sinkhole and Anna pulling me back toward the bog. Cannot confess that even though it feels like a betrayal, I am afraid of what Anna might be. I am afraid that the village is right.

Witchcraft.

Spirits.

The bog has done something evil again.

My stomach flips and twists as we stare at each other. The secrets and my own danger lodge under my skin like the thinnest of splinters. Impossible to root out.

"I have to go." She says it like a question, and I nod again.

It takes her another minute, but eventually she opens the door, darts another glance back at me and whispers, "Please don't go to the bog," before leaving.

Shame washes over me, heavy like the mud that can suck you down into the bog's inescapable depths. She still doesn't trust me. She still thinks I killed her daughter once and could do it again. I'm dangerous, and the truth of it slides through me like poison.

I'm suddenly terrified that Anna's gone again, that she's woken up while we were standing here like two broken fools and she's fled back into the trees and it's all my fault. All my fault again.

I run back to our room, and my chest loosens slightly at the sight of her breathing evenly in bed, a slice of sunshine between the curtains falling across the arm she's flung above her head. She looks so different in sleep, her face so peaceful. So *Anna*. For one moment, it's like she's really back—without all the questions and secrets and missing memories.

I have the terrible thought that she's a mirage, that my eyes are playing tricks on me, so I place two fingers on the side of her neck. Holding my breath, I feel for a pulse, some proof of life. It flutters strong beneath my fingers, but I keep them there while I count her breaths, just to be sure. *In, one-two-three, out, one-two-three. Alive, alive, alive, alive.*

I slide into bed beside her and try to stay awake, to keep counting those breaths. But after a night of so little sleep, I drift into my own dreams, carried by the rhythm of the counting. *Alive, alive, alive, alive. Here, here, here, here.*

⁓

I wake up with my hand in my pocket, lightly resting on the cards. When I pull them out, the Rain card is upside down on top of the deck—the inky silhouettes of trees just visible through a gray downpour. Upright, the card means rejuvenation: the coming of spring, a seed bursting forth into a precious, fragile baby plant. Inverted like this, though, it implies exhaustion and hurt, a deluge that drowns instead of giving life. I hear it in the distance, the sound of that torrent.

The meaning settles dark in my center as I realize that the warmth of Anna at my side has gone cold. The space where she was: unoccupied.

Again.

Don't let her out of your sight. I've failed Mama. I've failed myself. Every single time.

I scramble from the bed, dread clawing at my heart. "Anna?"

The only answer is a loud *BANG* from the other room. My body uncoils slightly. A bang means she isn't gone, hasn't faded into the trees again. She's only gotten up. Maybe to get a glass of water.

Yes, I hear water running. That must be it.

I try to slow my breathing as I step into the hall—and the brief relief evaporates from my skin.

In the living room, the rug has been flipped up at the corners, the cushions pulled from the couch, shoes knocked askew from their tidy line by the door. Another *BANG* sounds from the kitchen, loud and metallic.

He's listening.

Could he be doing more than listening now? The bangs not the noise of Anna getting water, but of *him*—whoever he is—crossing the line from bog to village, village to house. Will I find Anna in the kitchen, or something else?

Don't let her out of your sight.

I might vomit.

"Anna?"

No answer still as I reach the kitchen doorway, the sound of rain beating in my ears even as I can see sunshine outside the window. I make it one step into the kitchen and freeze in my tracks.

The kitchen is worse than the living room. Drawers flung open and left that way. Cabinet doors too. Mixing bowls litter the floor. Spoons pile on the counter. The oven door is open, the knobs turned all the way up. Heat pulses through the room. The faucet over the sink is on—the sound of torrential rain, not rain at all but cold water pumped in from the well, overflowing our tiny sink and creating a waterfall into the floor. Like the bog has come inside, forcing its pools upon us instead of luring us into them.

The puddle snakes from sink to cabinets to floor and then into the center of the room, where Anna stands in the heart of the growing pool, surveying it all. She's the fox that got into the henhouse. A bird trapped indoors, knocking everything about until it can escape. Her eyes are distant. Her hands wet.

There is no sign of anyone else.

I unfreeze and rush to turn the tap off, then stand in front of Anna, opening and closing my mouth involuntarily until I drop to my knees to search her eyes. Water soaks through my skirt, and I notice her socks are bloated with wet.

My throat is tight, my chest tighter, as I search her face. "Anna, what did you do?"

She blinks, darts a glance over her shoulder before answering. "I'm trying to find them."

Goose bumps prickle on my skin. "Trying to find what?"

She pauses, her voice gone even softer, barely audible. "His eyes."

My throat burns. Eyes? She's searching for *eyes*? What happened in the bog that spit her back out searching cupboards for eyeballs? I reach for any answer, but nothing presents itself. The only eyes that we're warned to beware are Soovana's. But that's in the bog, not in the house.

Not in the house.

Even a house with a pool at its center, growing more bog-like by the second?

"Whose eyes, Anna?" My whisper is pinched. She glances around the room as if she's already said too much. Her chest rising and falling too fast.

Not knowing what else I can do, I stand, lift her into the kitchen chair, and struggle to put everything back into place. Mama can't see it like this. Can't see that I let her out of my sight. Failed again. Can't ask the questions I've asked, get the answers I've gotten. About hidden eyes and spirits listening. And most of all: I don't want her to realize that nothing Anna does seems like what my little sister would do. That nothing she is seems like what my little sister would be.

That something is deeply, irrevocably wrong with Anna.

Now she pulls off her socks and drops them to the floor, tucking her legs onto the chair with her and staring hard at the window, as if the eyes she's searching for will blink to life there.

I shudder, and I clean.

When the mop is drying on the back stoop and the kitchen looks like our kitchen again, I sit on the couch facing her. Serious. "Anna, I need you to tell me what happened. Where were you? Why—"

Before I can finish, Margit flings herself into the house like she owns it. The door smacks shut behind her, and Anna startles off the couch like a wild animal.

"Da said to come keep you company. Let's go for a walk." Margit's tone is no-nonsense, like she hasn't noticed the way Anna flew from the couch. Like she's over the novelty of my sister being back and still being five and no longer speaking Estonian. Like everything is normal.

I scowl at Margit and move to Anna, slipping my hand into hers. "You startled her."

"She's easily startled." Margit shrugs.

"Mama said not to go out," I say, though that's not quite true. She just said not to go to the bog.

Margit raises an eyebrow. "All right, then I'll stay here with you."

She moves toward the kitchen, and my insides spike with panic. Did I clean well enough? Will she notice something's wrong? Will Anna warn her about eyes in the house?

Margit, the world's worst secret keeper, wouldn't keep any of it from her da or my mama. Would Uncle Silver cart Anna off somewhere for testing, seeing all this as proof that something is

69

psychologically wrong? He runs an asylum; he believes in sending people away for their own good. And Mama—I can't name what would happen if she knew. It's an unknown terror in my belly, a certainty that wherever she goes behind her eyes might one day steal her entirely from us. I cannot let these secrets break her.

If we go with Margit, the villagers might see Anna. If we stay, Margit will see the kitchen. But it's working hours; there will be fewer people out.

I make the decision before Margit gets to the kitchen. "Wait, we'll go. Let's walk. You're right. We could use some fresh air."

Margit nods, as if she knew she was right all along. Then she crosses the room in two steps, leads Anna—who throws me a panicked look—to the door, and starts putting on her shoes.

"It's all right, Anna." I switch to Russian, realizing how scary it must be for us to speak Estonian if she doesn't understand it. How scary it must be to understand nothing and then—without warning—be taken away.

"We're going for a walk," I reassure her, pulling on my own shoes.

She nods mutely and reaches out to lace her fingers through mine again. Breathless relief washes over me like a warm bath. Like her tiny hand was all I needed to think that maybe everything will turn out right in the end. Maybe we'll solve the mysteries of where she went and what happened. Maybe in a few days—a few weeks—she'll speak Estonian and laugh like she used to. She'll answer the questions, and everything will snap into place.

We take a path through the low green-yellow shrubbery between houses, Anna's hand tangled in mine. Margit leads the way with the kind of march a soldier would be proud of (or, at least, a *sober* soldier; the ones around here are mostly drunk and look nothing like the dignified men they show on TV).

"Did your da say anything about her?" I ask in Estonian, thinking that if anyone might have theories about why she's still five years old, it'll be Uncle Silver. Maybe there's a medical explanation. Or something he'd know about as a party member.

Margit narrows her eyes at me. "Why would he?"

"I don't know. He's a doctor. She didn't age." I whisper the words, even though Anna can't understand my Estonian. "He didn't...have any theories?"

Margit startles, then scowls. "*No.* He's not that kind of doctor. You know that. He's more of a scientist. Besides, if Da knew how to keep people from aging, believe me, there'd be party members lined up around the block for his secret. Your mama's the one with theories."

She says *theories* like it means *idiocy*, and my hackles rise.

"What do you mean Mama has theories?"

"She hasn't talked to you about it?" Margit's tone is unbearably superior. "I overheard her asking the witch if there are herbs that can stop aging. As if Anna's been in the bog for five years gorging herself on some magic plant." She laughs, but the sound is hollow, and for just a second, I wonder if she's as scared as I am and just hiding it better.

"And you have a better idea?" My words are sharp-edged.

A muscle twitches in her jaw. "It's impossible. No theory needed. The world gives to you, and it takes from you. There are no reasons. There's just what you do about it. I make perfect marks, volunteer with the Pioneers, join the party, and nobody will take anything from me again." Her tone changes at the end, bitterness seeping through the usual disdain on that odd statement: *Nobody will take anything from me again.*

"What do you mean *again*? Who's taking things from you?"

She startles in a way that makes me think she didn't mean to say that out loud, then walks faster. I guess that means the conversation is over, but I keep mulling over the question.

Who's taking things away from Margit? Privileged, confident, party-daughter Margit who gets an orange every time her school marks are good. She had a Western teddy bear, bright white and feather soft, unlike our own drab, gray, rock-hard Soviet versions, and a VCR when none of the rest of us could afford one. She's right that she's a party darling, doing all the right things—basically running our local chapter of the Pioneers youth group where kids learn about Communism. She'll get every advantage. She'll go away to university. What in the world has anyone taken from her? What does she have to be bitter about?

When I emerge from my thoughts, we're nearing the edge of town—one of the last houses before the tree line and the bog—and my skin flashes with heat. Margit may be able to pretend things are fine, but *I* know that everything about this situation is ominous.

I can see the trees from here, staring me down, daring me to come too close. They'll take Anna again if I'm not careful. I know it in my stomach, in my throat, in the ache in my jaw.

I grip Anna's hand tighter. I should turn around and march straight home. Instead, I only slow, staring into the shadows past the tree line, questions burning in my chest.

What was it that took her? I feel like the answer is going to swallow us up. *Witchcraft*, the town keeps whispering. *Monster*, I heard my mother murmur once. *Ghosts*, she suggested another time when she didn't know I was listening.

Soovana, my mind adds. Bog thing. Trickster. Faerie. When we were little and Margit wasn't above that kind of speculation, she suggested maybe the forest was a portal to another world, like in a story. That makes as much sense as anything else.

I may not know what it is, may not have been able to coax an answer from this strange version of Anna. But I do know *where* the answers are. Portal, spirit, or monstrous thing—

The bog. Its shadow-dark trees point their fingers. Its boulders stand at attention.

It tugs at me. Heart and gut and body. My neck, my navel, my arm—

No.

It isn't the bog tugging at my elbow, I realize.

It's Anna. Again.

Her eyes snag on the tree line, her lips set in a determined frown. She's pulling me toward the trees.

I stop, dig my heels in. *Not again*. Frustration and fear cycle in the unending question: *Why is she trying to pull me into the bog?* I try to find any explanation for why Anna would want that, why Anna would do that. But I come up empty.

Anna *wouldn't* want that.

But a bog thing might.

I hate the thought the moment it skitters across my brain. Hate myself for doubting her.

But what else makes sense?

"What are you doing?" I whisper.

"Shhh, he's watching," she whispers back.

Violent chills shudder up my spine as I whip my head around to stare into the trees. *He*. She said *he*. Not *it* or *they* or some other idea altogether—not monsters, not ghosts. *He's watching*. Soovana. My eye twitches involuntarily with the unsettling truth of it. The thing I've known in my gut all along.

Soovana took my sister.

And this isn't over.

"Why are you stopping?" Margit's voice is impatient as she whips around—and I straighten, a new fear emerging from the shadows of my mind.

Margit telling Uncle Silver doesn't just risk him thinking Anna's crazy. It risks something else too, doesn't it? Would he report us to the party? Report her strange behavior, put us under scrutiny?

The fear is a thousand crawling things unearthed from the

accidental shifting of a rock. They ricochet in a thousand directions on a thousand crawling legs across my mind, my heart, my skin. And the shame follows again, hot and thick. I'm the worst family member. Believing the worst of Anna, believing the worst of my uncle.

I open my mouth to tell Margit it's nothing when I notice Anna is no longer tugging me toward the trees. Instead, she's statue still, sweaty palm clutching mine as if we're both hanging on for dear life.

I follow Anna's gaze away from the trees, the bog, the place I expect to find danger. It's not a watching spirit in between the birches that has stopped her, scared her. It's not a set of lantern eyes. A whisper through the night. A figure with cranberries growing from his beard.

No. Whatever dark magic keeps us from the bog has skipped out of the tree line and brought its mischief to the village. I wonder, distantly, if it was I who conjured it by falling past that invisible line just before Anna appeared or if it was Anna who broke whatever unseen thread kept it back.

Whatever the answer, now it's here. Across an open patch of grass, the ancient well in old Agnesia's backyard is doing a thing that wells should never do.

It's overflowing.

Water escapes the top and cascades down the stone sides, as if the earth is vomiting, trying to rid itself of poison. It roars as it escapes its stone prison, scraping the silence like the crack of a branch behind you when you're walking alone in the dark. The air above the well clouds with mist, rising white above the fast-flowing water. And the ground around the well is pooling, dark with mud and bright with reflected shards of open sky.

I think of the kitchen, the overflowing sink. Anna standing in the middle of a growing puddle, reflecting the chaos. What does it mean that everywhere Anna goes, water breaks free of where it should be?

Riina's voice echoes across the years, from when she used to walk Liis and me through the village and whisper legends that came before the Soviets. *When the well overflows, the witches are angry. They're fighting and stirring up trouble underground.*

Witches. Angry. Stirring up trouble.

This is a warning. A portent. Our kitchen must have been too. Anna is trying to get to the bog; the bog is trying to get to Anna.

One moment I'm frozen, watching, and the next I'm dragging Anna away. Margit can fend for herself. Something is wrong here. Everything is wrong here. Anna can't be here. We've come too close to the trees; whatever is inside them sees us, hears us, calls to her.

Anna's right. Something is watching.

IX
THE MOON

By the time we make it home, I realize it's not only my skin that's flushed with heat. Anna is an ember, a fire, pink-faced and sweating.

She's sick, I think, and the thought is—first—a strange relief. Fevers can make a person delirious. Illness can confuse our minds, can't it? Is the fever why she's been dragging me toward the bog instead of away? Not because she isn't her, not because the trees are whispering her name. Could she simply be confused? Too feverish? Too ill to know what she's been doing?

Has she been sick this whole time, and we were too distracted by everything else to notice?

Then panic rises, drowning out the relief. Mama is going to blame me for taking her out. For going too near the bog. And I'm ashamed to even think it, because this isn't about me. It's about Anna. Who cares what Mama thinks of me? But I do.

I do.

I give Anna some broth and then tuck her into bed. I wonder if I should get Riina's help, but the thought of leaving makes me think I might pass out. What if the forest comes for Anna? What if she dies? I'm suddenly certain that if I leave her for even a second, she'll be gone again. I can't go get Riina. If I hadn't pushed Liis away, she'd be here. She could go get her mama. The knowledge cuts at me, every day another reason I can never get it right. Keep Liis close and put her in danger; push her away and now that I need her, Anna's in danger.

Damn it. Where's Margit when you need her? Sweeping in to save the day when no one needs saving, then abandoning us when I could send her for help. I wonder if she's back at the well, watching the water creep toward the little house. Watching it take over.

"Vik?" Anna's voice is fragile as a bird's wing. "Will you read my cards?"

Her Russian is perfect, and my stomach does another flip. Even Margit has a slight accent, and she's at the top of our class. Still, I force a smile and answer, "Of course, my love."

I reach into my pocket and take out the cards. The relief of seeing them, touching them, shuffling them is overwhelming. My heart stretches like a cat in the sun, releasing some of the tension coiled throughout my body. The *thwwtt* of the shuffle, the feather-like edges of a well-worn deck remind me that I'm here and now. Anna is here and now. The well can't get her. The bog can't get her. And a fever is a normal thing. Everyone gets fevers sometimes. Someone will come by, and I'll send them for Riina. All will be well.

I spread the deck beside Anna, and she points to a card.

"What are you asking the cards today?" I ask her.

I've been too scared to ask her these last few times. Scared of what, I don't know. But now I ask, pausing before I flip her chosen card.

"If I'm going to die."

I don't know what answer I expected, but it wasn't that one. The comfort of a moment ago vanishes, and where my skin was flaming, now it's cold. The cold of a starless winter night, so dark you can't see your hand in front of your face.

"Why would you say that?"

"Because it's what happens. You feel bad and then you die."

"No, *no*, Anna. You feel bad and then you get better. Liis says a fever is your body's way of fighting. It means you're strong."

Anna looks unconvinced, taps the card twice, and I flip it.

The Moon. It means illusion and fear, but that doesn't seem like the right answer to Anna's question, so I choose a prediction more comforting but still close to the truth.

"The Moon means you're going to discover truth, Anna. Which means you can't die."

Her eyes soften and she nods a little. I feel the weight of her trust in me like I'm carrying the whole forest on my back, and guilt threatens to strangle me. I've been so busy asking myself if Anna is Anna that I didn't notice she's sick. I wonder how I can still breathe through the thick, choking shame of it. Still the question stays in the back of my mind, an unwelcome guest.

Someone knocks at the door, but I can't tear my eyes away from Anna, so I shout for them to come in, hoping it's not some nosey villagers here to warn me my sister is a witch. I don't think I can bear to hear it right now outside my own head.

Only slightly better, it's Margit.

"You know," she says in the superior voice she favors, "you didn't have to go running off like a stepped-on cat. It's just a well."

"Tell that to the neighbors who think she's a witch," I hiss.

That muscle twitches in her jaw again. "Superstitious nonsense people. I can't wait to get out of this hell village and go to university in the city."

"Good for you. But for now, since we're here, can you go get Liis's mama? Anna has a fever."

Margit darts a startled glance at Anna. And that's when I realize: *Margit hasn't looked at Anna once today.* Not really. Never for more than a second or two. She hasn't hugged Anna either. Or cried with us. Or asked about what happened. Did she speak to Anna at all?

"Margit?" Her name comes out a question, but the rest of what I want to ask lodges in my heart like a splinter.

Through all her bravado about superstition, does Margit secretly fear Anna isn't Anna too?

I open my mouth, close it. Then Margit turns and starts out of the room, throwing the next words over her shoulder while retreating as fast as she can. "I'll get Riina."

B y nightfall, Anna has had every herbal and folk cure I've ever heard of—and a few I haven't. Her belly is full of peppermint tea and garlic bread. Her feet are wrapped in socks soaked in vodka, which are, in turn, wrapped in a towel, which is, in turn, wrapped in cellophane to keep the vodka in. Everyone knows your feet heal your whole body, and I can't believe I didn't do the vodka socks before Riina arrived. I didn't think of the garlic either, though I should have.

I have a sinking feeling that I've failed Anna again. If I'd done more earlier, she'd get better faster. And perhaps she'd give us the answers, stop saying that Soovana is watching and finally tell us the truth of what happened.

Riina seems to read my mind. "None of this is your fault, Viktoria."

I hum an unconvinced acknowledgment.

"Sit, have a cup of tea. You can't help Anna if you're all tense."

I hum again, sit at the kitchen table, and sip the cup of tea she pushes toward me without tasting it. I can see Anna on the couch, asleep with her feet all wrapped up and her hair damp with sweat. She's so small, so fragile. A twig too easy to snap. A flower petal too easy to tear. She was lost to me once, and I can't breathe through the fear that she's slipping away again.

I don't know I'm crying until Riina wraps her arms around me. She's soft and warm, and I realize that I haven't been hugged like this in years, which just makes me cry harder. The tears are for Anna and then they're for me and then they're for every bad thought I've had in my whole life, releasing the pressure inside me like the well overflowing, expelling pain for everyone to see.

I don't want Mama to see me like this, so as soon as I can bear it, I pull away and go to the sink to splash cold water on my face, rearrange my expression like I'm confident that everything will be okay.

Liis's mama comes up behind me again, hugs me around my shoulders, and kisses the top of my head.

"You're a good big sister," she whispers. "You did everything right."

The words make the tears rise up again, but I push them back down, try to hold the pieces of myself together.

When Mama gets home from work, it's a relief to pretend. To sit here quiet, calm, and let Riina explain. It comes as a surprise, though, when she finishes reassuring Mama that Anna will be all right, takes Mama's sharp shoulders in her hands, and says in a voice threaded with worry, "You and the girls should stay with us awhile."

My stomach turns over. Is Anna really that bad? I think about her asking if she's going to die, and I want to run out the door screaming to attack the bog with my fists and teeth and fingernails. To rip the bark off trees and throw the stones from their places and fill the puddles with broken branches so they can never suck another person in.

"Why, Riina?" Mama's voice is as raw as my thoughts.

"People are talking. They're scared. Agnesia's well overflowed today. Yesterday, a sinkhole opened in one of the pastures and swallowed a horse."

My heart seizes. These things are connected—or the village

believes they are. They might know Anna was at the well, and it won't matter that they don't know that she was there for the sinkhole too. They'll connect those dots. They'll trace the lines of improbabilities. That's what Riina is saying. Me running away hasn't helped Anna at all. It hasn't saved her from their suspicions.

It hasn't even saved her from mine.

Riina goes on. "You know how this village is. You know they suspect witchcraft. And you know the first unusual thing that happened in what they'll see as a trio was Anna coming back. Three bad omens that trace back to a little girl."

Mama sits beside Anna on the couch and runs her fingers gently through the sweat-damp curls. My heart feels like a bruise, and I hate myself for thinking she'd never touch me like that. I should be worrying about Anna.

"No, Riina." Mama's voice is strangely steady. "People will calm down. It's just overflowing wells and sinkholes. We've had both here before."

"We haven't had this, though." I'm surprised to hear my own voice join the conversation. "Haven't had anything like Anna."

Riina motions to me with her eyebrows raised. "Exactly. The bog has never returned one of our own—and one of our own *who hasn't aged*. If you and I think it's creepy, imagine what people who have no connection to Anna think."

I wonder if I should say more. About her searching the house, what she said about dying, the way she keeps trying to pull me back into the bog. But if I think Anna might not be Anna, what will Mama think? What will she do? Would she tell Uncle Silver? Would he take Anna to a lab? I can't get past the questions, so instead I let myself fade back out of the conversation. Listening, watching Mama wrap a finger around Anna's spiral curls.

Riina goes on, her words echoing my worries. That the more people know, the less safe we'll be. "Maarja. I'm telling you logic goes out the window when people are scared like this. When they don't understand."

"*I* don't understand either," Mama whispers. "But we'll stay here. What will anyone do about it?"

I look to Riina to find out what she thinks the village might do, but she's quiet now, her lips pressed together in an unhappy line. The expression reminds me of Liis and pushes at my heart like a thumb on a bruise. Where is Liis now? What would she say if she were here? I don't know the answers anymore. I used to know them all.

Riina steps to Mama, laces her fingers through the hair at the back of Mama's neck. She leans down to kiss Mama on the head like she did before with me, then murmurs—her tone equal parts care and warning—just loud enough for me to hear.

"Not knowing what they'll do is the problem."

X
THE EMPEROR

With Mama watching over Anna, my own need to watch her lessens and a pull toward the bog fills me to the brim, tugs under my belly button, simmers beneath my skin. I wait until they're folded together on the couch, asleep. Then I slip out the door and to the tree line, rubbing my thumb against the cards in my pocket.

What will the neighbors do to us? I ask the cards as I walk. *Where was Anna for five years? Why is she still five? What happened to her?*

What will happen to her?

I know I'm asking too many questions. Readings are best when you focus on one. But this is a world with too many questions, including the one I've been avoiding:

Is Anna really my Anna anymore?

She was a flower when she left, petals so easily crushed. But now could she be a flytrap—one of those delicate-looking plants just waiting for a bug to crawl into its honeyed arms? When they whisper, *Witch, witch*, do they know something I don't?

If I don't go to the bog and read the cards now, I may never know the answers.

"Pah! They're superstitious fools!" Uncle Silver said when he stopped by to check on us after work. "Sinkholes are a natural part of living near the bog. Not magic. Just science. That well overflows every few years. It's just unfortunate timing."

Do I believe him? I hate myself for even asking. I've been waiting for Anna to come home, longing for it. Now she's back and I'm doubting her. I—*the dangerous one*, the one who led her into the bog in the first place—am doubting her.

What a terrible person I am.

I reach the tree line, settle onto the soft, spongy ground, and shuffle the cards while I breathe. *In, one-two-three, out, one-two-three. Shuffle, one-two-three, cut, one-two-three.*

I stare into the trees as my hands beat out their familiar shuffling rhythm. Something shifts at the edge of my vision, and I think of the stories about oaks and alders uprooting themselves to attend a wedding. I wonder how trees move if they do move. Do the forests that disappear because of the ungrateful villages simply vanish into thin air, or do they wrench their roots from the ground, rip themselves violently from the landscape where they grew, and leave behind a torn-apart devastation? If our forest left, would it take Soovana with it? Would it take the danger—and the answers?

I stare at the shifting space, but nothing moves when I look straight at it. I breathe long and slow, trying to keep my heart steady.

Tell me something true, I ask the cards.

The deck doesn't have time to answer. Because something true is already here. Announced by the crunch of leaves underfoot, the surprised "Vik" tumbling off her tongue, the *kak-kak* of a fox close behind.

Liis.

She drops to the dirt beside me, so comfortable here. Like I used to be. Like I never can be again.

"What are you asking it?" She motions to the deck in my hands.

I bite my lip. For so many years, she asked questions like these, and I couldn't answer—all the things I wanted to say bunched up in my throat, stuck. Because if I said them, she'd get close again. And if she got close, she'd get *hurt*. And if I said them, they'd be true. If I said them, they'd crush me into nothing. Crush us all. My questions are weapons, safer inside my head.

But today something is different. Like the questions piled up in my throat have hit their tipping point. There are too many to keep in.

So I answer.

For the first time in five years, I *really* answer.

"I'm afraid that Anna isn't Anna. That the bog made her… something else."

There it is. The terrible thing. Outside my own head.

My eyes meet Liis's as she visibly shudders back, her usual curiosity and humor erased by shock and fear and something else. Something like I stabbed her straight in the chest.

My shame is fire, searing in my throat, my chest, my gut. Liis thinks I'm a monster. I *am* a monster. I want to disappear. To fly away. To bury myself in the deep, black dirt and sleep and sleep and sleep forever. To be anywhere but here, anyone but me.

I look away to keep from crying.

"Why would you say that?" Liis's voice is as tiny as I've ever heard it. I press my fingernails into my palms as if I can force the terrible words back inside me.

This time, I cannot tell the truth.

"Sorry. It's nothing. I didn't mean it."

"What would she be if she isn't Anna?" Liis presses.

I choke on the answers. Bog thing. Spirit. Witch. Ghost. Magic wearing my sister's face.

"I shouldn't have said anything."

A heartbeat. Two. Three. Each of them unbearably long. Then Liis shifts beside me, and I chance a look. She rises to her feet, her expression still wrong.

"I have to get home." Her voice is wrong too. An octave too high.

She whistles for Kaos, turns. And that's when I fully face her, watch the tight, stiff lines of her body as she walks away. I made those lines, that tightness.

I was right before: all these terrible, ugly things inside my head should stay there.

I force my gaze back to the cards, shuffling again with shaking hands. I need their answers more than ever. New questions crowd in with the old: Does Liis hate me? Has she finally seen what Mama knew five years ago? That I am dangerous. Dangerous. Dangerous. And every time I forget for even a second, something horrible happens again.

The card I pull is the Emperor—a wolf with an inky scar across its snout. Authority. Security. Rules. Boundaries. I don't know what it means right now. That I broke my own rules by telling Liis the truth—and there are more consequences to come? That Anna is secure or that no one is? That the forest boundary will keep us safe or that it has been breached? That I've broken some other invisible rule? That Anna has?

"I don't understand," I cry, staring at the cards as if they could answer me.

Of course, they don't. Pressure to scream builds in my chest like lightning gathering in a cloud, and I imagine myself throwing the cards into the forest. Stomping them into the mud, tearing them into pieces. The thought turns my fury to horror, and I squeeze the deck as hard as I dare to keep myself from doing the unspeakable thing, destroying my only friend.

Friend. Yes, I suppose that's right. The cards are my friend. The only thing I tell my secrets to ever since Anna disappeared and I ran away from Liis. Now especially, when I know that my secrets disgust Liis. That my questions horrify her.

I breathe in through my nose and out through my mouth, waiting until I feel certain I won't hurt my cards. Until that fear passes, replaced by another: *What if Anna got worse while I was gone?*

As soon as the thought occurs, I slip the cards back into my pocket and run. If I can get there in time, I can save her. I can make sure she's all right. I can make it up to her—the doubting. The need to check her breathing chafes me like a bad seam in a too-tight coat. My feet pound the familiar path back home, incautious, bone-jarring.

When I get home, it's midnight, and they should still be asleep. But instead the house blazes with light from every room. The door is wide open. And in the doorway: the silhouettes of men. A dozen or more.

I know who they are the moment I see them, and the cicadas must too, because they've stopped their nightly jamboree. Even they know that you don't draw attention to yourself when these men come calling.

These are the men you never want at your house. The men you make jokes about and then look back over your shoulder to be sure you haven't conjured them out of thin air. The men who take our daddies and our granddaddies and our great-granddaddies when the forest and the vodka don't.

The men nobody ever invites in.

My house is full of Soviet soldiers.

~

Ш ho have you told?"

The highest-ranking soldier is also the most terrifying, his chin and cheekbones sharp enough to cut glass, his skin the color of ice. If he didn't have the power to destroy everyone with a single snap of his elegant fingers, I'd call him beautiful. Like a painting someone might do of a wizard. Like a character in my oracle deck. I think of the Emperor card I pulled just minutes ago. Is this what the cards meant? Authority. Security. Rules. Boundaries. The USSR army stands for all those things.

I'm angry at the cards again, because what good is a prediction if it doesn't tell me what to do? What good is being right if it can't save any of us? Not Anna, not Mama, and certainly not me, as I'm marched uncomfortably into the room with a soldier's hand like a steel trap around my shoulder.

Anna curls on the couch in the tightest spiral, a pill bug startled into the shape of a wheel. In front of her, skinny and insubstantial, Mama tries to block her from the soldiers. If they knew Mama, they'd know how hard she must be trying to hang on to herself, to not retreat behind her own eyes to wherever it is she goes when the fear comes knocking at our door.

"Who have you told?" The soldier's voice is even sharper the second time he asks.

"Told what, sir?" Mama's voice trembles.

"About the little girl! There are already rumors as far away as Tallinn that a ghost girl has walked out of a haunted forest. It's superstitious nonsense! It's un-Communist! And I demand to know who you spread these rumors to!" His icy skin reddens now—with anger or exertion or some combination of the two.

Mama lowers her eyes to the floor, murmurs, "No one. We haven't told anyone. Someone else in the village must be talking about Anna…"

"And is it true she disappeared five years ago?"

"Yes, sir." I can taste the fear in Mama's words from across the room, sharp and sour like moonshine made in bathtubs. My own fear spikes in response, pinching my gut like it's wrapped in brambles.

"And it's true she came back this week?"

"Yes, sir."

"Do you know where she was?"

"No, sir."

"Where did you tell everyone she was?"

"Nowhere, sir. We've been home with Anna, treating her fever. We haven't told anyone anything." Mama struggles to keep her eyes focused. Anna is a silent, sweaty spiral on the couch.

The soldier runs his tongue over his teeth, deciding if he believes us. I wonder what he'll do if he doesn't—hurt us, take us away, kill us here and now? And I wonder why he cares so much about Anna.

Is it because anything that seems even the slightest bit supernatural, mysterious, or unknown reeks of religion, and religion—as we're all taught—leads to immorality? Or do the soldiers feel they've been made into fools by something they can't explain? Or is this bigger than the soldiers—some higher-up thinking that if stories like this get out, all of the USSR will be the butt of a worldwide joke? Superstitious, they'll call us. Hypocritical with our atheist government and our ghost-believing, spirit-pacifying population. With our secret stories of lakes made of tears, and girls turned into stars, and spirits who share a heartbeat with the bog. Foolish to believe in mysteries even if we see them with our own eyes.

"You know what Stalin said," the leader says, his voice low now. " 'Death solves all problems—no person, no problem.' "

People aren't supposed to like Stalin anymore, but the soldiers clearly do. They all laugh like this threat is the best joke they've heard in weeks. I feel sick. Mama looks like she might faint.

"Are you a problem, ma'am?" the soldier asks.

Mama shakes her head.

He opens his mouth, probably to make another terrifying joke, but instead I hear Uncle Silver's voice behind me. "What in the name of Lenin is this about?"

Thank heavens. If there's anyone who can save us, it's Uncle Silver. He ranks much higher than these soldiers. He runs the whole government asylum at the edge of town, the one that reaches a little too far into the forest for anyone's comfort. It's the first time I've ever cared that he is an important doctor and scientist. The first time his position seemed like anything more than a reason for him to try to steer me toward better behavior.

I let out an audible breath, and Mama does the same. A chorus of relief. Only Anna still seems as tense as she was.

"Well," Uncle Silver demands. "Explain yourselves."

"Comrade Sokolov!" The soldier closes his mouth and stands up straighter. "We were investigating a rumor. Seems these folks have been spreading trouble."

"These folks"—Uncle Silver waves a hand toward Mama and I—"are my sister and niece."

Nieces, Uncle Silver. *You've forgotten there are two of us again.* Or maybe Anna is the one he means; now that the angel is back, the dangerous rebel can be forgotten.

The soldier shifts on his feet, as uncomfortable as a child caught throwing rocks at chickens or sneaking vodka from the still. "I'm sorry, sir. I didn't realize."

"Well, now you do. I'll take care of this from here."

The soldier bobs his head, crow-like, and motions for his men to file from the room, their sharp elbows and the sharper angles of their guns disappearing through the door before it closes almost deferentially with a soft *clack*.

Mama and I chorus our sighs again, and I watch as the thing she's been holding back all along takes her, her eyes losing focus, her movements going sluggish.

"Maarja, it's all right, really." Uncle Silver moves to help her sit on the couch.

I kneel at the other end of the couch, run my fingers through Anna's hair. "You can relax now, love. They've gone."

"Agnesia's well overflowed. A sinkhole swallowed a horse. They think we're a curse," Mama murmurs, half-coherent.

"Who's Agnesia?" he asks distractedly, glancing at me.

"The old lady who lives at the edge of the forest. You know her, Uncle Silver. She waves to you all the time…"

He waves a hand at me, as if the explanation is too much for him. "I don't have time to memorize the names of everyone in this village, Viktoria. I don't know someone just because they wave at me."

His eyes catch on Anna, and he frowns. "She's sicker."

He says it like an answer instead of a question, but I nod anyway.

"Mm," he grunts in a way that means he's about to tell us what to do. Not that Uncle Silver or Margit are ever *not* about to tell us what to do. It's their most defining feature. Ours is that we ignore them.

"Maarja, I need you to focus." Uncle Silver is facing Mama now, his hands hard on her shoulders.

She blinks rapidly at him, and I wonder if this is a special twin power—the ability to call her back from the depths. I've failed too many times myself to believe it's something I can do. The first year after Anna's disappearance was the worst. I tried everything. I screamed. I cried. I ignored her. I sang and joked and tried to smile, like I was someone else altogether. Anything to bring her back.

But I could never get her back. Not even a little. Not like those few words from Uncle Silver. The thought lodges in my chest like a shard of glass, making it hurt to breathe, and for a moment, I hate her. Then I go back to hating myself instead, wishing I was worth coming back for.

She's listening with all her might when Uncle Silver continues. "You can't take her to the hospital. The soldiers will be back if you do. It'll be worse. I outrank those men, but there are people higher than me who'd think you were stirring up trouble. Do you hear me?"

Mama nods.

"Do you understand the full implications of what I'm telling you, Maarja? I need to hear you say it."

I understand, and I climb up onto the couch to curl myself protectively around Anna as Mama answers.

"They'd take her. They might take us all," she whispers. "We'd all disappear."

Another way to vanish. Like Da, we'd become only memories here. Only a space where a person used to be.

XI

WINTER, INVERTED

The things I'm afraid of could fill the sinkhole that swallowed the horse. Fill it maybe three times over.

I'm afraid that the soldiers will come back, that Uncle Silver's protection won't be enough to save us, even though it's been two days since they filled our living room with their sharp chins and sharper guns.

I'm afraid of the well overflowing at the edge of the bog, the sinkhole appearing out of nowhere, the storm brewing overhead. Afraid, even more, of the storm brewing here in the village. *Witch, witch, witch*, they whispered as I walked past this morning, on my way to the always-mostly-empty store with our coupons for rations. One of the usually drunk men who cluster on the corner whenever they're not working stared me down across the street. A collection of shoemakers on their way to work rumbled like thunder, growling, *Witch, witch, bitch, bitch*, under their breath.

I'm afraid of those growls.

I'm afraid that Liis is dead. That Mama is dead. That everyone is dead, and I just haven't heard yet because I let them out of my sight. I dared to pick up rations. I dared to stop counting breaths.

I'm afraid that Anna isn't Anna. And I'm afraid that she *is* Anna and that Mama was right five years ago: I've killed her. Because even though she's back, now she's slipping away again. Eyes fluttering. Face clammy. It's been days since the illness started, and now it's like it'll never stop.

I'm afraid that Liis hates me. That I told the truth and now she *knows*. She knows that I was never worth loving at all.

It's nearly dinnertime, and I can smell the rain outside and the rye bread baking in the kitchen from my perch on Anna's bed. With my hand on her back, I can feel the alarming heat beat off her skin, the subtle rise and fall of her breaths.

I think about her asking if she's going to die, and I wonder if she knows something I don't. If there's a question I should have asked that would have unlocked the truth. I tried so many of them; I got no answers. *Why are you five still? Why don't you speak Estonian? What's in the bog, Anna? What's past the trees?* Witches and magic, sinkholes and pools to swallow us up and spit us back out without having aged a day. Soovana, Metsavana, Kivialune, keepers of marshland, trees, and boulders.

Would knowing the answers heal her? Or do I just want answers because I want to know how I feel about her return?

Does it matter if there is a perfect question, an unlocked answer? That's the question that topples all the rest. Would knowing what happened change how I feel about the fragile little girl whose breaths I've been counting?

Tears gather at the corners of my eyes as I curl around her like a cat, because this is all I know how to do. Because somehow my body knows the answer to those questions before my mind: *It wouldn't.* Knowing what happened to Anna wouldn't change this moment. Wouldn't stop my heart from reaching toward her. Wouldn't stop my body from involuntarily curling around her, tugging a white-blond curl as if I could gently coax her back to us fully. Wouldn't stop me from loving her.

The certainty is a sip of water on a sun-bleached day, a crackling hearth fire when you come in from the snow. My heart expands with it; the tears drop silently down my cheeks and into her hair. I press my lips to the back of her head.

I've been so busy wondering if Anna is Anna that I missed this in myself. The certainty. In my body. In my heart.

I love her.

Not just the Anna of my memories. Not just the Anna who spoke Estonian and remembered her life. Not just the Anna I took into the bog.

This Anna. This precious, scared, delicate little girl. No matter how she's changed. No matter what the answer is to her mystery.

I pull her closer, count her breaths. *In, one-two-three. Out, one-two-three.* Match them with my own.

Something in my heart shifts, and I speak the promise brewing there out loud, though Anna may not be conscious enough to hear me. I say it in Estonian because Estonian feels like a promise.

Then I say it in Russian because I am saying it for her: "I will change your vodka socks a hundred times if I need to. I will stand over you when the soldiers come. I will drag you away from the bog no matter how many times it calls to you."

I send the promise into the air, and I send it to the bog, and I send it to Soovana, wherever he may be—watching us like Anna said or haunting the mirror paths of the deepest part of the bog.

If this girl is a bog thing, then she is *my* bog thing. And what am I if not a bog thing too? Shape-shifter, changeling, ghost. Like a deck of cards, I have been inverted shuffled, moved, *made different* in every way by those wizard-shaped trees and dew-sticky leaf beds and angry hallucinogenic plants and whatever hides among them.

"I'm sorry," I whisper. Because it's so clear to me now that it never mattered whether the village was right. She is a hurt little girl slipping away from us, and she deserves for me to focus on saving her, not defining her.

I reach for my cards and pull one. The Meadow. A grassy space with a woman at its center, her head encircled by a wreath of flowers. She's Muru Eit—the meadow queen. Mother of grass. Keeper of home.

Home.

The card means home.

And whatever else is true, that is true too: Anna is home. I will do anything to make sure she stays here.

As I slip the card back into the deck, another flutters onto the bed.

Winter, the only card in my deck that's abstract. The snowflakes are sharp-edged triangles unsettlingly out of place among the artistic flourishes of the rest of the deck—elegant wolves and jokester foxes, girls flying from trees, women in flower crowns.

Upright, the card means rest and meditation. Inverted, it's another sort of rest altogether. Illness. Burnout. The kind of exhaustion that makes you forget things, like where you left your house key or which year Lenin returned to Russia or who you're supposed to be.

I pull Anna tighter. Because from this angle the card isn't clear. Is it an upright promise of healing or an upside-down omen of more pain to come? I lift the card and press it back into the deck, as if my palm on its face will protect us from the worst possible answer.

In the next room, the front door opens and closes, and then Riina, Liis, and Kaos are in the doorway. It's the first time I've seen Liis since she left me at the forest's edge, and I search her face. There's no trace of the shock or hurt or disgust from before. Just Liis. Curiosity and cleverness and concern.

"May I?" Riina motions to Anna, and I move from the bed. My stomach pulls uncomfortably at the prospect of letting go of my sister, as if my hand on her back is what's keeping her in this world. As if the promise I whispered into the air requires me to stay beside her for its magic to work.

As if I'm the real witch here.

I force myself to stay standing, even though every part of me wants to lie back down with Anna. Liis moves beside me, bumps me in a friendly way with her little arm even though I don't deserve her joviality. I can't tell if I want to cry from relief or shame. Kaos takes our distraction as permission to curl up on my bed on the other side of the room.

It's strangely comforting, Kaos choosing my bed. Kaos choosing my space as her own feels like another invisible thread still connecting Liis and me, however thinly.

"Kaos!" Liis scolds, and the fox opens her mouth in defiance, ducking her head and screeching to let us know she plans to defend her choice.

I snort, the first time I've laughed in days. The sound is shocking.

"I'm sorry I ran off before," Liis says, as if she was the one who did something wrong. She nudges me again. "You okay?"

My throat pinches around the answer. I am not okay. I am never okay. But I can't tell Liis that. I can't see that horror on her face again, can't see the worst of myself through her eyes.

I open my mouth, even though I'm not sure what I'll say, but before I can speak, the night rips in half with screaming, and all three of us conscious humans jump at least a foot in the air. From the bed, Kaos hisses, her eye aimed at the front of the house, her lips curled back to show her full canines.

The scream comes again—from our front yard. Not a scream of pain, but of rage. And then there are words.

"Come out, Maarja, and bring the devil with you!"

XII
GULL

Anna barely stirs at the noise, but Kaos relocates to Anna's bed, hissing toward the raised voices, poised to fight off attackers. I've never loved anyone as much as I love that fox for being ready to go to war over my feverish little sister.

The rest of us rush from the room and out the front door—and I stop in my tracks, my heart in my throat.

Because *war* is exactly what's about to happen outside.

A village full of people has emptied itself into our yard. Most of the men are already drunk. I know because they're *always* already drunk—on homemade vodka, cucumber aftershave, even gasoline when they can't find anything else—and because they have that stumbly, faraway, irrational quality. They growl and lose focus in their eyes and step slightly to the left when they mean to step straight forward.

There aren't as many women, but the ones who came are either drunk themselves or beady-eyed with anger. Their hair is an identical shade of unnatural orange from a bad batch of the supposedly blond hair dye that's the only color the shop in town carries, and no wonder they're angry: they look like they're on fire. They clutch brooms and sticks and—my stomach catapults to see it—kitchen knives. They're the screaming, open-beaked gull of my Seagull card. Anger. Conflict. Broiling bad will. A storm itching for a fight.

I have to get Anna out of here. The thought is electric across my skin, raising a thousand goose bumps.

I try to make myself small as I ease back toward the door and into the house, slip into our room, and lift Anna—who is too ill to help me—into my arms. Holding her like this is harder than I thought, and I'm afraid I'll drop her. But I can't think of what else to do. I'm certain they've come for her, and I can't think of a single good outcome of our drunk neighbors standing in the rain with kitchen knives clutched in stress-white knuckles.

Liis appears in the doorway, and Kaos hops off the bed to butt her head against Liis's leg.

How can I help? she mouths, all steady urgency, and I tilt my head for her to follow me into the hallway.

"Bring out the child." A man's voice booms from the yard, more terrifying than the thunder.

Mama is clearer—and louder—than usual when she replies, "For what purpose, Maks? You've come to my house in the middle of a storm to demand I bring a sick child into the rain—*for what?*"

"You know that isn't your child, Maarja! It's a bog thing. An omen. If it ever was Anna, it's not anymore." This time the answering voice is feminine, and my heart twists. The men here—well, it's easy to imagine them out of control. We've all seen the fistfights, the drunken brawls, the black eyes like decoration (the one fashion accessory in this town that isn't a hand-me-down). They're unreasonable on the best days, capable of anything. But the women? This is the first time I've thought they might be dangerous too.

This time, Riina answers the mob. "Ulli, be reasonable! This is a lost child returned home. Think about what you're doing!"

"If lost children return from the bog, where are all of ours? Where's Karl, then? Kristel? Eliise?" Ulli's voice is sharp as the knife I imagine clutched in her hand. "We've all lost someone to the bog. If they turn up at all, they turn up *dead*. What's so different about her—unless she's a curse sent here to taunt us, torture us, kill us all?"

The crowd grows louder in response, its thunder building in time with the increasingly urgent pounding of rain on our roof. Imagining them all soaked through and unmoving sends a shiver down my spine.

They're not wrong about one thing: So many families have lost someone to the forest. The school is full of empty desks. The houses full of empty beds. And nobody's gotten someone back. The bog takes; it doesn't give. But the idea that they'd hurt Anna because she's the exception to that rule tightens my throat until I'm barely breathing.

I peek from the hall into the living room, struggling under Anna's limp, unwieldy weight. Our back door is through the kitchen, and I'll have to cross the living room to get there. The front door is still open, though, and anyone looking past Mama will be able to see us. If they try to cut us off around the back, there's no way I can outrun them with Anna in my arms.

I realize I need to find a way to push the door mostly closed, and I turn to tell Liis. To my relief, she has already noticed and is army crawling across the room, low enough that no one can see her through the windows. I want to tell her not to close the door all the way, in case Mama needs to make a quick escape, but I don't need to. Just like when we were little kids, Liis and I are on the same page. She nudges the door until it's cracked, pulls a blanket off a nearby chair and wedges it under the door just enough to keep it from blowing wide open.

I'm so grateful for her, I could cry.

"If she's not a curse, explain the well overflowing!" A voice shouts from the unruly crowd.

"And the sinkhole!"

"My lost horse!"

"The trees burning behind my house!"

"The viper that came into my kitchen!"

Every bad thing that's happened in the village this week comes screaming out of the crowd in succession. Vipers and natural disasters, sick children and marital disputes. Anna is, apparently, responsible for them all.

I struggle across the living room with Anna, bent over as far as I can be and hoping no one notices through the windows. The lights are off inside and the storm is dark outside and the rain is falling harder, hopefully obscuring their view.

Liis is already holding the back door open, motioning me forward with her little arm. Kaos stands beside her, hissing toward the front of the house.

"If she's not a curse, why are the Soviet soldiers hanging around town?" Ulli's voice is back to booming.

The crowd growls agreement. And then I'm out the back door and stumbling through the rain and too far away to hear any distinct words.

Thunder peals, and lightning follows quick behind, lighting up the sky as I struggle around the nearest neighbor's house, out of sight of my own. The relief is almost as cool as the rain.

Then the screaming takes on a new tone, and I catch Liis's eye. My own face must be a mask of terror, because she reaches out to squeeze my shoulder, motions for me to go on, and then darts back toward the house to see what's changed.

I keep stumbling, Anna's body hot even in the now-pouring ice-cold rain. She feels heavier with every step. I didn't have time to get my shoes, and small stones and twigs pinch at the bottoms of my feet.

I'm at the next house, slipping around the side yard, when Liis catches back up to me.

"They're burning it," she says as if she still can't quite believe it. "They're burning the house."

"Mama?" I whisper.

"My mama will take care of her. I promise. It's Anna they want. We have to run."

Fear spikes through me, and Anna's heaviness is no longer a factor. I'm stumbling and then running, barely noticing the burning in my arms.

If they catch us, will they burn Anna too?

I am afraid they will. When people decide you're a monster, they treat you like one.

XIII
SPRINGTIME

I didn't see my house burning, but I can picture it in my mind's eye. Flames reaching from room to room, swallowing the couch, the beds, the books, the pantry. Eventually, the rain will put it out, but not before it eats our life whole.

I wish I could push it from my mind. I imagine myself shoving the thought away. I hold my breath and try to picture something—anything—else. But the thought is still there, just out of sight, and I know the fear is going to haunt me. The ghost of what has happened, could happen, will happen again.

Nowhere is safe now. I feel it in my very marrow. Our house is gone. The village wants us dead. And the bog keeps calling Anna back. With overflowing wells, sinkholes, flickers, and murmurs in the night.

Her body is still heavy in my arms, my every muscle tense and screaming as Liis motions for me to follow her into the bog.

I freeze as the day Anna disappeared flashes before my eyes. One step, two steps, ten steps in—a few short sentences, and Anna was gone. All week she's been pulling back toward it, tugging my hand, whispering those knife-sharp words: *He's watching*.

Soovana. Watching. Is the flicker in the corner of my eye distant lightning, or is it him?

My body is stone, my breathing thin. I can't take her in there again. I can't lose her again. Not after I promised that I would do anything to keep her safe.

"Come on," Liis shouts above the downpour as Kaos zips past her into the trees and disappears.

I stare after the fox, and Liis follows my gaze. "She'll be fine," she yells as lightning illuminates everything around us for half a second. "She's not a pet; she's a wild thing. She knows her own mind, and she'll be back."

She puts her hand on the bark of a nearby tree, and I cringe. She's not afraid. She's never been afraid. But I am. Afraid of what, I don't know. That the bark will reach out and wrap itself around her. That the touch will make the bog angry, as if it's a living thing. It will clear its throat and announce its intentions—to take everyone I've ever loved.

"Come on." Her voice is as loud as it goes, but still barely audible above the hammer of thick raindrops all around us. "We can't stay here."

We. But it's not we. Not Liis who is in danger. It's me. It's Anna. We have to run. We have to hide. And Liis is running with us not because she has to but because she is Liis. Because she keeps showing up when I don't know how to.

Which makes all of this hurt even more.

"I *can't*." I choke the words through a tightening throat. "We can't go in."

"Yes, we can. We have to." Her face is solemn, rain streaming down it from every angle, her normally curly hair plastered to her forehead and cheeks.

"We can go to your house." I want it to sound like a suggestion, but it comes out like I'm begging for my life. Which I suppose I am. But not mine, really. Anna's. I shift her in my arms.

"That's the first place they'll look with my mama standing beside your mama." Liis takes two steps toward me and puts her hand on my shoulder again, like she's anchoring me to her. "We have to hide out until they think we're not there. Until they sober up. This is the safest place, I promise."

Safe? As if the forest could ever be safe. As if going into it with *me* doesn't make it ten times more dangerous.

"We can't stay out here in the rain. It'll just make her sicker," Liis pleads, kissing my temple the way she used to when we were kids. "You can do this. I know you can do this. We won't let Anna out of our sight."

I'm frozen with terror. Terror of what's in front of me and terror of what's behind, like I'm surrounded by a ring of fire. Any way I run, I'm going to get burned. My muscles coil into tight little knots without my permission, and my eyes squeeze shut. Even my toes are curled tightly against the mud. Everything inside me screams to stay put. *Don't cross the tree line. Don't kill your sister.*

"There's shelter and it's not far. I promise. You just have to trust me. Nobody else. Nothing else. Just me. Do you trust me, Vik?" Liis isn't giving up on me, and that's what breaks my trance, unroots me from my fear, and lets me take the first step, then the second.

I'm at the tree line.

I'm through the trees.

And then Liis is reaching for the side of a mossy mound of dirt that comes up to our shoulders and opening a door. A door in the forest, so well hidden my brain didn't recognize it until she'd already pulled it wide. My mind spirals in nameless alarm, and it takes me too long to realize it's a bunker. The government puts them in the strangest places — insurance against an American nuclear attack. Places every important person can hide, scattered across the USSR. I suppose this one is here because of Uncle Silver. They'd want to save someone like him if the Americans attacked. To them, no one else here would be worth saving.

I watch Liis disappear inside and follow her awkwardly in, glad that it's a slanting floor and not a ladder. My arms twitch with the effort of carrying Anna, and I know I wouldn't make it down if I had to do something more than duck and stumble in.

I lower Anna to the floor in the dark, my back and neck protesting with the strain. Liis strikes a match, lights a candle. I wonder if it's a supply left here for someone like my uncle or something Liis has stored for herself. I wonder how often she comes here. And I realize as I wonder that the wondering has replaced the fear. The bog feels unsafe, but this man-made place, dusty and dark with a single candle, somehow doesn't. It wasn't made for us, but it was made for safety. And I guess that's enough for my stretched-out nerves. I feel like I've passed a test. I haven't killed my sister.

Yet.

I have the sudden, horrible thought that my relief has jinxed her, and I rush back to feel her breath and place my hand on her forehead. Her breathing is strong, and the fever is the same as before, and I'm ashamed of my own panic.

"What is this place?" I ask when my heart stops trying to beat its way out of my chest. It's obvious that it's a bunker. What I really mean is how did she find it? What does she use it for? Is someone going to find us here?

She seems to get my meaning. "A bunker — but it's been abandoned for years. Nobody checks on it, so I keep things here. It's a place to come if something bad happens. Like tonight."

"You never told me about it." The moment the words leave my mouth, I know they're ridiculous. Of course she didn't. I wasn't listening. I wasn't *there*.

"I wanted to." Her words have no edge, but they cut me anyway. She hands me a blanket. "It's not a towel, but it's the closest thing I've got here."

"Do I leave her in the wet clothes?" I ask, uncertain, hoping Liis's mama's healing skills have given her the answer.

She purses her lips. "I'd get her out of the wet clothes and wrap her in the dry blanket."

Relieved someone knows what to do, I follow her instructions, wrapping Anna in the blanket like a cocoon, settling myself—still soaked through, now shivering—against the wall, and propping her head on my leg instead of the concrete floor.

Liis drops to the floor beside me, and we sit in silence for a long time, watching the candle's wax soften and liquefy and start to bead at the edges. I try not to think about how close she is, how much I want to tell her everything, how much I *can't*. I try not to think about how if this were five years ago, I'd lean my head on her shoulder. We'd be laughing. This bunker would have been something we'd discovered together. Our hideout, not only hers.

I try not to think about Anna, burning like an ember. I try to pretend I don't know what the angry, drunk mob would have done to her. What they *have* done to my house. I picture it turning to ash, and my stomach flips. Everything I own could be gone now. Clothes. Shoes. The curtains I sewed with the little pieces of lace Mama brought home. The pictures.

Oh, the pictures.

Da. Will we forget what he looked like now? I didn't even know that was something I could lose. His face.

I reach into my pocket and pull out my cards, searching for comfort. And I find it. The edges are damp, but otherwise they seem okay. The relief of it warms me. Anna's body pressed up against me must have kept most of the torrent out of my pocket. One thing I haven't lost. Two things, counting Anna.

"Are you going to do a reading?" Liis asks, her voice shivery.

I shake my head. "They're too damp to shuffle. I think I need to pull them apart and let them dry."

"Here," Liis offers, scooting closer to me. "You go do that on the other side of the candle. The floor here is too wet from us sitting on it. I can sit with Anna."

I'm embarrassed to realize I've started crying, warm tears shocking on my storm-wet face. Everything is so much worse because Liis is nice to me. Because I *want* her to be. Because I miss her like I'd miss a part of my own mind. I don't know why she wants to take care of me—the girl who almost killed her own sister. The safest thing for Liis would be if she hated me. But I also need her not to.

I don't say any of this out loud. I don't know how to. But Liis sees my tears and turns to wrap herself around me in a hug.

"It's going to be okay," she says, even if it won't.

Still, I wrestle back the tears, then scoot out from under Anna's head, careful to hold it up until Liis can scoot herself into my spot and cradle Anna's head on her own leg.

I'm not doing a reading, but it feels like it as I gently pry each card from its fellows, lay them out on the ground to dry. The card with the worst water damage is the one at the back of the deck: Springtime. The art is a kitten on its back, batting at a long-stemmed flower. The meaning: innocence, beginnings, freedom. It is puffy with wet, the art distorted so that the flower is too fat and inky, and I think I might start crying again. Everything is falling apart—my house, my life, my sister, and now my cards. Not gone, but damaged.

How is it that life manages to get worse and worse? I thought losing Anna was the worst that could happen, but now it's like the bog has given her back just to let me lose her—and everything else I love—all over again.

The thought is so physically painful that I don't know how it doesn't strike me dead here and now, like a bolt of lightning or the fire sweeping through my house as we speak.

I turn from the cards. If I keep looking at them, I'll break down completely. Instead, I focus on the room. The concrete walls, dusty floor. The way when Liis closed the door behind us, it shut out even the roar of the rain. Shut out the bog, the village, the danger.

"Thank you," I say as I lower myself to sit cross-legged across from Liis.

"For what?"

"Bringing us here. Coming with us. Knowing there was somewhere safe."

Her smile is a wry one. "'Safe' is an interesting word choice."

The cold knot of fear in my stomach returns, small and hard. "Is it not safe?"

She reaches across the space and squeezes my fingertips, banishing the knot. "Oh, I don't mean it like that. We're safe here. I just spend a lot of time thinking about why."

"Why … what?"

"Well, there's a bunker here precisely because the Soviets don't think we're safe from the Americans. And there's only one, one tiny room, not enough to fit even a dozen families—because they think there are only a few people in this town worth keeping safe."

"Uncle Silver." He's the clear answer, the only one that the party might want to protect. I wonder if that means we'd survive too, if the Americans dropped a bomb. Would Mama and Anna and I live through it—not because we matter to them, but because of our proximity to him?

Liis shrugs. "Or the bosses at the factory, or any high-ranking soldiers who pass through. The only thing for sure is that it's not us. So it's keeping us safe now, but it wasn't made to."

Anna shifts in her sleep, and I press closer, putting the back of my hand against her still-too-warm forehead. I think about the soldiers, the fact that we can't take Anna to a doctor—how even something like a hospital, which should be for everyone, isn't for us either.

"Nothing is for us," I say after a long pause, and the words hurt like picking off a fresh scab. Not the village, where flames are engulfing my house as we speak. Not here, where feverish Anna is wrapped in a blanket on the cold floor. Not hospitals or factories or the shop with barely enough to survive on. Not the bog that keeps calling her back.

"Maybe some things could be." Liis brushes a rogue curl from Anna's sleeping face.

I have the wild thought that if only I could curl up in Liis's lap and let her brush my hair back, the world would somehow right itself. That I'd find one place, one thing, that is for me.

"Like what?"

"Did I tell you about the demonstrations?" Liis's voice does what mine cannot, expanding warm, hopeful, into the space.

I shake my head, return to the wall, and slide down beside Liis and Anna. It's been so long since Liis and I have really talked. More than me blurting out the wrong things over and over again these last few days. She hasn't told me about anything. I've seen her so much more with Anna back, but our conversations have been fleeting. Gratitude at the familiar spark of her voice, the rebel excitement at its edges, warms me, settles some of the panic skittering across my skin.

She goes on. "In April, there was a demonstration in Tartu to celebrate Estonian history and culture—the first one where the police haven't gotten violent."

That's a surprise. Normally any demonstration, any sign that we think of ourselves as *Estonian* rather than Soviet, ends in police violence.

Something hopeful flutters in my chest, and Liis continues. "People brought flags—blue ones, white ones, black ones—and flew them beside each other."

My eyebrows raise at this subtle rebellion. We're forbidden to fly the Estonian flag with its blocky blue, white, and black stripes. But *technically* a single-color flag wouldn't be illegal. *Technically*, you could fly the three colors together as long as they weren't on the same flag. A clever loophole. You weren't really breaking the law, but everyone knew that you meant to. Everyone knew Estonia was in your heart.

"You were there?" I ask.

"No, I heard about it on Radio Free Europe. Mama and I secretly listen together in the evenings sometimes. There's so much nobody tells us about, but it's happening. Uprisings and protests and people who say that it's wrong we can't fly our flag or speak our minds or travel to Finland or Italy or even the coast without permission."

I nod, because it *is* wrong and because I don't have anything to add. I'd heard of the protests, of course. They're too huge not to hear about, growing too fast to ignore. But it's hard to focus on something that feels so big, so far away, when there's so much to worry about right here. Like the threat of American bombs, the hope of a revolution barely touches me here.

Liis pushes her now-drying curls out of her face and continues, her voice shimmering with hope. "Because the police left people alone last year, Mama took me to the September festival. It was even more spectacular. It's so hard to describe, Vik. Ivo Linna was onstage singing patriotic songs, and the police told him we had to leave, so we did—*all three hundred thousand people walked to the festival grounds to keep on singing.* Nobody went home; nobody gave up.

"And then this man sped by on a motorbike with an Estonian flag! Not three flags—*one*. And suddenly there were flags everywhere. It must have been planned, flags stashed under shirts or in handbags until the right moment."

She sighs in awe, like she's forgotten where we are, forgotten the cold and the hard concrete floor, forgotten everything except those flags popping up around the festival grounds. "I've never seen so many happy people in my life. Everyone was so *hopeful*."

I can picture them: hundreds of thousands of people singing, the man with the flag. The wild recklessness of being ourselves when we're not supposed to be. Where would Anna be if we lived in the world the protestors want? At the hospital, probably. Safer, maybe. Or perhaps the world would have been so different that she never would have disappeared at all.

Liis sings a few lines of our unofficial national anthem, the one we're not supposed to sing but everyone knows anyway. *"Mu Isamaa On Minu Arm"*—"My Fatherland Is My Love."

The song is a comfort, a memory of Mama's nighttime lullabies whispered across the years. Even a vague memory of Da, his voice a low baritone.

My body untenses, and I lean more heavily against the wall. Liis nudges me and grins. "There's another protest next week. They're calling it the Baltic Way. The plan is to create a human chain across three countries—Estonia, Latvia, and Lithuania. Three countries who want to be free."

"Why?" I whisper.

"To tell the Soviets we stand together, and there are too many of us for them to stop. To tell the world they can't ignore us."

"To tell the world that we matter." I test the words.

"To tell them Estonia is *for us*." She laces her fingers through mine.

I don't know how long we're in the bunker, drifting between sleep and conversation, but eventually Liis cracks the door and says the storm has stopped. We wait another hour—or two or five; it's hard to tell—and when Liis is convinced that we're well into morning and it's safe to go back to her house, I gather up my now-dry cards, double-checking to make sure I didn't miss any. I wrap my arms around Anna in her feverish blanket cocoon and—tense and sore and feeling watched—step from the stale air of the bunker into the earthy, wet-leaf smell of forest after rain.

Liis is a few steps ahead, face pointed resolutely toward the village, when my foot slips on something loose that feels like a rain-slick fallen branch and I almost drop Anna. I just manage to keep myself upright.

"Vik?" Liis calls over her shoulder, concerned.

But I'm no longer paying attention. I've turned to see what tripped me—and my heart freezes in place, like the whisk of a wave in the dead of winter, when the edges of the sea turn to ice all at once. The hope of the bunker disappears into the reality of the forest. The reminder that *this place is not safe*.

The thing I tripped over is a skull.

Not just a skull. My mind stumbles over the not-quite-rightness of it. It's the shape of a skull, yes. But it's not simply one skull. It's a dozen of them, more than a dozen. The bleached-white bones of a dozen little animals. Rabbits or squirrels, bats or birds, rats or moles. They've been arranged in the shape of one large skull. One *human* skull.

Its jaw aims menacingly toward the bunker door. Facing us, watching us.

Is it a warning? A sign? Arranged for us—to scare us, show us, expel us from this place where we should never have been—and by what…or who? Or was it here all along, meant for someone else, meant for everyone, never about us at all?

Liis sucks in a sharp breath behind me, and I know she's seen it too.

He's watching.

Anna's words echo back to me even as she is too delirious now to repeat them.

My eye twitches, my throat so small it's a wonder I'm still breathing. I can feel those eyes, and I suddenly understand why Anna ripped every drawer from the kitchen cabinets, every cushion off the couch.

It's terrible to know you are being watched. If I thought I could find Soovana's eyes—force him to look away—I'd tear apart every house in the village. Every skull on this storm-drenched ground.

Kaos slinks into the center of the skulls, grabbing what looks like a former bird in her jaws and crunching it to pieces. There's something sacrilegious in it, and I want to scream. Because I'm suddenly convinced that if we touch the bones, something terrible will happen. Something even more terrible than all the terrible things that already have.

My arms burn from holding Anna, and my throat burns as I try not to be sick. "We have to get out of here."

"Let's go." Liis turns and leads me through the slice of forest that just last night allowed us our escape but now feels like it's full of eyes, mouths, malice. Knives at the ready around every corner.

I barely breathe until we are out, dragging tired feet along dusty path instead of leaf-soft forest floor. My heart only restarts when we open her front door and then close it behind us. Safe.

For now.

Liis's house is just as I remember. I will my heartbeat to return to normal as I step inside. Most of the village houses feel the same. We have the same couches, the same tables, the same chairs, the same hand-me-down cookware. Sometimes the village shop is lucky enough to get a shipment of pretty teapots or blankets in a new design, but you have to know someone to score one of those, so they're rare unless you're from an important family. Our individuality is in the details: Margit's collection of plastic bags with foreign logos, washed with care and used as handbags; Anna's collection of empty, cleaned plastic yogurt containers that she used to play tea party with; Da's hand-carved figurines; Mama's hand-drawn sheet music; my oracle cards.

The memories scrape at me. Da's figurines. Mama's music.

Was Mama able to save any of it? I step deeper into the house, try to push the thoughts away. Focus.

Liis's house—Liis's house has always been different. The couch is the same model we all have, but the cushions have been resewn with a patchwork of old fabrics, each patch representing a different rescued animal's failed attempt to make the couch into a meal. We used to name the fabrics after the animals: Ilu green, Metsik floral. I wonder if the faded pink patch on the right is Kaos pink.

The TV is on in the living room, the camera zoomed in on someone eating a steak, its meat rich and red inside. The propaganda channels don't have anything like this, so it must be Finnish TV. No one is supposed to have it, but when people realized the signal travels across the Baltic Sea if you have a good enough antenna, better antennas started showing up at any home that could afford them. The big debate in school is whether the things in the shows and commercials are real. The greens are too green, the reds too red, the shampoos too foamy, the clothes too colorful. Most think they must all be plastic decorations, costumes, food painted to make your mouth water. Real food, after all, is mostly brown.

Liis's kitchen is a jungle of dried and drying herbs hanging from strings across the ceiling. The shelves are lined with jars full of the usual—preserved jams, dried berries—and the wildly unusual—alcohol-soaked vipers, healing concoctions gathered from the bog, something that looks suspiciously like hair. Funny how in the bog the berries feel like danger, but here they feel like home.

Liis's room is the best, of course, every wall painted with elaborate nature murals. Assassin plants and rare flowers. Moss-covered stones and the trees we used to look for our fake wands underneath. There are new additions to the art since the last time I was here so many years ago: a pile of baby foxes under a tree, the faint shadow of a girl behind a boulder, playing hide-and-seek. Another evolution of Liis that I missed. It's a little like my cards, all forests and animals and the shadows of girls. Beautiful and dangerous, empowering and uncontrollable.

Kaos is curled in the corner on a bed of fabric scraps and old clothes that will someday, I assume, become part of the couch.

Liis's room is where Mama and Riina settle Anna under a blanket, in a set of Liis's old clothes, her feet wrapped again in vodka socks. Mama is crying without a sound as she plays with Anna's curls.

Liis stands in the doorway with Riina's arms around her shoulders. She presses her face to Liis's hair and murmurs, "I'm proud of you," before kissing the top of her head.

My heart wrenches and I look away. What must it be like to be someone a mother can be proud of? What must it be like not to be cursed? For the second time in twenty-four hours, I wonder how I'm still alive when all I can feel is pain.

XIV
ECLIPSE

"If we knew what happened to her, maybe we could save her." Riina's voice is low, the despair as drenching as yesterday's rainstorm.

I was asleep, and now I'm wide awake. *Anna.* Riina is talking about Anna. My hand is on her back, and I'm curled around her like a cat protecting kittens. She breathes in, *one-two-three*, out, *one-two-three.*

Mama's voice is low too, coming from just above us where we've fallen asleep on Liis's bed. "There has to be something else we can try."

I keep my eyes closed, will my breathing to stay steady. They wouldn't be talking like this if they knew I was awake.

"Maarja, she won't last another week like this. She's gone from bad to worse so fast...you have to take her to the hospital."

"You know I can't. The soldiers will know..."

"If she gets any worse, you'll have to risk it. Can't Silver call the soldiers off?"

I open my eyes the barest sliver. Riina has her arm around Mama, and Mama has her chin tucked up on Riina's shoulder, murmuring into Riina's neck.

127

"He said they're right—we can't take her. It'd be worse for all of us. They'd cart her off to an asylum or do experiments on her…" The sentence ends as if her fear has bitten it off abruptly.

"We're going to wake the girls. Let's go talk in the other room."

I close my eyes fully—and almost jump into the air when I feel Mama's hand warm on my shoulder, her lips light on my cheek.

The two of them shuffle off, but I lie there a long time with my eyes closed, trying not to cry. Mama kissed me. It's been years since she's done that. Now that Anna's back, has she forgiven me? Even with Anna delirious and hot as an ember?

I push the thoughts away. This isn't the time to think about me. Anna isn't getting better. Even Riina is worried. I count my breaths and keep my eyes closed, as if pretending to be asleep could make this all a dream. I try to picture waking up to find that everything is fine. Anna is well again. Anna speaks Estonian. Anna can tell us what happened.

Instead, a sinister part of my heart whispers, *Or you'll wake up and she'll be dead.* Because Anna was right to ask me if she was dying. She is. And we can't take her to the hospital.

She killed her sister. I can hear the words in my mind as clear as if Mama said them aloud again. It's my fault. It's always been my fault.

I wrap my fingers around Anna's tiny, fragile ones and open my eyes. What was it Riina said? *If we knew what happened, maybe we could save her.* I turn the words over in my mind, examine them from every angle. Anna needs to be saved. If I want to save her, we have to know what happened. And if Anna can't tell us, only the bog can.

Only *Soovana* can.

He's been hovering at the edge of my mind since she disappeared. The only explanation that makes sense. A flickering lightning bug set of lantern eyes in the distance, coaxing my little sister into the bog. And then doing—what?

That is what I need to know.

What has he done, and can he undo it?

The logic is somehow calming. The truth of what I have to do is clear, and it smooths me out, straightening the corners of my fear, replacing panic with purpose. Anna has been trying to pull me in since she got here. And if that's what Soovana wants, that's what I'll do. There's nothing else left to try.

"Anna," I whisper into her hair. "Anna, I'm not going to let you die. I promise."

I say it as if the words are a prayer, as if I can infuse them with magic if I say them with enough conviction. But I also mean it in a way that isn't *just* a prayer. Because if the answer is to find out what happened, that's what I'll do. Not hope and wish and curl myself around my dying sister.

I'm going into the bog again.

And this time I won't come back until I have answers.

I wait until the hall light flickers off; then I wait some more. If Mama or Riina catch me, they'll stop me, and I cannot risk that. *In, one-two-three, out, one-two-three.* Anna breathes and I breathe with her. Every breath a promise.

When I think enough time has passed, I unwrap myself from Anna and slip from bed, bare feet whispering across the wooden floor. I pad into Riina's room, where she and Mama have fallen asleep with their arms around each other. Mama's forehead is against Riina's lips, as if Riina fell asleep halfway through kissing it. My heart stretches toward them. What would it be like to fall asleep with Mama kissing my forehead or with my arms around Liis? What would it feel like to let someone who mattered that close now?

Both their chests rise and fall in the low light. I watch the rhythm of it for a few minutes, counting, letting my own breathing match up with Mama's.

I'm going to save Anna, I wish I could tell her. *I'm going to save you.*

I tiptoe back into Liis's bedroom, where Anna's still asleep, twitching with fever dreams. I press my lips to Anna's forehead like Riina did to my mother's. I hope she knows through the fever how very loved she is.

I reach into my pocket and slip a card out from the middle of the deck. The Eclipse—the barest circle of sun hinting around the edges of an inky-black orb, ferns indistinct in shadow below. The card means abandonment, and I suppose that's appropriate. I *am* leaving. But I'm not leaving to abandon Anna; I'm leaving to save her. I hope that distinction matters.

I steal around the room like a thief—which I suppose I am now, because I'm taking Liis's things. All of mine are destroyed—burned to ash or drowned in rain. So I slip on Liis's canvas summer shoes, tuck her flashlight into the waistband of my pants. There's something comforting about it, taking a piece of Liis with me even though I plan to sneak past her into the night.

My stomach pangs at the thought. I'm leaving her *again*. Always, ever leaving her behind. But what else can I do? I can't be the one who killed Anna, and I can't be the one who loses Liis. She's safer here than she'd be with me—no matter how much my selfish heart wants her to lead me into the trees again, wants to borrow my courage from hers.

There's a slice of brown bread beside the bed. Mama brought it earlier when I refused to leave Anna over dinner. I eat a few bites in an attempt to shore up my courage, even though I'm not hungry.

I slip into the living room as quietly as I can, not sure if I want to laugh or cry at the sight of Liis and Kaos on the couch. Liis with her mouth open in sleep and Kaos somehow tucked up into a ball beside her head. Kaos is pretending to be smaller than she is, spilling her back legs and tail over onto Liis's shoulder.

I'm halfway across the room when Kaos screeches at me and I freeze, waving a hand at her as if she's a human who understands that I mean she should be quiet. Instead, she makes an agitated hissing sound, like how dare I disturb her sleep? Liis bolts upright on the couch, staring straight at me.

"What are you doing?" she asks too loudly.

I wave my hand again, frantic, and whisper, "Don't wake them."

She glances toward the hall, then back at me, taking me in. "You're going into the bog."

It's more statement than question, but I nod anyway.

"All right. Let me get my shoes." She stands.

My heart drops into my stomach like a stone. "No, Liis. You can't come."

"Yes, I can, and yes, I am."

No, she can't. My mind flails for an explanation, a way to keep her here. "I need to do this on my own."

"That's the most foolish thing I've ever heard. Give me a good reason, or I'm getting my boots." She crosses her arms.

"Someone has to take care of Anna."

"My mom. Next."

"You won't be safe with me."

"Pshhh." Her huff reminds me of Kaos's irritated hiss. "I go into the trees almost every day. Don't act like you know more about the bog than I do."

Kaos hisses at us both again, and the scowl on Liis's face moves toward mirth.

"We're disturbing the queen's beauty sleep," she whispers.

I crack a grin of my own, but I can't let the distraction change things. Liis *can't* come with me. I can't be responsible for her. I can't be accountable to her. I know in my bones and teeth and the pit of my stomach that she cannot come. That if I face Soovana, I face him alone.

"Please stay," I try. This time my voice cracks. I stop trying to make her understand why. *I* don't understand why—not really.

She purses her lips, tightens her eyes. "That's how it is, then? Again?"

I don't know how to answer that, but I think it means she's going to let me go. Something loosens inside me at the thought, and I know I must be right. What I'm doing must be right.

I turn toward the door, but then turn back once more.

"Don't tell," I whisper, the words somewhere between command and question.

Liis, who's never been as good as I am at hiding her emotions, looks extravagantly insulted. "I would never break our pact."

My chest catches. *Our pact.* The promises so simple, so impossible: Always share our secrets. Never tell each other's. And never leave each other behind.

The first two are important in a Soviet country. We all have stories of grandparents or even parents carted off by the Soviets because a neighbor, a friend, even a family member reported them for some infraction—real, imagined, or fabricated. Liis's grandfather was taken for joking that the great Soviet Empire couldn't make a good sausage. A boy in our class lost his father to a rumor about banned American books.

133

I know because when we weren't in the bog as kids, Liis and I were spying on the adults. Under the floorboards, cramped into vents. We heard things, knew things.

In theory, people don't report like that anymore. We're free to speak our minds now. Though the soldiers at my house are a reminder that freedom has limits. The party is still listening. And we all still feel those reports in our blood. Trusting someone with a secret is a dangerous, subversive, sacred thing.

The kind of thing that entrenched our closeness as children. The kind of thing that led to pacts sealed with crushed cranberries, a nod, a promise to Soovana.

And then there's the third promise. *Never leave each other behind.* The rule I broke the day I ran back into the bog for Anna without Liis—and every time I left her behind in the five years since.

I broke the pact. I broke it over and over. But Liis never has. She's never left me behind. She's never told my secrets. And me asking her not to now feels like an insult.

I open my mouth. I should apologize, tell her to come with me. But the thought still twists my gut, so I only do half.

"I'm sorry," I whisper.

The look on her face tells me that my apology is not accepted. I've broken the pact one too many times. When I slip out the door and into the night, it cuts the last fragile thread of friendship between us.

XV
THE HEALER

I used to think of the bog as the Healer from my oracle deck—a card whose meaning is infused with femininity, beauty, the magic of nature. But now I think of her as every dangerous card combined. She's the Devil and Storm and Fire and Ice. She's unwelcome surprises and sudden endings, loss and heartbreak that hollow you out. She's darkness and shadows and hidden things that howl in the night.

I face her now, and the trees stare back. Clumps of dirt topped with moss jut from the ground like a giant is buried here and reaching upward. Like if you stepped into the circle, a hand would burst from the mud, wrap around you, and drag you down.

My body doesn't want to do this.

I know because it feels so heavy, so sick. The few bites of thick brown bread I forced down before leaving were a mistake. My stomach still screams at me an hour later, like I've given it shards of glass instead of food.

I almost laugh. *I just did this*—followed Liis into the bog. I stepped in and stepped again. We all came back out. It's fine. I'm fine. Anna and Liis and Kaos are fine. The first steps shouldn't be so hard.

But they are.

And it doesn't matter how hard they are. I have to take them. I have to save her. And if I can't save her, then I guess I'll join her—be swallowed up by whatever monster snatches through the birches and boulders at girls who dare wander too far.

I click the flashlight on and force myself to move. One step, two steps, three and four. Breathe in, breathe out. Past the wizard tree's judgmental glare, around the giant's hands, over a patch of mud so black in the dim light that it looks like I'm standing on a dark night sky.

It takes a long time for my heart to stop pounding in my ears, for me to regain my senses and remember that I'm not just walking into the forest—I'm looking for answers. Looking for magic.

Looking for Soovana.

A flicker of his lantern in the night. The hovering mist that's said to hide his passing. A cluster of cranberries that might be the ones he wears in his hair, like the ones in Anna's pockets, the ones we offered up to him as children. Anything unusual here might be a sign of him. A hunched birch, twisted pine. They say he blends so well into the landscape that human eyes rarely perceive him. Unless he's flickering his eyes to lure you deeper in.

I walk slower, sweep the flashlight beam over the ground and the trees and the mounds of dirt that come up to my knees or elbows or even armpits. I think of Liis's bunker and run my hands along the sides of the mounds, checking for handles, gaps, anything that might indicate a door. Perhaps it isn't just bunkers hidden in the mounds. There are plenty of stories of spirits and witches underground.

If Liis were here, would she know what to look for? The question pulls across my skin, tugs at my center. As if the thread of our friendship is still there, like the aspen trees, connected even when we're far apart.

I wish she were here. Then I hate myself for wishing.

A branch cracks behind me—the sound like a gunshot that sends the murmurs of night creatures into an uneasy silence—and I whip around, sweeping my flashlight through the trees.

Nothing.

A deer or a fox, maybe. I hope it's not a wild pig or worse—a lynx, a bear, a territorial moose. When I was a kid, I would have found all those prospects thrilling. To see a moose with my own two eyes would have taken my breath away. Now the thought makes my stomach swoop as if I've missed a step. Any one of those animals could kill me like it was nothing.

My flashlight stutters, goes out.

I suck in my breath. And it hits me now how foolish I've been. I'm alone in the forest with only a useless flashlight and a small canteen of water. I didn't bring anything that could serve as a weapon against an angry moose or a hungry wolf. I didn't bring food in case I'm stuck here for days on end.

What was I thinking? That the animals would leave me alone and the only danger was whatever took Anna? That I could fight it off with nothing, without even knowing what it is? That having the courage to go farther in would somehow force the trees to answer my questions, force the giant to climb from the dirt, force the mysteries to reveal themselves? As if the bravery to take a few steps was all it took to solve a mystery, unearth a spirit, conjure Soovana. I don't have any answers for myself, and I feel sick with my own failures—to save Anna the first time, to save her again now.

Another crack rings through the night. *Please, don't let it be a moose.*

I swing the dead flashlight again, and it stutters back to life. Unreliable, but not yet fully broken. Nothing appears in the flickering beam.

My face grows sticky with unwanted tears as I continue on. The trees thin as I press deeper in, toward the true bog, which is mostly low shrubs and peat moss, blue pools and stunted, gnarled trees standing sentry beside them. The forest I'm in forms a ring around the bog, where few things grow and fewer things thrive because of the acidic water and the lack of nutrients in the earth.

The plants there are smaller, fewer. Twisted, prickly, hardy things determined to survive no matter what.

As I step slowly toward them, it's like the world is shrinking. Trees shorter and shorter, more and more twisted. The sounds of night creatures nearer to the ground.

The moon is bright enough to see by without my flashlight as the trees thin and block out less light, so I switch it off to save whatever's left of its power.

Focus, I hum inside my head. *Focus on Anna. Anna, Anna, Anna.* Anna who used to love dancing whenever Mama sang. Anna who thought pickles looked like snakes and tried to pet them instead of eating them. Anna who needs me now if I ever want her back for real.

Another crack—this time far to the right—followed by a grunt.

Animal or spirit? The sound is unnatural, a growl but not a growl.

I wipe my sweaty palms on the front of my skirt and switch the flashlight back on, sweeping it toward the noise.

A pair of eyes flash in the beam—high off the ground, taller than me.

I drop the flashlight. *Heaven help me.* I fall to my knees and grab it, my thoughts racing, trying to place what I've just seen.

Tall and brown and white and twisted. Horns or antlers or branches. Too tall for a wolf or a wild pig. The wrong shape for a bear.

Soovana, my heart whispers. He can appear as a tree, a man, a twisted moose-like thing. Eyes shining in the night. Antlers or branches reaching around him like a crown.

Have I conjured him by coming? Was Anna right that he was watching all this time? Ready to meet me when I dared step past those first trees?

My throat is tight, and my breaths burn. Every muscle stands at attention.

I fumble the flashlight and point it wildly toward the eyes, straightening to my full height.

What did you do to my sister? I form the words in my head, but they never make it past my teeth.

Because this is no Soovana. No twisted tree. No manlike figure.

This is a moose.

A real moose.

Twice the size of a horse, twice the weight too. Antlers spread as wide as I am tall. It could crush me with a single step, destroy me with a sweep of its head. Moose don't bother you until you bother them. But I have dared to shine my flashlight in its eyes—several times.

And after it growl-grunts again in that inhuman way, it charges.

Laughter rises involuntarily in my throat. Being trampled by a moose and bleeding out between the trees is not the end that I imagined for this story.

She killed her sister—and herself.

At least I didn't kill Liis.

I tighten my hands around the flashlight, ready to bludgeon the charging wall of moose, to go down swinging. Where I've been sick and terrified this whole time, now everything is clear, everything is calm. My vision narrows on the animal. My knees bend of their own accord. I brace for impact.

And then—out of nowhere—another animal flashes out of the

forest behind me and crashes toward the moose. Reddish fur and white-tipped paws. A flash of white teeth in the moonlight.

It's a fox. A *one-eyed* fox, her mouth open and hackles raised.

Kaos has come to save me.

Liis. Here even when she isn't here. Saving me even when she cannot save me.

The moose's scream is an unearthly thing. The primal rage of an animal surprised. Its voice goes higher, shivers through my bones.

Kaos stops between me and the moose and screams a warning—*kak-kak-kak* like an angry bird—and then darts away toward the bog. If redirecting the moose's charge was her goal, it succeeds. The moose forgets me entirely, its attention locking on the place where Kaos vanished into underbrush as I step slowly, oh so slowly, back and back again. Away from the agitated animal and its echoing cries.

I keep going until I hear the moose moving in the opposite direction, its alarmed cries quieting. Another shuffle of noise comes from my left, but I don't even have time to stay scared. It's Kaos again, returned to scold me with a *kak-kak-kak* and an open mouth.

"Kaos." I sigh the word and drop to my knees again in relief, pressing my hands to the cold dirt, tipping my face toward my furry rescuer. "How did you find me?"

When the answer comes, I startle so hard that I fall backward.

"I brought her."

XVI
RAVEN

Liis!" My heart is in my throat as I turn to face her. I have the unreasonable thought that I conjured her with my longing. Liis in danger—my fault yet again.

"Wh-what are you doing here?" I stutter out the words.

"You never gave me a good reason not to come."

Kaos sidles up to us and head butts Liis's leg. Liis reaches down to scratch her ears, then shifts her backpack as she straightens up.

"So, you followed me?" I try to piece it together, and I wonder how foolish I sound, trying to catch up.

"Yeah, you dope. You can't go wandering around the bog without backup—as you have now proved." She gestures to where the moose was and makes an I-told-you-so face.

"No, I'm fine." My shaky voice is unconvincing, and I know it. "You should go back."

"That's ungrateful." Irritation overtakes her half-joking tone.

"What? No. I just don't want you to get hurt."

"I'm not the one in danger here."

"Don't be foolish. You know as well as I do that everyone's in danger in this bog. Twenty people have disappeared or died in eight years. That's not exactly the hallmark of a safe place."

"Look, I come into the bog almost every day—"

I cut her off. "Not this far, you don't."

She shrugs in a way that lets me know she's angry and trying to stay calm. "At least I know the bog a little bit. You don't know it at all."

"It's dangerous!"

"Of course it is! But not in the ways you think. It's dangerous if you don't know it, don't respect it! *I* know it."

"You can't know it! It's unknowable! It's Soovana's! It doesn't belong to us!" My voice is desperate. My feelings are tangled. I want to hug her, and I want to scream at her, and I want her to not hate me, and I want her to hate me so much that she leaves.

"It *does* belong to us. It's not either-or, Vik. It belongs to the spirits and our ancestors and the old stories and the old rituals. *All of those belong to us.* The spirits and the mysteries, the stories and the truths. The bog is mystery, and it is danger, and it is *life*. You know how many people would have died without the herbs in here? Without the berries, the food? You've turned it into your personal boogeyman, but it's more than that. You're right that it's dangerous. It's just not dangerous in the ways you think it is. And you marching in here *alone* is going to get you killed—not because of Soovana but because of your own stubbornness!"

I open my mouth to reply, but Liis cuts me off. "It was a moose this time—but it could have been a bear or a lynx! What happens when you walk into a bear den or step in a sinkhole like that horse? What would you have done if Kaos hadn't been here?

I love you, you fool. I'm not trying to talk you out of this, if that's what you're worried about. I just want to help."

"So you're mad because you think I'm in danger?"

"I'm mad because you left me behind—again! I'm mad because I love you."

How can she still love me, after all this? I can't fight with her anymore, and I can't explain, and it's clear she won't leave. The dread tugs at me, and I sound defeated when I answer, my words a mere whisper. "You don't get it."

Liis's voice stays confident, her eyes on my face even as I turn it toward the ground. I can feel her gaze, feel the certainty like heat pulsing off her skin. "That's what I'm telling you. It *doesn't matter* if I get it. I'm here."

Where I felt only dread moments ago, now I feel too many things to count. Some of them are terrifying—the scratch of the unknown, the sense of doom, the sensation of a belly full of glass.

But one of those feelings is not terrifying at all. It's a splash of cool water in a heat wave. It's air finally filling your lungs when you realize you've been holding your breath. It's the feeling of being loved.

Relief.

It's a sense of relief.

When I was little, I assigned everyone I knew to a card in my deck. Uncle Silver is Ivy—ambition in its purest form, creeping undeterred up walls and through tiny cracks. Riina is the

Lynx—keeper of sacred knowledge. Mama is the Lovers—a card in my deck that would shock most Estonians because it is two women kissing in a grove and here that's illegal. It's a card I'd remove from the deck if I were doing readings for strangers. A card that marks me—and perhaps marks Mama, who gave it to me—as an outsider. Other. Because the card doesn't shock me; it comforts me. It's softness and enchantment and secrets, but the beautiful kind.

I think of Mama when I see the card because one of the women reminds me of her. Something about her cheekbones, something about the way she holds herself. The card is tenderness and grace in the same way Mama used to be.

And Liis…Liis is the Raven, a card that's all confidence and determination. In my deck, it even looks like her, a woman with a raven perched on her hand—wild hair, dark eyes, wide stance. She's courage personified against a backdrop of birch trees. And I realize that relief comes hand in hand with hope. Because if anyone can save my sister, perhaps it's Liis.

"So, where do we go from here?" Liis squats in the dirt, absently stroking Kaos's head. Kaos turns her head to direct the scratching.

"I don't know." My shoulders tense as I say it. This is why I didn't want her here. I don't have answers. I'm groping in the dark for them.

"Well, what were you looking for before you ran into the moose?"

"I—" I pause, hesitation bunching up inside me. I search for the reason why and find too many: Will Liis believe me that Soovana is the culprit? Do I sound foolish for saying it aloud? Worse, there's a dark certainty here that saying it aloud will make it real. Will bring his wrath down on our heads.

I can feel the boulders watching, the trees straining to hear.

I swallow, force the words through sand-dry throat. "I'm looking for Soovana."

It sounds even more ridiculous when I say it out loud, and I wonder if it's possible for a person to hate themselves more than I do right now.

Liis doesn't react, though. She nods as if that answer is at all adequate, then stands to face me. Kaos gives her a look of betrayal at the abrupt end to the ear scratches, but then loses interest and goes to investigate the roots of a tree where they jut above the earth.

"So, is that what you think happened? Soovana took her?" Liis asks.

I've thought about so many scenarios—witchcraft and trickster spirits and portals and Americans kidnapping her—but yes, this is the one my heart believes. The one it always believed. "I don't know," I hedge. "I don't know what disappears a girl, freezes her in time, and then spits her back out having forgotten her language, her house, her life."

Liis shakes her head. "Me neither."

"The only explanation that seems remotely possible is magic. Spirits. I can't think of a non-magical explanation. Can you?"

Liis shrugs. "Magic is just shorthand for 'things we don't yet understand.' And since there's nothing we understand that could possibly do this, seems fair to call it magic."

"Is that something your mama says?" I ask, because it sounds like a lecture Riina would have given us at nine or ten while we gathered berries at the edge of the forest.

"Yeah." She smiles.

Then we both pause for a long time. Me because thinking about her mama makes mine seem even more distant, and both of us because if it is magic, I still have no idea where to start and I imagine she doesn't either.

"Why Soovana?" she finally asks.

I bite my lip. The real reason is too flimsy. I think it's Soovana because of some cold certainty deep in my gut. Not rational. Not explainable. Saying that out loud would make me feel exposed in a way I can't quite put my finger on. So instead I list the supporting evidence I didn't even realize I was keeping tally of. "She arrived with cranberries in her pockets. She says he's watching her. Watching us. He's the trickster, known for leading people astray. What other spirit or magic does that? None that I've heard of."

Liis takes it all in, then adds, "And he was Anna's favorite. Her favorite story. I remember you telling me."

Something about her remembering that detail makes me want to cry.

Liis goes on. "If she saw Soovana, she would have followed. She would have gone after him."

I do start crying, then. Because it's true and because Liis remembered and because yet again it's my fault. I didn't warn Anna against Soovana; I worshiped him. I told his stories in reverent tones. I didn't tell her to be afraid.

Liis breaks through the thorn-sharp thoughts. "I think we need to visit the sacred oak grove."

"Oh?" I sniff back the tears, try to steady myself.

"If the old spirits are magic, that's where the magic lives. It's near the asylum. Mama takes me there sometimes to pay our respects to the bog, the trees, the plants that keep us alive. People used to pray there a lot, she says. Before the Christians came, then the Nazis, then the Soviets. If we're looking for magic, that's where we should start."

I nod and motion for her to lead on, but before she does, she cracks a smile. "What would you do without me, Vik?"

I'm not sure if I want to laugh or cry as I answer, "Get gored by moose and miss out on the most sacred place in the whole bog, apparently."

The unspoken part, what I'd do without Liis, is what I've done for the last five years: wander in the dark, waiting for the impossible, so alone I could barely breathe.

XVII
THE BAT

The way to the grove is marked by a faded blue comb nailed to a tree just above our eyeline. We stare at it, cocking our heads. Is it an offering for the bog? A signpost to the grove? Proof that someone else was once brave enough to come in this far?

Or, more sinister, breadcrumbs marking the way out—a warning screaming *run, run, run*?

I have the urge to touch it for good luck, then the sudden thought that if I don't, Anna will die. I wait until Liis starts walking again, and then I reach out to tap it. I still don't feel right, so I tap again. Twice. Three times. I start to feel panicked—to burn with shame—because I know this is me being a weirdo again. Any minute Liis is going to turn around and see me and think I'm losing my grip.

I am, but I don't want her to know that.

I used to think everyone had thoughts like these—the sudden realization that if you don't do something, something terrible will happen—until I told Margit about them a couple of years ago. She looked at me like I was a viper curled up in the pantry, a spider in the oats. I tried to explain that if I didn't turn the tap off right, Anna would never come home. But when I said it out loud, it made so much less sense than in my head. And the look on Margit's face told me just how ashamed of myself I should be. I never want anyone to look at me like that again.

I tap the comb again, willing the tightness building in my chest to uncoil. AURGHHH, why can't I be normal? I reach up and press my whole hand against it, try to slow my breathing, counting one-two-three, one-two-three. This feels better. This feels like it'll work: banish the bad luck, protect Anna.

The tightness uncoils just a little, and I start walking again as Liis turns back and gives me a confused look. "You okay? Did you see something?"

I shake my head. "No, it was nothing."

Thank heavens she didn't see me. What would she have thought?

I walk fast to catch up, and it doesn't take much longer for us to reach the grove—a raised hill with a circle of oak trees tangling into the sky, their roots tumbling over one another into the empty center.

Liis spits on the ground and drops to a seat in the center of the trees as Kaos circles them suspiciously, sniffing at each trunk and then digging randomly at one. I start to join Liis, but she stops me with a raised hand and wide eyes.

"Spit first," she says. "It's protection against the spirits that would want to lead you astray."

I forgot about that one, another protective spell gifted to us by Riina when we were little. My stomach turns with the thought that perhaps that's where I went wrong: I didn't spit on the day I sat on the forest floor to read Anna's cards.

I spit now, then lower myself to the earth. Then, at the same time, we both push our hands into the dirt, curling fingers around dead leaves and gritty earth still damp from the drenching rainstorm of the night my house burned.

My heart reaches toward Liis so hard that I'm surprised it doesn't leap from my chest. This is how we became friends—by digging in the dirt until our fingernails were black, stuffing wild blueberries into our mouths instead of the bucket Riina sent us out with, worshiping the deadly dewdrops of the assassin plant and the silk-soft petals of wildflowers and the wonder of the plants that can give you headaches and visions. We were wild things, bog children, curious and wide-eyed and best friends the moment we laid eyes on each other. Two explorers who knew each other on sight.

The other kids didn't understand. All we wanted was papery birch bark against our cheeks and rescued baby birds drinking sugar water from our fingers. All they wanted was to make fun of us—for our dirt-stained skirts, for Liis's arm, for my tics, and for both our weirdo mothers.

Best friends. Only friends. I miss her like I miss myself. Like I miss that feeling I had, before Anna left, that anything was possible. Everything was magical. Someday we'd find a way to be free. It's the feeling that started to flutter in my chest again when Liis talked about three hundred thousand people singing Estonian songs in unison, flying illegal flags.

My longing is so thick you could cut it with a knife. It smells like springtime rains and soft beds of pine needles and the mud you can't quite get out from under your fingernails. It tastes like secret patches of wild strawberries and herbal tea we gathered with our own hands. It takes my breath away.

If this grove were an oracle card, it'd be the Bat—a visionary place. When I first got the cards, I asked Mama why a bat when bats are color-blind. She told me they see more than we think and sense even more than that. Watch them fly and see how they never ever collide, even as they come so close to their fellows.

This grove feels like that. A place that knows things outside my own vision. If just sitting here could take me so vividly back in time, what will it do when we ask for its magic? Hope sputters to life in my chest like a wild thing ready to take flight: bat or songbird or dragonfly, iridescent, fragile, alive.

"We're not the only ones who come this far." Liis's voice is as magical as the grove itself, a sound like running water.

She turns to me and motions with her little arm toward a cluster of things at the base of a tree to our left. She's right; they're offerings. The remnants of fruit, a hair ribbon, a small glass jar, a figurine like Da used to carve. Something smells antiseptic, and I wonder if someone poured out vodka as an offering too. I wonder how many people brave a small slice of forest to get here, to pay their respects, to ask the bog not to take their own—or to give them back.

"What now?" I ask.

"A ritual, I think," Liis answers. "Perhaps you could do a

reading for the grove? Maybe the magic will amplify the reading? Or maybe like calls to like?"

It's as good a suggestion as any. I pull my cards from my pocket, shuffling until it feels right, the *thwap* of the cards calming me.

I'd normally spread the cards in front of us before choosing, but the earth is still damp, so I fan them toward Liis in my hands instead.

"Ask a question," I instruct. "Then pick a card with your left hand…"

Liis laughs out loud and waves her little arm toward me. "Yes, let me just pick that with my invisible left hand."

I let out a mortified snort. After all these years of knowing Liis, my fool brain still assumes everyone has a left hand. She can do anything, and somehow my brain translates that into being the same as everyone else. "Sorry. Um, pick a card with your *right* hand and intention in your heart."

The reason you're supposed to use your left hand is because that's the side your heart is on, but intention is just as good, I'm sure. She reaches out and flutters her fingers above the cards.

"What comes next?" she asks the cards, then decisively pulls one from the right side of the fan and flips it onto her leg.

The Meandering Path. It's a pretty card with a path winding along low hills into the distance. A tree stands in the foreground with three branches pointing toward the path. A fox stares up at the branches.

Upright, the card means progress and movement. The branches say, *This is the way, this is the way.* There's a breakthrough coming. A clear path forward.

The card is facing me, though, which means it's upside down for Liis. Since she picked it, that must mean the reading is inverted. My heart sinks with the thought. Inverted, the card is its opposite. Instead of movement, it's unexpected delays, unclear paths, no tree branches to point the way.

The clearing—so brimming with hopeful magic just moments ago—feels cold now. The offerings dull and dirty. Rotten fruit and wasted liquor. A trick of the trickster Soovana. Hope flickering and then stolen.

I explain the card's meaning to Liis—my heart pinching at the smallness of my own voice—and she scrunches up her face. "Should we try again? Maybe you should ask and pick a card?"

I feel no hope at the prospect but open my mouth to agree when I hear a low murmur in the distance and instead shove the cards in my pocket. I hold up a hand, asking wordlessly for silence. Liis leans to the side and pushes herself up with her right arm. I scramble to my feet right behind her.

I turn my ear toward the murmur, trying to hear better, trying to determine the source. Soovana isn't known for speaking unless spoken to, but sometimes the trees whisper in the night, if you believe the old stories. Perhaps it's the forest clearing its throat again. The thunder from the earth itself, described by past generations.

But no. As I listen, the noise comes again, sharper this time. Masculine and boisterous and very much human.

Men. More than one of them. Here in a forest where few dare tread. My worry-pinched mind trips over the questions: Who are they? Why are they here?

They are getting closer. Laughing and talking. I press myself against one of the trees, and Liis does the same two trees over. We peek around the trunks and wait. I can see flashlights beaming, hear them laughing, and then one man shines the light full in the face of another. The second man swears; the first bends over laughing. And in the flashes of brightness, I realize who they are.

Soldiers.

They're heading this way, and the grove isn't thick enough to hide in—not if they come anywhere near us. The oaks aren't close enough together. There's no real brush along the ground.

I turn my face to Liis, hers pale in the moonlight. "We need to hide."

She doesn't answer—just uses her chin to point at a knife-thin animal track leading out of the grove and away from the men.

XVIII
MEANDERING PATH, INVERTED

When my foot comes down on a half-rotten branch just one step outside the grove, the crack reverberates in my ears. And I'm not lucky enough to be the only one who notices.

"Hey, what's that?" A single soldier silences the laughter of the others.

I brave a slow step, every muscle in my body tense. Liis is two steps ahead, crouching as she creeps forward too.

"Who's there?" A threatening, masculine boom.

"I see something moving!" Another, and my heart stops.

Liis stares back at me through the darkness, eyes wide. Then the noises of the soldiers are moving faster—forcefully—toward us.

She mouths the word *run*.

The trees thicken as we rush away from the center of the bog. I crash into more than one of them as clouds roll over the moon. Thunder hums in the distance—a low growl of warning.

"Did you see where it went?" Their voices are too close behind us, even as the words tell me they don't know where we are. I try to move quieter, breathe quieter, my body a tangle of nerves as the soldiers press from behind and the thickening forest slows our progress. Like she wants us to be caught.

I almost laugh at how, for just a moment, in one tiny spot, the bog seemed almost *safe*. Magical in a way that could bring back a little girl instead of swallowing her up. Now it's all threats again: thorns snatching at my arms, spiderwebs broken across my face, sticky and ticklish with fat yellow-orange spiders that I try to flick from my hair without slowing my pace.

Even as the soldiers' voices fall the slightest bit back, we don't dare turn on the flashlight for fear that they'll see it, and we both stumble more than once.

They can't catch us. That's all I know. Not after they came to our house and warned us to keep a low profile. Not when we're not supposed to be in the bog. Not after what I heard Mama say about them carting Anna off to an asylum or worse.

My skin is full of knives, and every step stabs me. We're not going that fast, but my heart races, and I struggle not to breathe in explosive gasps. My face and hands tingle, and my vision swims. I wonder if I'm going to pass out.

Then we break through the trees, and I realize we're at the back corner of the asylum grounds. To our left, a tall fence topped in barbed wire stretches unbroken toward the front of the large, square, concrete building. To our right, the fence turns sharply and butts up against a smaller building, an annex.

Both buildings remind me of the shoe factory where Mama works and the hastily constructed concrete apartment buildings around it on the outskirts of the village. That's where the Russians live, hundreds of them carted in to work the factory floor. And to

Russify us. To make us less *Estonian*, as if being Estonian is distasteful. We're supposed to be equal. We're supposed to be comrades. But the truth is that the Russians keep to themselves. Even in grade school, if you try to sit with the Russian kids in the back of the class, they'll beat you up—a fact that Margit learned the hard way when she was ten. You can sell your soul to the party, but you will never be one of them.

The asylum is as Russian and as ugly as Margit's bruises.

I don't remember the annex from when we tried to break onto the grounds as kids, but then again, that was winter, when it's dark almost all day long. And back then we weren't running from anyone.

Liis sprints toward the annex with Kaos at her heels. I turn to follow her but pull up short when she starts pressing on the windows one at a time.

"What are you doing?" I whisper.

"We need to hide. I can't tell if they are still following us. We're too exposed here." When neither window opens, Liis drops to her knees in front of a heavy metal vent cover and pulls a piece of metal from her pocket to hand to me. It's a screwdriver without a handle.

Hide...here? I didn't think my heart could beat faster, but it proves me wrong. "What if someone's inside?"

She shakes her head. "The windows are dark. And we'll be quiet. If your uncle catches us, he'll just send us home."

Home. My heart trips over the word. I know Liis means her

house, but she just reminds me that my home is gone. We haven't been back there yet, so I don't even know if there's anything salvageable in the wreckage. Or if the fire and smoke and rain and mob have destroyed every inch of the only home I've ever known.

I force myself to focus as Liis goes on. "If the soldiers catch us, though…"

I don't know if she stops talking because she has no idea what the soldiers will do or because the idea she has is too terrifying to voice. But either way, she's right. I'd rather face my uncle or an asylum security guard than the men who laughed when their leader stared Mama straight in the eyes and said, *No person, no problem.*

I take the screwdriver. "Where did you get this?"

"I always carry it with me," she whispers back. Then, glancing over her shoulder: "I'll tell you about it later. Unscrew the vent cover."

Sweat trickles down my back and pools behind my knees as I work, listening for the soldiers, hoping—impossibly—that they will stop, turn around. One screw comes loose and drops into the dirt. A second, a third. Then I have the vent cover off.

Kaos disappears into the hole first, and Liis follows fearlessly, headfirst into the darkness. I try not to imagine the whole thing collapsing on us as I back myself in and pull the vent cover as close to the hole as I can, hoping no one will notice it's hanging by a single loose screw.

There's no way to turn around, so now I'm forced to shimmy

backward into space. The vent is tight and so is my throat. The tingling in my face and the firefly spots before my eyes return. What if the vent ends abruptly and I fall and hurt myself? What if the annex is unstable and the vent collapses? I try to shove away the image of myself and Liis and Kaos tangled in sharp, broken metal, but it makes my breath come faster still.

"You okay, Vik?" Liis's whisper echoes through the small space.

"Mm-hmm."

"Do you have my screwdriver?"

"What? Oh yeah." I wedge myself upward and reach into my pocket, then try to peer back over my shoulder.

"I can't see you," I say into the darkness.

"I think you're safe to turn on the flashlight," she answers, and I realize I forgot I had it.

I set down the screwdriver and pry the flashlight out of my waistband at the small of my back, then click the button and point it toward Liis. She's facing the other direction, pressed against one wall, bracing on her little arm and reaching her hand as far toward me as she can. I brace myself equally awkwardly, inching toward her until our feet are touching, balancing myself with my flashlight hand and tossing the piece of metal to her with my other hand.

It clatters to the ground just out of her reach, and we both wiggle back up the vent so she can get it. Liis giggles nervously and then starts working at the vent cover on the other end with the

160

little metal tool. The screws unscrew from the inside of the annex, so on this side, all Liis can do is use the screwdriver like a tiny crowbar, wedging it between vent and wall, trying to loosen its grip. *Clank*, pause, *clank*, pause.

The sound of metal on metal makes my teeth hurt, but eventually screws ping from the vent cover to the ground inside the annex building. There are no other sounds and no lights, just like Liis said, and I hope we were right to come here. Hope that it's empty. Hope we're not dropping in on the guard's favorite nap spot or—worse—my uncle's office.

By the time I switch off the flashlight and lower myself to the ground inside the annex, I'm dizzy and nauseous and the spots in front of my eyes are worse. I press my back against the cold concrete wall and slide to the floor.

"What's wrong?" Liis is beside me, pressing a cool hand to my cheek. I lean into it, close my eyes, and try to still my breathing.

"I don't know. I think I might…pass out."

"Kaos, come here." Liis's voice is commanding and Kaos, uncharacteristically compliant, climbs into my lap, warm and strong.

A thrill of surprise runs up my spine, and I shiver. I'm holding a fox. A fox who saved my life, no less.

"Pet her, tell me how she feels." Liis's voice is soft.

"What? You know how she feels." What is Liis doing? I don't understand.

She laughs. "I know, you dope. This is what Mama does when

someone's having a fear attack. When you're so scared you forget how to breathe. It helps, I promise. Tell me what she feels like."

My pulse is already steadying as I answer. "She's soft. Warm. I can feel her breathing."

Breathing. Thank heavens. There's something I can latch on to. I start to count inside my head, match my rhythm to Kaos's. Her breath is fast, but mine is faster—too fast. *In, one-two-three, out, one-two-three.* The spots fade, and the tingling in my face is replaced with warmth. Embarrassment.

"I'm sorry," I murmur, darting a glance at Liis. She's still kneeling in front of me, her hand now on my knee.

"What for?"

"For…being a broken weirdo."

Liis laughs—a soft, gorgeous sound in the empty building like the low cackle of a raven, the trill of the first chorus of twilight-drunk bugs. "Are you serious? First off, literally everything we've done today is the scariest thing I've done in my life—every minute gets worse than the last one. If you weren't scared, I'd be afraid you were a robot. And second, I *love* that you're a weirdo. I've always loved that you were a weirdo. Who said I wanted you to be like everybody else?"

Something loosens in my chest, then my shoulders, which I hadn't realized were tight. I blink away tears, but I can't find any words to answer, so I just say, "Oh."

"Are you feeling better?"

"Yeah, I am."

She nods, scratches Kaos behind the ears. The fox flips over in ecstasy, lying on her back in my lap and squirming back and forth. Her tail wags wildly, and she presses her head against Liis's hand, making a *kak-kak-kak* noise. I laugh and press my lips together to try to keep the sound from traveling.

All our noises are soft, yet all feel impossibly loud in this tomb-like space. But no one has come. No soldiers; no guard.

"So, what do you think this place is?" Liis gives Kaos one last scratch and stands, glancing around the dim space.

"I don't know."

We walk through an empty, doorless doorway. The annex appears to be made up of three rooms. The one we're in has two walls of file cabinets and one side stacked with desks, one right on top of the other, with a tangle of chairs haphazard in front of them. A layer of dust on everything sends warm relief through me. This place must not be visited often. We're probably safe here.

In the next room, which is about twice the size of this one, other supplies line rows of shelves and lie in messy piles. There are cots in the corner with old mattresses leaned against them. One shelf is loaded with heavy rubber gas masks, an ominous reminder of the recent Chernobyl nuclear meltdown, and beside them a pile of the flimsy cloth masks those of us without military gear sewed to try and keep ourselves safe. A table near the annex's front door is stacked with boxes of what looks like broken medical equipment—vials and jars and pill boxes. Reminders of pain and suffering and death past, tossed so casually aside.

The third room—separated from the main room by a door with no knob—is a small bathroom. Thank heavens. Though it too is covered in dust and is apparently home to a family of spiders, we're deeply relieved it's here and scramble for who gets to use it first. Kaos decides she doesn't like us play fighting and hisses her displeasure from a perch on the creepy gas mask shelf where she unceremoniously knocks the cloth masks to the ground.

"So, why do you always carry a screwdriver?" I ask a few minutes later as we both start to circle the big room, exploring the mess. We lift dust-caked objects to examine them and peer behind shelves, into corners.

"Remember when we figured out how to get under my house to spy on Mama?"

"Yeah."

"Well, I never stopped. Eventually I figured out that if I carried some tools with me, I could get into most places. The vents at school. The bunker in the woods behind my house. It's never a bad idea to have something you can use to unscrew a screw or pry open something metal." She shrugs in the dimness, and I see the white flash of a smile.

"Where'd you get it, though?"

She shrugs again. "Traded some vodka to the guy who sets up the TV antennas."

Ah, that makes sense. The TV guy would have plenty of tools, especially because he's pretty rich right now. Ever since the whole

164

country figured out that with the biggest, fanciest antenna package we can pick up Finnish TV stations.

The minute we discovered that the premium antennas offered a window outside the Soviet world, people with the skills to set up those antennas became the most in-demand workers in Soviet Estonia. They charge fifty roubles to install one, which is two weeks' salary for most people. But it's worth it. Otherwise we couldn't have seen the full Olympic Games. We wouldn't know about Levi's jeans. And nobody would have watched and understood what it means to have democratic elections. Just imagine! Choosing your own leaders. Choosing your own world. Apples so red they must taste like candy, trips to the sea without waiting for special permission instead of cold, dark asylums and soldiers tracking your every move, waiting for the barest hint of dissent.

"He gave me the broken one, but it works fine even without a handle, so what do I care? *Oh!*" Her voice pitches high at the end, and I jerk around to face her.

Her face shines as she stands before a shelving unit piled with lumpy masses that might be uniforms or old clothes, holding something out to me. I move toward her, my heart beating fast. Could it be something to do with Anna? A clue?

Something shifts inside me with the question. Why would I even think a clue could be here? Magic is the only thing that can freeze a child in time, and magic lives in the bog. This place is a prison. Dangerous criminals kept away from the rest of us. There's no reason a clue would be here.

Could a clue be here?

What if I've been wrong all along, thinking the answers are hidden in the whispering trees, the sky-deep pools, the spirits hovering over unburned bones? Could the answer be something more mundane and just as insidious: a sickness, a biological weapon, an American nuclear facility experimenting on little Soviet girls? Uncle Silver and Margit are always going on about the Americans. Could they have come for us in this way we least expected?

Could the asylum be a place with answers? A place to find out what the Soviets know, what perhaps Uncle Silver knows and never shares? The secrets of enemies locked up just as tight as the prisoners?

"What is it?" I whisper, reaching out, my heart a stutter.

She hands it over, her voice almost tearful with awe. "It's a pilot's cap!"

Disappointment and confusion sink into my gut. What does a pilot's cap have to do with anything? I'm not sure what I'm supposed to say, so I just stare until she goes on.

"Sorry, how could you know? Mama got me a book about the Night Witches—a group of women who flew planes in the Great Patriotic War. They say the Nazis were so afraid of them that any man who drowned a Night Witch was automatically given a Medal of Honor. They dropped *twenty-three thousand* bombs on the Germans and helped win the war."

Her voice is breathless with excitement now, and she hugs the cap to her chest. "I really want to be a pilot. Can you imagine? Flying free? You could go anywhere. You could do anything. You'd be almost invincible. And you'd matter. You could win a whole war."

"That's amazing," I say, and I mean it so much the thought fills my whole body, pushing out the disappointment in favor of Liis's joy, of something from my own soul that I recognize in her words.

Then I throw my arms around Liis. I know what it means to want to fly away. My dreams were never so specific—and I didn't know about the Night Witches. But I've imagined myself as a bird a thousand times. I've imagined myself the girl from the Fire card. I've imagined myself collecting feathers. I've imagined myself away, away, away.

She hugs me back, but when I pull away, her voice is different, fraying at the seams. "Girls can't be pilots anymore, though. They were only allowed because it was an emergency, because the motherland needed all the help it could get. Hitler had to be stopped at all costs, even the cost of letting women fly." She laughs bitterly.

I want to comfort her, but she's not wrong. Women aren't allowed to fly. If there's a statement truer than that one in Soviet Estonia, I've never heard it. They'd probably also take issue with her little arm, say she has to have two hands to fly a plane. Liis doesn't need two hands for anything, but if the kids in school think she does, I don't think the Soviet military would offer her a pilot contract. Even if the Nazis came back and they let women fly again.

The thought makes me flush with anger. Anger that we were born here instead of Finland, where the people in TV shows make their own choices. I shouldn't think this and definitely wouldn't say it out loud—but the Soviet motherland, like the bog, always takes and never gives. I think about Liis's protests and wonder if they mean that someday things will be different. Someday we can wave an Estonian flag, sing an Estonian song, fly a plane, or just live without fear of the Soviet soldiers on our doorstep.

I hug Liis again because I don't know what to say, and I hope the hug means as much to her as it does to me. That I'm on her side. That we're in this together. That it's wrong. Wrong, wrong, wrong.

For them to keep her from her dreams.

Just like they're keeping me from answers.

XIX
THE SEEDLING

The thunder is a rolling boom growing closer, and the annex is too dark to see much now. Still, we work our way through the room, sorting through boxes of medical equipment and examining gas masks. Even though the pilot's cap was nothing, the idea that the Soviets might know something we don't lodges in me like the thinnest splinter—impossible to get out. Even if I am right about Soovana being at the heart of this mystery, maybe there's some answer about him here. Notes from a security guard on the night shift who witnessed a twisted, treelike man at the edge of the trees. Notes from my uncle about inmates reporting flickering eyes or flashes of white-blond hair outside the fence. I can't believe I didn't think about asylum records before. It's the closest place to the forest, the place most likely to witness whatever is happening deeper in the bog.

If we're hiding out here anyway, I need to know if there's anything that might point us toward answers.

Liis has tied the pilot's cap to her belt and retreated into the smaller file room to sift through papers, aiming the flashlight away from the windows as she reads.

She reads portions of the papers out loud, translating the

Russian to Estonian. Patient numbers and names. *Fits of mania. Suicidal. Grief.* The words run together, all similar, none relevant to the questions I'm asking. Though I do wonder what these people did with their mania and their hallucinations and their grief that landed them here. Turned them into the kind of people who needed to be contained.

"Do you think there were any babies born here at the asylum?" Liis asks as I join her in the file room—a distant departure from my own thoughts.

"No idea."

"Do you think they even take in pregnant women?"

I shake my head and shrug. Why would that even occur to her?

"It'd be awful to be pregnant here." Her voice wavers. "What would they do with your child?"

"Liis, are you pregnant?" I ask, alarmed.

A look of horror crosses her face, and then she laughs like an explosion until she devolves into a coughing fit. Kaos hisses her displeasure at the noise. "No, no, dear god, no! I was…just thinking out loud."

Was she? Her laughter seems off somehow. Nervous. And this doesn't seem like something Liis would worry about. Then again, what do I know about Liis's worries these days? I who've barely asked her anything about herself in five years.

She holds out a file to me, but I wave it away. I can't imagine patient files will tell me anything about Anna. She wasn't a patient here. Nobody in our family was.

My stomach drops at the thought. I shouldn't be here at all. I should be out there, in the bog, looking for clues. We've gotten sidetracked and it's unforgivable. We haven't found any notes on strange occurrences outside the fence. Just masks and broken-down medical equipment and hundreds of files.

"We need to go," I tell Liis. "There are no answers here. We should go back to the oak grove and try again. I bet the soldiers are gone now."

Liis opens her mouth to answer, but thunder crashes overhead. Kaos skitters from the room, hissing, and hides under a shelf around the corner. Then comes the deluge. The rain, heavy and fat, pours down so hard that it rattles the windows and drowns out Kaos's unhappy-fox noises.

Liis tilts her head toward the window. "We can't go out in that."

No. Guilt squeezes me like a hand-me-down coat that won't quite zip. "We have to. Anna's dying."

At that, Liis raises her eyebrows, and I realize I haven't told her about the conversation I overheard. I explain as fast as I can, then motion toward the door. "We need to go."

"Vik, there's no way you can see through rain like that. And it's pitch-dark now. You could pass a cave or a bunker or a monster two feet away and never see it. Going out in this won't help Anna. You'll just make yourself sick or run into soldiers or fall into the bog."

I want to argue because it feels wrong to stay, feels wrong to stop looking for any reason at any time. But she's right about the rain. I won't be able to see anything. Including soldiers and sinkholes and spirits.

I try to will my body to be as logical as my mind, to stop feeling like I'm doing something wrong for waiting out the storm. But maybe it doesn't matter how logical things are. Maybe I can't control the way I feel. The thought makes me feel even more like a failure.

Liis is standing now, wedging files back into their cabinets.

"Are you hungry?" she asks, and I realize I am. Ravenous.

She leads me into the larger room and pushes one of the mattresses over onto the floor. I follow her lead and pull a second alongside the first. From her backpack, she produces bread, two boiled potatoes wrapped in paper, and a small jar of wild blueberry jam. I almost cry with gratitude. Yet another thing I hadn't thought of: food. How could we go on searching for answers, possibly for days, without food? She passes me a canteen of water, and I realize I haven't drunk all day, despite the small canteen I brought. No wonder I feel dizzy and nauseous.

We finish off both potatoes and have some bread and jam, saving the rest for tomorrow. Then exhaustion descends on me like the rainstorm—heavy and thick and debilitating.

I lie down on one of the mattresses. Liis goes to the bathroom, and I'm so close to sleep that I startle when she returns.

She lies down on the other mattress, facing me. "So, how are you feeling?"

"What do you mean?"

"You just told me Anna's probably dying. We are hiding from soldiers. You had a fear attack an hour ago. It's a lot. How are you feeling now?"

My face collapses, scrunching to hold back tears. I feel so many things. How can I explain them? Frustration. Confusion. Fear. Always, ever fear. Guilt so bright white I can't see anything else.

"I feel…small." As the words come out, I know they're right. The frustration, the fear, the guilt—they all make me feel small. "Powerless," I add.

Liis pauses for a long time, then whispers, "You're not, though. Powerless."

"Don't say that. What can I do? Other than ruin people's lives? I ruined Anna. Mama. I hurt you—the only friend I ever had. So, okay, maybe I'm not powerless. But if your only power is to ruin everything you touch…" I don't finish the sentence because I don't know how to.

"It's not your fault, what happened to Anna, whatever's going on with your mom."

"It is, though. I took Anna to the bog. I broke the rules. I'm bad luck."

"That's not how luck works." Liis's voice rises. "Whatever hurt Anna is the dangerous thing. Not you. You couldn't have known what would happen!"

But I could. *I could, I could, I could.* Everyone told me.

Literally every adult I knew told us to stay away. I shake my head at the ceiling, unable to even look at Liis.

"Vik, you did hurt me when you left. You were my only friend. You were my only friend and you just…left." I can hear the tears in her voice now, and it's terrible. My heart is ripping into shreds. My terrible, traitorous, dangerous, bad-friend heart that never deserved her in the first place.

I'm crying in earnest now, a flood of shame exiting through my eyes.

"But I know you didn't mean it." Her hand wraps around mine, firm, strong. "You were sick. You lost Anna. I just wish you'd stop pushing me away." The last words are a whisper—as soft as moss, fragile as a dewdrop.

"I'm sorry." I'm not sure she understands the words through my tears, and I press my free hand to my face to try and stop them. "I didn't know what to do. I was so afraid I'd lose you too, and"—I laugh through the sobs at the irony of what I'm saying—"so I pushed you away because I didn't know what to do and I was so afraid you'd get hurt too."

So, I hurt her in order to not hurt her. I laugh-sob again. What a fool I have always been.

She's sitting up now, pulling me up with her and leaning across the space to wrap herself around me in a hug. "It's okay, Vik. It's okay. I forgive you."

I just sob harder because I know I don't deserve it.

"I love you," she whispers into my neck. "We're going to do

this together. Whenever you feel powerless, remember you have me. Together we're not powerless. Together we can break into air ducts and march through the bog, and we're going to figure this out. Together we're like the protesters—flying our flags, singing our truth. Together we're strong. Just stop leaving me, and we're going to figure this out."

We stay like that for a long time, until my eyes are so heavy and my grip on the waking world so fragile that I start to fall asleep on Liis's shoulder. We pull apart, and where her skin was now feels unbearably cold. The rain is still pounding on the windows and the roof. Kaos is still hiding under the shelves, refusing to come out. And I'm drifting, half asleep, half-aware, when Liis starts talking again.

"I keep thinking about how the world wants to change us. How, according to them, I shouldn't want to fly, and you shouldn't want to leave, and I shouldn't have been born without a hand, and our mothers should be traditional and married and boring and never doing things that scare people. How everyone wants us to follow the rules. Stay home. Don't protest. Don't go into the bog. Don't make the soldiers mad. Don't watch Finnish TV. Don't wish you had Levi's jeans. Don't wish for anything except perfect Leninism."

She pauses and I float through dreams. The rain pounding. Trees waving. The bog calling to me, telling me it's going to give up its secrets. *Come, come, and I'll tell you everything.* I dream of the Seedling, the card of childhood memories. The

Toadstool—progress. I see Liis climbing into the small opening under her house and beckoning for me to follow. I see Anna eating the lilac flowers and making a wish. I have a vague, blurry memory of Da laughing, tickling my belly when I was little before he left. I remember the feeling of finding that first assassin plant.

Then I hear Liis again, and I don't know if it's a dream or reality. Either way it's treason. Either way it's beautiful. Either way it's an echo of my own heart. The thing I used to believe. Before the bog was dangerous. Before the spirits were. Before *I* was.

"But that's the thing: I don't want *us* to change; I want the world to."

XX
THE TOADSTOOL

I startle awake, dislodging Kaos where she'd curled up beside me. She gives me the most disgruntled look a fox can manage, then settles back into the warm spot I vacated.

Something woke me, but I don't know what. Liis is still asleep just inches away. The annex is quiet and dim. No sounds, no movement. Through the closest window, I see thick, dark clouds obscuring the sky, the rain continuing its relentless downpour. But no sign of life. Nothing outside that should have startled me.

Still, my heart skitters. *Something wanted me to wake.* The certainty is a prickly, creeping thing.

I take a few long, slow breaths and ease myself off the mattress before sliding into the second room and glancing around. Nothing moves. Nothing is out of place. Only my nerves. Only a feeling.

I press my hand to my chest and breathe for another moment before reaching out to open the file cabinets lining the wall of this room. The files are the only thing I didn't look at yesterday. Liis started to, but I don't think she made it through more than a few folders. In my panic, I dismissed the files as nothing. Now I realize—with a sharp jab of shame—that if there is a report of something unusual in the bog, it could easily have been slipped in between patient records. Without checking, I'll never know.

I open the first cabinet and pull out as many folders as I can manage, then sink to the floor to go through the papers one by one, as fast as I can. The moment the rain clears, I want to have every answer this place can give me. Anything that might tell us where in the bog to look, what to look for.

Each folder seems to be the records of a single patient. Intake form, some hard-to-decipher medical information, and in the first one—my stomach does a flip to discover—a death certificate. Artur Kask. Dead two and a half years. Cause of death listed as unknown infection. Age: twenty.

I don't know why I never thought about people dying here, but something about that fact smashes another crack in my already-so-broken heart. I know the people who come here are dangerous, but does anyone deserve to die trapped between gray walls and barbed wire fences away from everyone and anything they ever loved?

I close Artur's folder and open the next. And the next. And the next.

Tamm. Kukk. Ivanova. The names start to blur together. The information is sparse. Mostly health checks, blood test results, initial intake forms with birth dates and full names and little to tell us who anyone actually was. What they cared about. What they did to get here. What they left behind.

I've almost stopped looking for notes about the forest, my

heart reaching out toward these people whose faces I will never know. Dangerous criminals, locked up, and yet—something about how much of them this place has erased feels tender as a bruise. I guess because it reminds me of Anna. The way some part of her has been erased too. Her language. Her memories.

I open the next folder, spread its contents across the floor in front of me. This time, instead of some faceless person, some unknown criminal, I see a name I recognize. A face I can picture. My breath hitches in my chest like I've run into an invisible barrier, my hand freezing above the intake form that has captured my attention.

An area for notes declares the person "in good health." There are some numbers and letters that must be more medical test results. The notes section has a single word: *depression*. Then there is a section for basic information. Birth date. Marital status. And name.

A deeply, terribly familiar name.

Margit Sokolova.

"That's your cousin's name, isn't it?" Liis says from over my shoulder, and I nearly jump out of my skin, involuntarily kicking my growing tower of folders across the floor.

"*Fakk*, Liis."

Liis grins. "Sorry."

"What did you say?"

"I said is that your cousin's name—on the form?"

I stare down at it again. Liis is not wrong. That is Margit's full name. But my cousin was named after her mother. So it's also my aunt's name—and my aunt's birthdate.

"It's Margit's mother," I say. "My aunt. She was a patient here?" I don't know if it's a question or a statement, so the inflection comes out all funny.

It's unsettling. My aunt—strong and no-nonsense, an important party member, always away on some vital business—was an inmate at the asylum? An asylum known for its dangerous inmates? An asylum where her husband works?

I have so many questions, I'm not sure what to ask first. Did Uncle Silver meet her here? Did he cure her and marry her? Or was he the one who admitted her? Why would they put her with so-called *dangerous* people?

I read the paper again. But there are no answers. Just more questions. Does Margit know? Has she been keeping secrets this whole time? What she said about people taking things from her—does this have something to do with that? Her life has always seemed so simple, all oranges and VCRs and plans to go away to university in Tallinn. But maybe it's *too simple*. Maybe she's good at pretending. Maybe her life is as complicated as everyone else's.

"Is there more?" Liis asks, dropping to a crouch beside me.

I reach forward and lift the second page, which drifted about a foot when Liis startled me into kicking the pile. "It's all blacked out."

I trace a finger along the page's thick black lines. Someone has marked out every word with a marker, nothing legible left. A history or a detail or a clue—a whole person even—erased by some worker with a heavy marker. Foolishly, I turn the folder over, as if I'll find the answers stuck on the back or tucked into an invisible pocket. I feel suddenly hot and uncomfortable—an unsettled, crawling feeling under my skin, frustration building like pressure in my chest.

"I don't know what it means." I stand, close the folder, and toss it to the ground beside Liis. "What does any of it mean?" I bite my lip, start to pace just for something to do. It's a weird find, but I can't see any connection to Anna.

Liis shakes her head. "I don't know either."

The question crawls across my skin like a thousand centipedes, the wrongness of it a bone jutting out where no bone should be. If my aunt was in an asylum where they keep dangerous people—murderers and violent protestors and dissenters plotting assassinations—and my aunt is not dangerous like that, *what does it mean*?

Is this a place for anyone they want to hide or accuse? A place for people who think the wrong things, who can't quite fit in the way they're supposed to? Is it not just our actions that can put us here but also our thoughts?

The questions unearth a worse one. A boulder lifted to reveal writhing, panicked crawly things.

Is this a place for people like me?

The question is unbearable, and I shove it from my mind, looking for something—anything—else to focus on.

"We need to focus," I blurt out, still pacing. "We need to go back into the bog. We're looking for what happened to Anna, not my aunt. Let's get our things and go."

I'm hot with shame, panic, confusion. We shouldn't have stayed so long. Shouldn't have rested. Shouldn't be digging through old files and random family secrets. Not now. *Anna, I'm sorry. I'm so sorry.* She's dying and I'm doing nothing.

Liis is standing now, reaching for me. "Vik, are you okay?"

My voice is small when I answer. "We've wasted so much time."

Before she can respond, I cross to the other room and climb onto a table to peer out the little window to where the rain stopped without me noticing. Thick fog drapes itself over the trees, daylight barely breaking through. Just a flicker. Just a—

Wait.

Two flickers.

Exactly the right height to be a tall man's eyes. Framed by crooked branches. Emerging from mist. Is what I'm seeing a thin and twisted tree with an owl in its perch or a too-thin, twisted treelike figure of a man? Hair and beard that looks like lichen. Narrow lips or a gash in the bark.

Soovana. Guardian spirit of the wetlands. Trickster. The reason I stepped over the boundary into the bog.

Anna was trying to pull me in. And now is he here to finish the job? Does he know that I will follow no matter what happens to me?

"Liis." I breathe the word like a cry for help.

Then I run. Through the room and into the smaller one where I hoist myself into the vent and crawl as fast as I can through it. He can't get away. I can't let him fade back into the mist.

"Vik, what the—" Liis calls behind me, but I don't stop.

I guess I haven't learned my lesson. I'll still abandon Liis—not to save her this time, but to save Anna, to get to that twisted figure and wring answers from its dark depths.

I wrench myself from the vent and drag myself to my feet outside the annex. I don't even think about the fact that the soldiers might be patrolling somewhere nearby, might see me. I only have eyes for the forest to my left—scanning for a gnarled shoulder, a contorted neck, a shining pair of eyes blinking through the dark to light the way.

Behind me, Kaos skitters from the vent first, followed by a breathless Liis, backpack in hand.

"Vik, what—" She tries again, but I hold up a hand to hush her.

I don't see him. But I know he was this way, to our left. The ground is pressed down in a pattern—ridges, angles, arrows—and I set off, following the grooves of it as Liis and Kaos scramble to catch up. Only after a few paces do I realize we're on an old vehicle track. Partly overgrown, but once carved out by some sort of tires. It leads straight behind the asylum, through the trees toward the bog.

I can't find him or anything like him, but I follow the tracks anyway—lead us into the ghost-white fog, thick and cool and wet against my skin. As if the bog is weeping on me. With me. For me.

Soovana, wait.

Soovana.

Wait.

XXI
ECLIPSE, INVERTED

When it's clear that I've lost Soovana—no trace of cranberries or flickering eyes—Liis convinces me to slow down. To walk slower than we normally would. Slower than I want to. Because the fog is thick, and walking too fast might just lead us into a sinkhole. Because they say Soovana can transform into mist, and too fast might take us right past him—through him—without our knowing.

So we're careful, methodical. In a way that makes every part of me ring with alarm. I agree with Liis in theory, but my heart screams that I'm losing him. I'm losing Anna. That if I go too slow, she'll die. If I go too fast, she'll die. And I can feel her dying in my bones and my gut and that hard center right below my ribs.

We follow the track because it's the only thing to follow in the general direction where I saw Soovana. I force one foot in front of the other, eyes on the trail, straining to listen in case there are more soldiers. Though I can't imagine they'd want to be out in this soup. I force myself to stop thinking about dying. That doesn't help anyone. Looking for Soovana does. Being sharp does.

Liis hands me some bread, and I eat it mechanically—barely

tasting it, barely registering that I am, in fact, very hungry. None of that is allowed to matter until we save Anna.

I picture her asleep on Liis's bed, Mama pushing back her sweaty curls. Our secret national anthem plays in the back of my mind, and I think about Mama singing it when I was little. I wish she still sang. My heart stretches out with the wishing. I bet Liis's mama sings. She's so *present*.

"Does your mama talk to you about things?" I ask.

"What do you mean?" She snaps her head toward me, sharp-edged panic in her voice, and I wonder what I've stumbled into.

"I mean, does she tell you when something's wrong? Do you know what's going on in her head?"

Liis looks extravagantly relieved, laughs breathily. "Yeah, I guess. Not everything, but she tells me how she feels about things. Yours doesn't?"

The question isn't really a question, and we both know it.

"No."

I want to say more, but I'm not sure what. That I've gotten used to missing people even when they're in the room. That Mama is there every day, but I still feel like she's abandoned me. That I'm not sure whose fault it is—if I've pushed her away like I pushed Liis, if she's disappeared into her own mind, or if both are true in equal measure. There are so many ways to lose people here.

Instead, I thumb away the tears that threaten at the corners of my eyes and ask, "What did you think I was asking?"

Because clearly she thought I was asking something else. Something that scared her.

She's quiet for a long time, placing each foot with care. Fog sweeps around her, rendering her wraithlike in the low light. Finally, she squares her shoulders, stops, and turns to face me, her expression determined and something else…

Scared.

"I've been wanting to tell you," she starts. "But it never seemed like a good time."

"Tell me what?" I study her face, but she ducks her head.

"I didn't come out here just to help you save Anna," she whispers.

"What?" If there's anything I thought she was going to say, it wasn't that. What other reason could she have?

Her face is etched with shame. Naked and unbearable enough to give me an instant stomachache. She darts a glance at me and wraps her arm around her middle, tucks her little arm against her chest like she's protecting herself.

"When I was a baby, someone left me in the bog. Somewhere around here—back behind the asylum. Mama found me and took me home and raised me as her own. But I'm not her own. Someone left me."

She pauses, but I only stare, trying to wrap my mind around what she's saying. *Left in the bog. Not her own.* The words sound so unreal, impossible.

"You look just like your mama." The first words I speak are simple disbelief.

"I know. It comforted me when I found out. Made me feel like I still belonged with her, like fate—or something—knew she was supposed to find me."

I open my mouth, close it again.

"When Anna came home, I thought—" She pauses and darts another glance at my face, then stutters on. "I don't know what I thought. Except that maybe the answer to her mystery is the answer to mine too. Maybe if we find out what happened to Anna, we'll find out who I am."

I stammer out a few words—*what, where, how, impossible*—my mind unable to connect them into a useful thought. Then, finally: "What do you think happened?"

Liis bites her lip. "It sounds stupid to say out loud, but I guess I always kind of thought something happened to my birth mama and a spirit brought me to Mama. That maybe the bog *saved me* somehow."

It explains why Liis is so unbothered by the bog when so many of the rest of us find it unsettling. She feels a kinship with it, or with someone or some*thing* inside it. Faerie or ghost or whispering tree, good-hearted hero in an invisibility hat.

"I had this idea that the trees pulled up their roots like they do in the stories, and they waded through earth and water and mud to carry me to where Mama could find me." She laughs, low and sharp.

I swallow hard. "Why didn't you tell me?"

"I didn't know." The words come out in a rush. "Not until I was thirteen. She said she waited because she was afraid when I was little I might blurt it out to someone and the Soviets would come take me away. I couldn't tell you when we were kids; I didn't know."

The confession undoes me, unravels me at the edges a little bit more. Liis—who I've known my whole life, who looks so much like her mama—isn't who we thought she was. Her life is yet another riddle of the bog. One more thing in this world that doesn't make sense. One more thread in my reality, snapped. She may not think it ominous, but I do. The bog not hero but villain. The source of a mystery yet again.

We both start walking again, following the track, even though no one ended the conversation. And as I walk, I feel cracks of doubt spreading across everything I know. Is there nothing in this world that I can be sure about? Is there nothing that's true? Who is Liis? Who is Anna? What did I see less than an hour ago, burning like lanterns through the bog?

And what does this new mystery tell me about what's going on in this place?

The questions are heavy, crushing me with their weight and number and impossibility.

XXII
ANCIENT OAK

Nothing is as it seems. Not Liis. Not Anna. Not the landscape, capable of swallowing a horse. Somewhere, someone must be laughing—but is it a spirit, the bog, the Americans, or some other villain I haven't thought of?

As we walk deeper into the trees, both too quiet, I think of the stories Riina used to tell us. About lakes that flew away in the night to punish greedy villagers and forests that wandered away, never to return. Trees demand respect, she told us. People used to tip their hats to the pines and feed hungry sinkholes with coins before the Russians called us fools and simpletons. I have the wild thought that if my motives aren't right, the forest might disappear from under my feet, taking its secrets with it.

Secrets—the things we're all carrying. Me. Liis. Anna. The bog itself.

It's hard to tell when we leave the outer forest and enter the true bog because the fog obscures the landscape. But eventually the path brightens, the silhouettes of trees thin, and the ground goes from springy to soft. Fewer things grow in the true bog because the peat-thick, mossy ground has so few nutrients. I wonder if we're walking on peat moss now, and my stomach swoops like I've missed a step. If this is moss, we're in the part of the bog that's most dangerous. Where a puddle could be a puddle or a ten-foot drop. Where plants can make you see things that aren't there. Where the stories of spirits might be real.

I keep my feet on the tire tracks, hoping that if a vehicle made it over this path, that means no gaps and sudden drop-offs.

There's a strange-looking tree in the distance, pointing upward at an angle. I wonder if half the root system has collapsed in a sinkhole, giving it that odd tilt. Then I wonder why the tree is so straight, stripped of its branches—just a smooth trunk rising diagonally into the sky like the bog is pointing a finger, blaming the clouds for something.

"What is that?" Liis whispers behind me, the first time she's spoken since her confession.

"A tree?" I answer, trying to sound normal.

"I don't think it is. Have you ever seen a tree like that?"

"No, but we've never been this far in."

The closer we get, the less it looks like a tree. It's more like a pipe. Or a round, steely fence post. Something metal, man-made. But how did it get out here, and why is it stuck in the ground at an angle? Who would have come so far in and put something so human out here?

The closer I get, the more fear buzzes beneath my skin. Everything is wrong. Anna is wrong. Liis's origin story is wrong. My aunt's name at the asylum is wrong. And something about this scene is wrong.

A minute later, I know what it is. It's no tree. No pipe. No fence post.

It's a tank.

A gray-green Soviet military tank.

Despite the fog, I see it clearly now. A tank made these tracks we're walking on. Then it plowed right into a pool of bright blue water. They must have tried to turn at the last moment, because the tank is lodged crookedly with its back end sunk into the pool and its gun pointing into the air.

Liis and I both stop a few feet from the edge of the pool. I slip my hand into my pocket and run my fingers along the edges of my cards.

"Why would they bring a tank out here?" I ask.

"To reroute the water," she says, and I give her a questioning look.

She explains: "Mama said they're doing it all over the country. Draining the bogs to water farms or something. It's killing the land. She didn't say they tried to do it here. But maybe they did. Maybe our bog fought back." Her voice is a little proud.

"Maybe the pools are like the moving forests, only instead of going away, they shifted to swallow up the tanks," I answer, and surprise myself with a smile. I may be afraid of the bog, but if there's a war between our land and the soldiers, I always want the land to win.

But then, am I scared of the bog anymore? I was when we were walking this way. But right now, I'm proud of it. Proud of our wandering forests and ocean-deep puddles, a land that fights back when someone tries to take its family.

Maybe the bog is only scary when you corner it, when you hurt it, when you steal from it.

Then again, it did take my sister—and I loved it back then. I thought it loved me too, sent me the gifts of assassin plants and lilacs and trees shaped like wizards. I would have never done anything to hurt it.

The fog is starting to clear around us, and more shapes come into view. A cluster of pine trees, their tops bristly and pointed. Clusters of low shrubs like porcupines huddled for warmth. Twisted trees like hunched-over old ladies. At least two other bright blue pools just past this one.

And something else: to the right, something boxy sunk low in the peat.

It's a trailer, jutting from the earth on the other side of the blue-blue pool where the tank met its end. Like it tried to go around the pool to pull the tank out and ended up stuck instead. There are dents in the earth beside one of the tires, like someone tried to dig it out before giving up, and now the mosses and low shrubs have started to grow into the hole.

"Look." Liis points to a tire beside the path, a rusted piece of metal lying beside it.

"I think you're right. They tried to take the bog and the bog beat them back," I whisper, because as the fog clears, I feel more exposed, as if anyone might hear me. "Do you think that's why there were soldiers out here? To retrieve things?" I ask.

"I don't think so. They were in the wrong place and didn't

have any trailers to pull something heavy like this out of the water."

"Then why are they here?" As soon as I say it, I realize that's the question I should have been asking all along.

Why are there soldiers in the bog? What business could they have in our remote, haunted slice of wetland? Why would the Soviets send them here, of all places?

And does it have anything to do with Anna?

The soldiers are often where we don't want them to be, but not here. Not in the bog. The bog is for creatures, spirits, not men.

There's something at the edge of the pool—a brown, muddy lump—and I move toward it, testing each step to make sure I'm not just walking on a thin layer of peat. I squat and reach out for the shape.

"Careful. Looks like an animal," Liis says from a few steps behind me.

"If it is, it's dead," I answer, holding my breath as I poke it and jump back, just in case.

Liis startles, and Kaos complains with an irritated clicking noise. But the muddy form doesn't move. And it doesn't feel like an animal. It feels like cloth. A bundle of clothes. An old jacket. A...

I lift it gingerly, and it unfolds into arms and legs, a head, a shiny pair of eyes. It's a child's teddy bear—a *Western* one. You can tell that it was once plush and full, detailed and beautiful. Expensive. The kind of thing you only have in our village if you know someone in the city or have something valuable to trade or have important parents in the party like Margit.

I stare at it, willing myself to understand. There's a reason for the tank and the trailer and the tire tracks if the Soviets have been draining bogs. What's the reason for a teddy bear? Some child's most precious possession?

My breath comes faster. It must have something to do with Anna. It's not hers. The only time we get special stuff like this is when Uncle Silver brings us presents, and that's usually chocolates or oranges. But even if it's not Anna's, it would belong to a child. Anna isn't the first kid who's disappeared here. So it's still a clue. Maybe every missing child came this way. Maybe somewhere around here another clue will tell us what happened, where they went next.

Or maybe something will happen to us too.

"What's that?" Liis says behind me, and I turn.

Kaos is nudging her, and there's something in the fox's mouth—something wet and muddy and small and—

"It's a shoe," I say aloud, and my heart triples its beating.

"A child's shoe," Liis whispers, her voice gone tight.

"A child's *left* shoe." I drop the bear.

"Anna."

And she's right. When Anna walked out of the forest a week ago, she was missing her left shoe.

My heart is in my throat when I state the now-obvious truth. "Anna was here."

XXIII
THICKET OF THORNS

Each time I learn something new, I think I should be happy, but instead I feel sick. Sick when we found Anna. Sick when she spoke Russian. Sick at the sinkhole, the well, the edge of the trees. Sick with Liis's secret. And now sick again—throat burning, head spinning—at the bear and the shoe.

Proof. Proof that Anna was here. There aren't many shoe styles available, so there's no way to know it's hers. Except that she arrived without her left shoe. Except that this is the right size.

Except that I feel it in my gut. The shoe is Anna's.

And that means she was here. Here near the tank. Here near the asylum. But also here in the bog. Does that mean the answer we're looking for is still tucked in Soovana's pocket? Or is it hidden behind the thick, cold walls of a tank? I feel like this truth should lead to another truth, but the mystery keeps shifting under my feet.

My mouth goes dry as dust, and I can't stop coughing. I drop to my knees beside the pool and cup my hands to drink. The water is strangely warm and tastes wrong, but it stops the coughing.

"Here," Liis says, kneeling beside me to share her canteen as I realize I must have left mine in the annex. "I filled it with rainwater last night. Bog water is acidic. It doesn't have minerals, so it won't quench your thirst."

Another thing I didn't know and didn't plan for.

I gulp the water down like I'm dying. Then: "What does it mean? What does the shoe mean?"

In the mystery shows on Finnish TV, it always seems so easy. You do the brave thing, walk into the bog, and the answers reveal themselves. You find a clue and—*ah-ha!*—it leads you to the next clue. So why does real life feel like walking in endless circles while your sister is dying back home?

"It means she was here." Liis's voice is steady, and I wonder how she can be so calm. I guess it's different when it isn't your sister slowly slipping away.

"What do we do now?" My voice is too loud, and I flinch *Don't forget, Vik, there are soldiers in the woods.*

Liis opens her mouth to speak, but I hold up a hand, listening. There's a noise in the distance, back at the tree line. I have no idea what it is. An animal? The soldiers? The fog is almost gone now, and the trees are too far apart to offer any hiding places. If it is soldiers, they'll see us the moment they step from the trees.

Another noise—sharp, a man's laugh. Soldiers, yes. Or at least people.

How is it that every villager who ventures into this place disappears, and yet the soldiers are just fine? Wandering around in here, laughing like the bog is nothing.

"We have to hide." My voice is an urgent whisper.

Liis is looking back up the path too, and I'm sure she heard what I did.

"Kaos, go!" she hisses, and the fox makes an irritated noise before moseying far too slowly away from the pool.

I search frantically for a place to hide. We could lie beside the low shrubs, but that only hides us if they don't come too close. If we huddle at just the right angle, they won't see us behind the trailer. But if they come close, we're trapped.

I look to Liis, but she's already made a decision. She slips into the pond with the tank, moving behind it. Submerging myself in the pool makes me feel uneasy. I played in rivers and streams as a girl, but I've never really been swimming—not like this. There's no choice now, though. I pull the oracle cards from my pocket and tuck them into a shrub. *Please,* tule taevas appi, *heaven help me, don't let the soldiers find them.* Into the water I go, my clothes billowing around me. It's strange that the water is so much warmer than the air.

As I slip deeper, another question worries at the edges of my mind. Like a fingernail scraping the same spot over and over again until it bleeds.

Why did the Soviets give up on a plan to drain the bog?

If that was the plan, why—in a world where the Soviets never give up—did they abandon this project? This is the same government that sent hundreds of thousands to Siberian work camps. The same government that won the Great Patriotic War. These aren't people who give up because they lost a tank. There must be another reason they stopped.

Something's wrong—so very wrong. And I don't understand what it is. Was there something else about the bog that pushed them back? Or something valuable about keeping it here?

Something valuable about keeping the bog. There's a thought. Perhaps whatever's happening in the bog isn't spiritual at all. Perhaps it's governmental. Perhaps the bog itself is hiding something Soviet.

Could it be that Anna saw something she shouldn't—that the Soviets had her all along? But that doesn't explain how she's five years old.

The situation won't let me linger on that impossible, frustrating thought for long. The voices grow louder, and Liis and I exchange silent glances behind the tank. They're coming this way.

Spots dance in my vision again, and I think about what Liis said at the annex. About fear attacks. About saying what you feel. I can't speak now, but I focus on what I feel: the cool, rough metal of the tank beside me, the balmy water lapping at my neck. My cards always comfort me, and my fingers itch for them. I wish they were waterproof. Instead, I hold them in my mind's eye.

If I were an oracle card right now, which one would I be? *The Thicket of Thorns*, I think, and shake my head at how much I hate that. It's the same card I'd almost always be: the worry card. The anxiety card. The card for people coiled up so tight they can barely breathe.

In my deck, the card is a thicket of thorns with a giant boulder in the middle. Five distinct thorns are stuck into the stone. Five thorns you can never pull out. It's the perfect metaphor for the way fear clings to me.

Liis presses her face against my shoulder, and I take the gesture as comfort. For me, maybe for her too. The voices are close enough to make out their words now, and I press myself against the metal of the tank, listening.

"This whole thing is a wild-goose chase!" one irritated soldier says.

"Orders are orders," comes another.

"Who cares about a little girl anyway?"

My heart stops at the words. *Anna.* They're looking for Anna! But wait, that doesn't make sense. They already came by the house. Uncle Silver scared them off. Would they have gone back so quickly? Do they know the house is burned and we're gone? Why would they assume we'd gone into the bog? And why are they only looking for Anna? If they thought we came here, wouldn't they be looking for Mama, Anna, and me?

Something is missing and frustration grates against me.

If they are looking just for Anna, is it because they think they know something? Have they decided, like the village, that she's something supernatural? That her mystery is one they need to solve? I know if they do decide that, they'll solve it by taking her away, locking her up someplace, questioning her, running tests on her. The fear is ice in my blood, knives in my bones.

"Hey, what's that?" The soldier's voice is excited now.

"A fox! Shoot it!"

No! Liis's eyes go wide with fear beside me, and I squeeze her shoulder. I can feel my other hand shaking on the tank. *Please, don't shoot Kaos.*

There's a pop of gunshots, and Liis folds her lips inside her mouth. I think she's trying not to scream.

Then: "Damn, you missed!"

"Damn fox got away!"

The men are laughing, and I wish I could yell. Why would you shoot at a harmless animal? I remember Kaos standing over Anna in the bed, ready to defend her, and I want to throw myself out of the pool and hurt these men who don't care about Kaos and don't care about Anna and don't care about anything except guns and booze and orders. Instead, I squeeze Liis's shoulder again and scream in my heart.

The voices stop somewhere in front of the tank, and I hold my breath.

Pop. Pop. Pop. Ping. Ping. Ping. The guns go off, and the bullets bounce noisily off the tank. Liis is shaking, and, not knowing what else to do, I squeeze her shoulder yet again. *They're shooting at the tank.* They have nothing better to do than shoot at the tank. I'm so glad it's a tank—bulletproof—instead of a car or a tree or a bush we're hiding behind.

"What's so special about this girl anyway?" There's a sound that I hope is the men shouldering their guns, then the *thwwt* of a match lighting.

The smell confirms my suspicions: they're stopping for a cigarette break. I sink a little lower in the water, pull Liis closer to me, my arm now protectively around her shoulders.

"The girl? Her uncle's some big deal in the party. The best Soviet scientist in a decade, blah, blah, something like that."

Uncle Silver. So they *are* talking about Anna. Looking for Anna.

"So, what? The girl is just some missing kid, and we're the dummies they tasked with finding her?"

Four words designed to crush a soul: *just some missing kid*. As if that isn't the scariest phrase a person could ever utter. They say it like it's nothing. Like she's nothing. But Anna is not nothing. Never has been, never will be. She is something even if she is changed. She is my Anna. She is the whole world. Every missing kid is.

"Yeah, we're the dummies." The voice is just as nonchalant as the one before it.

"*Fakk*, what a life we got handed."

Everyone laughs, five male voices tumbling over one another like stones in a river. Liis presses her shoulder against me, and I hold her tighter. I'm not sure if she's trying to comfort me or if she's scared, but either way, it feels good to have my arm wrapped around her shoulders. It anchors me to my body when my thoughts want me to fly away with them.

"So, why are we supposed to take the kid to the asylum? Why not the village if she's just somebody's niece?"

Uncle Silver's niece. That's what saved us from the soldiers last time, and it seems that it's what's painted a target on us now. The thought prickles. They let us go because of Uncle Silver; they come for us because of Uncle Silver. He is a reprieve, never a permanent shelter.

The soldier goes on, voice muffled, and I picture a cigarette between his lips. "Is she a dissenter? Crazy?"

My heart cinches at that last suggestion. Oh, Anna. I've been called crazy before, and I can take it. But Anna's fragile, and it's a word that cuts deep. Deep and wrong and *unfair*. What has she done? Is she crazy because she disappeared? Crazy because she came back? Crazy not because of anything she's done but what's been done to her.

Is that what everyone in the asylum is, really? Crazy because of what's been done to them. Crazy because someone simply says so. I've been so focused on the bog that I never thought about the asylum as a place where I might disappear. But that is what crazy means. That is what they are asking. Is this a girl who should disappear?

Too late, boys. She already did.

"Who knows? Not like we can ask. You try asking why someone gives you an order, see if you don't get shitter-cleaning duty for a month."

The men laugh again, stomp their feet on the ground. They're putting out their cigarettes, I think. Getting ready to leave. *Oh, dear heavens, please don't let them walk this way.*

I squeeze Liis gently, then release her so that she turns her head toward me. I'm not sure how to make a suggestion without words, so I nod at her and slip down in the water until only my face shows, pointed toward the sky. I hope she knows I mean she should do the same. Disappear as much as possible into the water while still able to breathe. If I see the men come around the corner, I'll go under and hold my breath as long as I can.

Liis looks scared but seems to get the point. She disappears from view, and I feel her shoulder bump against mine underwater. I can still hear her soft breathing near my ear.

We wait like that, breathing as quietly as we can, while footsteps pound and male laughter rings out and the sounds move farther and farther away. They never come around the pool. They must have followed the tree line into another part of the bog.

Still, we wait. Much longer than we need to. Because there's something very real, sobering, about how close they were. How close they still could be.

Finally, I lift my head and look around. I move around one side of the tank, and Liis goes around the other. We're both as silent as a starless night, a windless day. And when we pull ourselves, dripping and now shivering, from the bog, we just stare at each other.

Danger from the bog was one thing. But knowing these men are looking for Anna, knowing they're patrolling and might find us at any moment, that's another. The danger from the bog is a slick and shifting thing you can't quite put a finger on, but the danger from the Soviets is clear. Clear *and*—I realize—not going to go away. Even if we get answers about Anna, we'll still have to answer to the soldiers. We'll still be trouble for them. We'll still be a problem.

As the soldier said that day in my house: no person, no problem.

XXIV
LYNX, INVERTED

hy are there so many soldiers in a bog that's supposed to be haunted and empty?" Liis squeezes the bog water from her hair, spilling torrents onto the mossy ground.

"Didn't you hear? They're looking for Anna."

"Or they're looking for you." Liis stops squeezing and searches my face.

"What? No. Why would they be looking for me?"

The tingling in my face is back, my breathing fast again. Me? Is it me they want to disappear? Like they can hear my dissenting thoughts, feel my utter indifference to being a good Soviet girl, feel how I will choose Anna—choose Liis, choose Mama, choose anyone else—before I choose a Soviet path. No, it doesn't make sense. How would they even know I'm gone?

"Maybe they know you ran away, or they know we were in the annex."

My heart stutters at that. I did leave papers all over the floor. I did leave my canteen. But no. That still doesn't fit.

"They were around here before the annex." A headache prods at the top of my skull as I try to focus on some truth just out of reach. Like standing on tiptoes to pick a too-high fruit off an almost-close-enough branch.

"*Oh.*" Liis is the one to pluck the revelation and hold it into the light. "You're right. If they weren't already here, they couldn't have gotten here that fast. They were here *before* us—why?"

Every word she says tightens my chest, like she's stretching a rubber band. Tighter, tighter. These soldiers might be searching for Anna—or me—but they must have already been here. And in our small village, there's no reason for that. No criminals (unless you count stealing, in which case everyone in the country is a criminal). No protest organizers. No targets the Americans might care about, not really.

Why did the Soviets give up their plan to drain the bog? The question presses at me again, the fingernail about to break the skin.

The only thing important here is the asylum. But they've always done just fine with a security guard and the fence. In my lifetime, there's never been a dangerous escapee running around the village. Never been a complaint. In fact, I've never seen an asylum inmate at all. Not in the village. Not on a walk. Not getting fresh air within the fence.

My stomach does a flip. "Wait, why don't we ever see the asylum inmates?"

Liis's eyebrows rise. "I assumed they were dangerous and

weren't allowed out—after your uncle yelled at you for trying to go under the fence that time."

"If my aunt was an inmate, they can't all be dangerous."

"Maybe they are now? Maybe when your aunt was there, it was different. Maybe she was there by mistake."

The reasoning seems weak, but I don't say so. My body hums with frustration. Why can't I understand what's going on? Why are we even talking about the asylum? I feel like I'm following the wrong clues, solving the wrong mystery. Anna is what matters. She's all that matters. Asylums don't kidnap little girls and freeze them in time. Magic does. Besides, my uncle works there. He'd know if Anna had been there. He'd know and he'd get her out. He directed the soldiers away from us before; he'd do the same again.

Frustration and despair tangle hot under my skin. There's something very wrong about the soldiers being here. There's something wrong about the lies we've been told about dangerous people at the asylum. But I can't make it fit with what's happened to Anna. I can't make it fit with the bones outside the bunker, the horse in the sinkhole, the overflowing well, or Soovana's eyes flickering through the night. Or the way Anna is drawn toward the bog as if pulled by an invisible string.

My mind is the bog, all mirror paths and trees that cluster closer and lakes that relocate in the night, and I want to cry and scream all at once. I can't find a way to tie what we've learned to a little girl who doesn't age and forgets her native language. A little girl who pulled me toward the bog, around whom wells overflow and sinkholes open like ancient jaws in the earth. A little girl who told me Soovana was watching her

He's watching me too. At the annex I saw it, *felt it.*

My heart is so small and tight I can't believe it hasn't burst. The answers are so out of reach, so impossible, every one of them.

I think about all the time we've spent out here, with the answers slipping through our fingers like water—like trying to carry a bog pool home in the palm of your hand. So much time wasted for nothing. Anna back at Liis's house, burning up. While we were out here going through files and hiding from soldiers and…

I think about Liis's confession, and my frustration flickers into anger like the tiny ember of a cigarette lighting a brush fire. Why is the whole world against me? Why can't one thing go right? Why am I going to fail Anna again, kill her again? Why are there soldiers out here ruining everything?

I want to scream, but instead I choke out the first words that come. "You knew I was going into the bog…Why didn't you tell me you were left here as a baby?" It's the one puzzle piece clicking into place for me. Liis's origin story isn't just another mystery; it's also a clue. A clue we could have been following all this time.

"What?" Liis blinks fast.

"We could have talked to your mother. She could have told us exactly where she found you. Maybe it's related to Anna. Maybe it would have saved us time." I feel sick.

"I—I didn't think of that," she stammers. "I wasn't sure how to tell you. I didn't want—I didn't want to lose you again."

"So Anna is suffering because you weren't sure how to tell me."

Liis's eyebrows draw together, and her chin dimples like she's about to cry. "I wanted to help Anna, really. But I also thought maybe it would help me. And I knew I should tell you, but I didn't know how."

"You lied to me," I whisper, so hurt I can barely get the words out. Then: "You broke our pact."

Even as I say it, I know things are more complicated than that. I broke the pact first. I pushed her away. I left her behind, again and again. But even as I'm not sure I'm allowed to feel hurt, I do. The kind of hurt that radiates through your body—an icy lake cracked in one spot with the damage spider-webbing outward.

A tear escapes the corner of Liis's eye. "Vik."

I notice the flight cap, soaked and still tied to Liis's belt—and the frustration squeezes, hot and heavy, at my throat, my skin, my rib cage.

"Why would you want to be one of them?" I ask, rubbed raw by the sight of it.

"What?"

"A soldier. Why would you want to be one of them?"

"I wouldn't." She looks perplexed.

"That's what it means to join the military." My voice rises without my permission. "That's what it means to be a pilot!"

She glances down at the cap, unties it from her belt. "You're mad that I want to fly? I just want to *fly*. Not kill anyone. Not shoot at tanks or hunt down girls in forests. What does it matter anyway?" Her voice goes hard at the edges. "I was born an Estonian girl. That's enough reason for the government to decide that I can't do anything."

She's holding the cap toward me, and I snatch it out of her hand, then throw it into the water. I want to scream, but instead I whisper, "I hate them. I hate them. I feel like they're keeping me from the truth."

Liis reaches for my shoulder, but I wrench it away. She doesn't know that she's chosen the exact wrong moment to remind me she's here—my best friend who was supposed to share her secrets and instead let me waste a whole day doing readings in oak groves and hiding in annexes instead of coming straight here. She doesn't know that inside I'm a brush fire losing control. That all the hurt and fear and anger are too much to contain.

"You broke the pact." My voice is rising, uncoiling, snapping back like a rubber band. Or a viper. "You broke the pact all along. And you made me feel like *I* was the one who broke it, who betrayed you. I was the bad one. I was the dangerous one."

"That's not fair. I told you, when I found out, *you were already gone!*"

The accusation smacks at me like branches in the dark. How dare she throw my mistakes in my face when she's been lying to me for years.

"We could have asked your mother if she knew more! She

could have told us something about where she found you, how she found you!" I'm so frustrated I could scream.

"We could go back," Liis whispers, reaching out again, then letting her arm drop to her side. "We could go back and talk to Mama now."

"I can't go back!"

"Yes, we can. Maybe Mama can help…Maybe…"

But before she can finish her sentence, I'm whisper-shouting again. "This is why I didn't want you here! I was never going back!"

I shock myself when I say it, but the words are the truest ones I've spoken in a long time.

The truth about Anna has always been out of reach. I never expected to find it, I realize. And if I didn't find it, I'd keep looking forever. Whatever happened to her would happen to me. I'd be gone, dead, a spirit, a vapor, a rumor for the villagers to scare themselves half to death with.

I expected to die out here in the bog.

The idea is a relief—a dangerous, terrible relief. No more disappointing Mama, Uncle Silver, Margit. No more disappointing myself. No more carrying the weight of what I've done all balled up in my shoulders, my jaw, the arches of my feet.

"I'm sorry," Liis whispers at the ground, and I'm sure she doesn't know what I mean, doesn't know what I've just realized.

She still doesn't see me. She still doesn't get it. It hurts me so much that I lash out again. "A lot of good that does."

"I wanted to help." It doesn't seem possible, but her voice has gotten even smaller.

"I don't need your help."

"Are you sure? Because I can lend you a hand if you need it… Get it? *A hand*, because I only have one…" Liis tries to smile, but her joke makes this all worse, and it's like all the things holding back my anger pop off my soul one by one.

"Are you seriously joking right now?"

"I—"

"Go home. I don't need you. I don't want you. You're a liar, and I can't trust you."

"Let's just go back, Vik—"

"GO!" Now my voice is far too loud, and the soldiers can probably hear me, but I don't care. I just want her to leave. Leave me alone and never come back. She broke the pact and let me feel like the jerk. She let me run in circles like a fool. If Anna dies, it'll be her fault, and I can't even look at her.

"Vik—" she tries again, but I cut her off.

"Leave! I said leave! I don't want you here, you liar! No wonder someone left you in the forest! *You're* the curse—not Anna. You ruined everything." I'm sobbing now, and I wish I could shove the words back down my throat. But they're already out, and Liis looks like I punched her in the face.

She doesn't say anything else. She doesn't have to. Because I've just said the worst thing I've ever thought, and now she knows I'm a monster and was never worth her love. She takes a deep breath, turns, and marches toward the trees as fast as she can without running. Before she disappears, I hear her whistle and see Kaos weaving toward her—a flash of red and white along the edges of the trees.

Then they're both gone.

I snatch my cards out of the brush where I hid them. On top, the Lynx is upside down, and I almost laugh at the terrible irony. *Secrets.* The Lynx means secrets. Mine or Liis's, take your pick. They're all destroying me from the inside out. It's like the cards were trying to warn me all along.

XXV
THE FOX

I don't need her.

It's what I tell myself, and it's not even a little bit true. I've always needed Liis, and I've just sent her away. Permanently, I think. Because how do you come back from saying your worst thoughts out loud?

I'm dangerous. I knew it and I proved it. I wasn't even mad at her, not really. I was furious at something else—something I can't scream at or lash out at or insult because I don't know what it is. The thing that took Anna—be it bog or spirit or soldier.

I've been standing here too long, dripping wet, watching the rest of the fog dissipate in the sunshine. What do I do now? Anna's shoe was here. Liis was found somewhere near here. There must be more answers nearby. *There have to be.* But I feel frozen. Where do I start? What am I looking for?

I run my thumb along the cards in my hand, and the feather-soft edges comfort me. Before I know it, I'm shuffling them. Cutting the deck, shuffling again. The movement brings a sense of focus, purpose. *What do I do next?* I ask silently, forming each word deliberately in my mind. Then I fan the cards and pick one with a small water spot on the edge.

The Fox. Her teeth bared, her eyes narrowed. Fierce and dangerous and furious.

Kaos. My worn-thin heart reaches toward the place where Liis and her fox disappeared into the trees.

If I didn't know much about divination, I'd think it was a terrible card, one that means death or evil or fear. But really the card is about releasing limiting beliefs—the things that hold us back. If you look closer at the fox, she is sleek, shrewd, determined: a thinking animal, a thinking card. I always interpret it as the card where things aren't what they seem, a card that promises somewhere—deep down—you already have the answers.

Release your limiting beliefs. The words settle in my mind. Which belief am I supposed to let go? I should be frustrated. It's another nonanswer. Another signpost that points the way to nothing. But instead of frustration or fear or hopelessness, calm descends. The knots in my stomach and chest unclench.

Because perhaps the answer isn't soldiers and tanks and Soviet lies versus bones and bog spirits and magic that crackles at the edges of the world. Perhaps, somehow, it's both. The bog's secrets may be Soviet or spirit. But they are the bog's secrets. And perhaps every tiny, seemingly unrelated thread weaves together into some kind of answer.

It doesn't matter which way I start, I realize.

If Anna's shoe is here, if this is the epicenter of whatever happened, then I'm closer to answers than I've been. And there are answers. I realize I still believe that.

Which means what matters isn't where to start. It's *that* I start. Every strange thing I've found so far, every lie unearthed, happened because I did something. Because I started.

My pocket is too wet for the cards, so I tuck them under the bush again, a flutter of tightness in my chest reminding me how afraid I am that they won't be safe. But they're safer there than in my dripping pocket, I hope. And saving Anna matters more than the cards, no matter how much I love them.

I start around the edge of the water to the right, scanning the ground for any other clues—shoes or teddy bears, spirits or the latch to a secret bunker underground. The earth is soft and uneven, the peat moss yellow and green, stark against the bright blue of the still water.

There are more pools beyond this one—pool after pool after pool cut into the moss. I have the thought that perhaps the whole world is blue-blue pools covered with a thin layer of earth, and the idea makes me dizzy. Maybe at any moment we could all sink into the ground and disappear. Maybe that's what happens to people out here. The answer to Anna's mystery isn't in the trees or the moss or the tanks or mud-slicked teddy bears. Maybe it's under the water.

A headache starts to throb at my temple, and I think about Soovana, his lantern eyes beckoning in the dark, leading people into the bogs where they get lost forever or fall through and drown. I can see him leading Anna here, chasing butterflies or dragonflies, his eyes like lightning bugs. Could he have taken her hand, dropped her into a pool, and suspended her in time? There are mentions in the stories of spirit time passing differently from human time. If that happens, it must happen outside our line of sight, and under the water is the one place we can't see.

I wonder if I should plunge into each pool—and if I want to because the answers are sunken in their depths or because of what I said to Liis. That I never intended to return.

Was I planning to die out here?

A normal person would feel fear, wouldn't they? But instead, there it is again: *relief*. Relief that warms me like the sun on my skin. Relief that uncoils my muscles and brings tears to my eyes. I'd never be responsible for hurting someone again—not Anna, not Mama, not Liis. I'd never disappoint Uncle Silver. I'd never feel the tightness in my chest that means something is horribly, breathtakingly wrong, that everyone's in danger, that if I don't do something, my whole world will end.

I wonder if my leaving would save them all. The thought has been lurking somewhere in the back of my mind, unacknowledged, for a while. It was something I could never look directly at—like the sun, but under my skin instead of overhead. Now I turn it over and stare its brightness straight in the face.

My feet press into the soft moss. Another pool looms into view. And I'm crying in earnest now. Because I've forgotten what it feels like to move through the world without the fear that I'll destroy everything I touch. Because I wondered if Anna was a curse, and I told Liis she was the curse, but *I'm the curse*. I've never really believed it was anyone but me.

The thought takes my breath away and my head pounds harder, and that's when I see him. Again.

Soovana.

He's like a mirage, distant, fuzzy, his edges indistinct as if I'm looking through glass. Manlike. Moose-like. And the lantern eyes—it must be him. Closer this time, clearer if indistinct.

I start running. I don't even think about it. He's the answer. The answer to what happened to Anna. The answer to what happened to Liis. I'm either solving the mystery or charging into its heart to disappear myself.

The mirage shifts and disappears, but I keep running. It's the only clue I have. The only—

My right leg sinks into the hidden pool first, then the other follows, plunging through moss that looks like earth into warm, muddy water—then deeper, into the mud itself at the bottom of the pool. The mud rises up to my knees, sucking me down, sucking me under.

And that's when I realize how very wrong I was.

I do not want to die.

XXVI
THE FOX, INVERTED

Panic freezes me like a sudden shock—but freezing is the right thing to do. I've stopped sinking, my legs trapped in cold mud, the water sloshing violently around my shoulders.

A headache throbs behind my eyes, and my face tingles, a thousand invisible needles nudging me toward oblivion. *Do not pass out.* At first that's all I can think. What did Liis say back in the annex? It's a fear attack. Just a fear attack. Focus on sensations. Kaos was warm, so warm, so soft. And now what? What do I feel?

Water. It's cold this time, tickling at my collarbone. What else? The mud is even colder, thick. The water is murky with debris—moss and grass and clumps of mud stirred up by my fall. Something taps against my thigh—a branch as thick as my arm—and the rhythm is a comfort. I reach out to touch the peat moss at the surface. It's somehow scratchy and soft at the same time. It smells thick and earthy, faintly like rotten eggs.

It's working. The spots in my vision grow smaller; the needles dancing across my upper lip are fainter. I imagine Mama asleep with Riina kissing her forehead—loved, safe—and I force my breathing into her familiar rhythm. *In, one-two-three, out, one-two-three.* The tingling recedes, replaced by a flush of urgent warmth across my face and neck.

I cast my mind backward, pulling at the threads of old memories. What did Riina tell us about the bog? Because she *did* tell us. She was the one adult who didn't pretend we weren't curious, the one adult who knew that left to our own devices, we'd push the boundaries of our mothers' fear.

Free one leg at a time.

The thought cools the hot panic on my skin. I lean tentatively on my left leg and, when the mud holds, start to pull my right leg—and something gives under my left, sucking me deeper into the mud.

I suck air between my teeth, stiffen in place. My heart races with the real possibility that freeing a leg will pull the other under farther—too far, far enough to close over my mouth, my nose.

But there's no other choice. It's either free a leg and free myself or stay here to die of drowning, exposure, or a rogue bullet from the soldiers shooting at foxes and tanks. What was it Riina said? Most people die because they panic or because they can't get out and hypothermia takes them, *not* from being sucked under. *Stay calm, move slow*, she'd said. No matter what happens in the forest or the bog, your best chance is keeping your head.

I take a deep breath and pull gently on my right leg again. This time I wrap my fingers around the moss to my right. I have no idea if it's connected to solid ground or just another thin layer of peat over this hole, but it's the only thing I can reach, so I tug softly for leverage.

My right leg inches toward freedom. I curl my fist around the peat and close my eyes to focus. One inch, two inches, three, five. The mud relinquishes my calf, the water dancing around it as the trapped tree branch knocks into me again.

With a jolt, my left leg sinks deeper again. I freeze, hold my breath, and grit my teeth. *Please*, tule taevas appi, *heaven help us.* I don't even know what I'm asking for, but the water is up to my chin and that's too deep. *I don't want to die.* I want to be free.

I want to live. I weigh the words in my mind, send them out around me as if they can reach Soovana or the bog or the mud that's treating my left leg as a meal. I. Want. To. Live.

I start to pull again. My ankle is free, my heel, my arch, and then my right leg. I've lost my shoe—Liis's stolen shoe—but one leg is free! Tears spring to my eyes, and I release the breath I've been holding.

I tug tentatively at the peat, but it shifts—it must not be connected to solid ground. I release it and try to the right, then the left. The left feels most stable, so I squeeze both my fists around the moss, keeping my right knee bent and tightening my middle as I begin to pull at my left leg.

At first, nothing happens. I have no leverage and exhaustion is starting to creep in, the muscles in my arm throbbing in time with a sickening twitch that starts in my right eyelid.

Don't vomit. Don't panic. Don't scream or the soldiers will hear you. I instruct myself in a rhythm like a song. *No matter how tired you are, you have to get out. You have to apologize to Liis. You have to tell Mama how much you miss her. You have to tell Anna how much you love her. You have to keep trying. You have to live.*

I clench my fists, my eyes, my heart, and I pull—slow, careful, with my abs. The action forces me to float backward, the back of my neck and head slipping below the water. *Pull, one-two-three. Pause, one-two-three.* One inch, two inches, three and five and ten.

When my foot comes free, mud devouring the other shoe, my face collapses in on itself. I sob, forcing myself to be as quiet as possible as I float on my back, knees tucked up so that the mud can't suck me back down, treading water to keep myself afloat.

Don't try to walk on the peat. Another lesson from childhood. Another reminder that I'm not safe yet.

I stretch my legs to turn over, knocking into the branch under the water and accidentally hooking a foot around it. The mud releases it, and it floats upward—surfacing near my face, covered in mud, slowly bobbing upward, larger and larger. Not a branch, but two, three, four. No. Not branches, but a whole tree. A tree with legs. A tree with arms. A tree with a mud-covered screaming face.

And then I realize what I'm looking at.

Not a tree, not a branch, not even a monster.

It's a body.

Don't scream.

The soldiers will hear you.

Don't scream.

XXVII
MIDNIGHT

Even covered in mud, hair slicked back, frozen in time, I know who it is. Something about the face, the shoulders, the height, the expression.

It's Liis.

The body is Liis.

Liis who taught me the names of the bog flowers, who rescues foxes, who loved me more than I've ever loved myself. Liis with her jokes, her habit of breaking and entering, her dream to fly away. Liis who I'll never be able to apologize to now.

When I realize it, I can't hold back my scream. Not just a scream, but the sound of anguish made real, the sound of loss so primal that it can shatter a living person into shards that can never be put together again.

Liis. My Liis. I called her a curse. I sent her away. I sent her to *this*.

I smash a hand against my mouth, shaking all over, straining to stay afloat. The soldiers must have heard. They'll be coming. I have to get out of here.

But Liis.

No. My mind pushes back against what my eyes are seeing. *It can't be Liis.* Liis went the other way. Liis went home. This body is covered in mud. It's been here for a long time. Days, months, even years. Not minutes.

Not Liis. It's not Liis.

Why did I think it was?

Because it's her face. Through the mud, *it's her face.*

Have I been suspended in time somehow, like Anna? Could it be her, jerked backward in time and slipped into the bog? If time can't be trusted with Anna, can it be trusted with Liis?

My mind struggles to find a thread of sense, an anchor to reality, but then it hits me. There's another reason it can't be Liis. The body has two hands. I didn't even notice. I forgot. But Liis's little arm ends above the elbow. This can't be her.

I'm choking on the relief of it, and I cough, too loud again, like a beacon telling the soldiers to come for me.

I have to get out of the bog.

Don't panic. Don't flail. Don't try to walk on the peat. Don't touch the body.

I shiver and tense, wrap my hands around the peat and pull myself toward it. Painfully slowly, too aware of the body floating beside me, tapping at me again with a mud-thick hand, I wriggle my way onto the thin moss. Some gives way, but it holds just enough. I'm army crawling now, elbow over elbow, never looking back.

It isn't Liis, I remind myself. *It isn't Liis.*

But why does it look like her? My stomach flips and flips

again. Does Liis have a twin? Were there two babies left in the bog and only one was rescued? Has the other been out here this whole time and, with one wrong step, she was lost? Or is this Liis's real mama? A witch, a monster, something that looks just like her? Is Liis even human?

The moment the thought crosses my mind, my heart screams no. *No.* Liis is the most human person I know. The only one who won't judge you for your pain and terror. The only one with enough patience to train a baby bird to fly. The only one who would still follow me into the bog even after I abandoned her a thousand times over the last five years.

Liis is human, even if I can't explain this body with her face. Like Anna is human, even if I can't explain why she's five years old.

No, something else is going on.

I don't stop crawling until I reach the nearest tree. I use it to haul myself to my unsteady feet. Then I run my shaking hands over my body again and again, flinging mud and water away with jerky movements—as if I can strip away the horror of the body with the mud. Coin-sized black spiders skitter away from my commotion.

My legs are rubbery with fear and strain, but I start toward the tree line. I need a place to hide, a place to think, a place the soldiers haven't heard me screaming. Now every step on the moss is a wince, a catch in my chest. *Please don't fall through again.* I wish I knew the route I took, wish I could retrace my once-safe footsteps, but the bog holds no trace of me. I was too busy running toward Soovana to pay attention to the path.

Soovana. My stomach turns over again. Did I see what I thought I saw? Was something leading me deeper in? Or was it a mirage? A hallucination courtesy of the pheromones of the headache plants? The result of too little food, too much fear, too much wanting?

The not knowing spreads through me like a poison. How am I supposed to bring back answers if I never know what's real?

I remember my cards, vulnerable, tucked beneath the brush, and turn toward the silhouette of the tank. I feel my way around the pools, shrinking back from their edges.

I collect my cards, holding their edges in mud-dusted hands, dry now but still dirty. One slips from the deck and flutters to the ground. Midnight—a sketch of a young girl trying to spin the moon—the card of turning points.

I pick it up and almost laugh. What turning point? I'm more confused now than ever.

When I reach the tree line, I'm no longer paying attention. My mind has settled into the rhythm of my footsteps, the feeling of bare feet pressed against earth, too exhausted to try and understand anymore. I need to find somewhere to rest. Somewhere safe. Somewhere to be alone.

But I'm not alone.

I know it with the shuffle of footsteps behind me. The crack of a single branch. And then, a voice.

So close that I jump through the air, my breath freezing in my lungs.

I turn, face the sound.

"*Thank Lenin*, Viktoria. *Thank Lenin* I found you."

Not Liis. Not Mama. Not even the soldiers.

Uncle Silver has come to save me from the bog again.

XXVIII
FALLEN TREE

Uncle Silver has never been a hugger, so it's shocking to feel him wrap his arms around me now. I stiffen, my body pushing back against the hug.

My uncle has come to save me, but he's also one of them. A Soviet Party member, tied to everything I've learned about them. Tanks in the bog from when they might have tried to drain it. Soldiers patrolling a forest that's supposed to be empty. An asylum for dangerous, crazy people who maybe aren't dangerous at all. Who are maybe just like my aunt.

Who are maybe just like me.

He's the one who saved me, pulled me from a tree, carried me out of the bog last time. He's the one who came for me now. Braved the place so many others would never. And he's crying, I realize as he pulls back from the hug, tears streaking his hollow cheeks. He looks sick. Has my running off scared him so much?

Still, my body doesn't trust him. Won't relax into his grip. Won't hug him back. Another thing the Soviets have ruined. They come into the bog, and the bog isn't safe. They come into the house, and the house isn't safe. They come into the family, and the family isn't safe.

He releases me. "Thank Lenin, Viktoria. I thought I'd never find you."

"How *did* you find me?"

"I heard a scream."

My heart clenches. If Uncle Silver heard me scream, the soldiers probably did too. He may be a party member, but he's also risking something being out here where none of us should be. The soldiers can't find either of us. No matter how much my body tenses under his arms, he's still a person I cannot lose. "We need to get out of here, Uncle Silver. There are soldiers out here—they'll have heard the scream too."

His eyebrows fly upward in surprise—and there's something soothing in it. If he's surprised, he didn't know they were here. If he's surprised, his connection to them doesn't run that deep.

He nods and puts a hand behind my back, ushering me deeper into the trees, toward the asylum. "What happened out there? Why did you scream? What did you find?" Uncle Silver wipes the tears from his cheeks and starts to sound familiar again, his questions commanding.

"I fell into the bog," I answer, my voice thin in my ears.

I should tell him about the body, but the horror of it closes around my throat. What good would it do? He doesn't need to know. At least not before I talk to Liis.

If Liis wants to talk to me, that is.

The thought hurts my heart so much that I miss Uncle Silver's next question, and he has to repeat himself. "And?"

"And I pulled myself out." The words come out small. I can feel myself shutting down. I never know why I do this, but answering questions feels like a heavy weight, a pointless exercise. What does it matter when you've already failed?

Uncle Silver's scared expression shifts so fast to irritation. "Did you find anything else?" He pauses. "Maybe you know something we can use to help Anna."

As if that wasn't the whole point.

"I don't think so," I answer. It feels wrong to tell him what we found about his wife being a patient at the asylum. It definitely feels wrong to tell him we broke into the annex. There's no way he'll believe me about seeing Soovana (and did I, or was it the bog playing tricks?). And the body—I push the thought away—I can't possibly tell him about the body. For a thousand reasons.

He's still staring at me, his face drawn, anxious, so I offer up the only other thing I can: "We found a tank and trailer sunk in the bog. We thought maybe the government tried to drain the bog once."

That nagging question is back: *If that was their plan, why did the Soviets give it up?* The one person I know who might have the answers is walking with me, so I try to push past the heaviness in my head and mouth and muscles to form the words.

But Uncle Silver's next question is out before I can start mine. "We?"

"What?"

"You said 'we.'"

"Liis and I. You've seen Liis—my friend." I wave my arm at him, wishing he'd be quiet so I could think, form my own question.

"I can't keep track of all your little friends, Viktoria." His voice is pure irritation. "Where is this Liis now?"

"She went home. Don't worry. She's fine," I say, and hope it's true. Then, before he can interrupt again: "Uncle Silver? Do you know if they tried to drain the bog? Do you know why they stopped?"

We're both quiet for a long time, our feet swishing through pine needles, Uncle Silver glancing around us, keeping watch, me barely keeping my eyes open. My head starts to pound again. He's moved us off the path toward the asylum, and I think we're pointed toward the village now. If he has a reason for changing his mind about our destination, he doesn't share it. And I don't ask. Knowing if they tried to drain the bog feels more urgent.

In the stretched-out silence, I almost ask the question again, but finally, he answers. "No. I don't know anything."

He's lying. I feel the certainty of it in my gut, twisting it tight. But that's to be expected, isn't it? Party members can't just tell us whatever they want, willy-nilly. And Uncle Silver is nothing if not a good party member. The frustration of that fact is a hard knot at my center.

I wonder if there's another question I can ask that he would answer, another way to find out more. But before I can form the words, he's talking again, his voice steady and certain. "Viktoria, you can't tell your mother about any of this. You'll only upset her. Tell her you didn't go very far in. You know how she gets."

My heart sinks. He's changing the subject, yes, but he's also *right*. I hadn't thought about that part of this—having to tell Mama, watching her eyes go further and further away, coming back with nothing. No answers. No cures.

She killed her sister. I haven't proved it wrong.

I'm going back to her with nothing. A pounding headache, a thousand new questions, and an exhaustion so deep I might drown in it. Just like last time, I have failed.

Every other truth is crushed under the weight of that one.

If everyone I know is a card, then I'm the Fallen Tree—a once-beautiful birch that's come tumbling down. Splintered pieces, papery bark spread across the forest floor, lost in the dirt and moss, swallowed by a giant's hand reaching through the earth. A card about failure, losses, girls who can't hold their worlds up anymore.

I've seen Soovana, but I don't know if he's real. I've seen the soldiers, but I don't know what they're hiding. I've gone into the bog with nothing to show for it but a near-death experience. And now I'm going home—with no answers, no cures. Only more questions, more reasons for Mama to hate me, more reasons I've disappointed Uncle Silver, more reasons to hate myself.

As we stumble out of the forest and into the village, Uncle Silver stops on the walking path that encircles our homes and faces me.

"All right, where is your mother?"

My mind trips over the question, the headache spiking fresh at my temples. "What do you mean?"

"I know you left the house. Where is she staying?"

I pause for a long time, letting my sluggish brain try to put the pieces together. "If you don't know where she is, how did you know to come save me?"

He shakes his head as if I'm being unreasonable. "She called. But she didn't say where she was."

I nod slowly, but it still feels off. I don't usually lie to Uncle Silver. I keep my secrets, hold things back—but when there's a direct question, I tell the truth. Tell him I went to the bog. Tell him I cannot let Anna go. But so many things are wrong here, and even though he's my uncle, he's also one of them. Would he tell the Soviets where we are in the end? If he couldn't convince them we weren't a threat, would he give us up? Are we safer or less safe with Uncle Silver knowing where we are?

It's a horrible, traitorous question, and shame rises hot to my face. He sent the soldiers away before. He's protected Mama before. He pulled me out of the forest twice. What more does he have to do to prove that his family still comes before his politics?

I push away the thought of telling him that Mama took us to a factory friend's house, take a deep breath instead, and say, "This way," as I start along the path toward Liis's house. "That's the house." I point when it comes into view.

Uncle Silver puts a hand on my shoulder to stop me. "I have to get back to work. You won't go running off again, will you?"

I shake my head. I feel barely awake, barely alive. I wouldn't even know where to start if I went back in. He nods, squeezes my shoulder with sharp, slender fingers, then turns and marches back along the path.

When I open the door, the house is quiet.

Too quiet.

"Hello?"

I wander from room to room, finding nothing, no one. No Mama, no Anna, no Riina, no Liis. The headache stretches its sharp, slender fingers across my body—cutting from temples to throat to the depths of my gut. It's hard to keep my eyes open. Hard to put one foot in front of the other.

Something's wrong, my mind whispers. *Something, everything, is always wrong.*

Maybe they had to run again. Maybe someone threatened to burn Liis's house down. Maybe they realized what a burden I am and finally went away. Worse, a theory snakes across the back of my mind, scales sliding over rock: While I was busy looking for Soovana, did he come for them? Did he finally pull Anna back into the trees? And Liis—the body—

I can't even form that thought.

I try to reach toward another answer. Maybe Anna is better, and they've all gone for a walk. Any moment, they'll be back.

And then I won't have to explain my failure, because someone else will have saved her. Riina will have figured it all out.

I'm too tired, too hollowed out to know whether I should hang on to that foolish hope with both hands or believe the twisting, writhing thing in my gut that says Liis's house—our last safe place—is no longer safe.

I lower myself to the living room floor because I don't have the energy to take off my mud-caked clothes and I don't have the energy to stand anymore.

Think, Vik, think. Where could they be?

Instead of answering, I start to drift. Half dreaming, half awake, half-aware that I've pressed my cheek to the slick wood floor. In my dreams, the bog body stares me down. My cards stand up from the desk, and the art steps out to glare beside her.

You killed your mother, the dark-haired woman from my Storm card says, her eyes wide with shock, before returning to the card and descending her staircase into the earth.

The Autumn card becomes a raven, feathers black and gray. Its beak turns into a knife, and the knife makes a noise that I know means *monster*.

Villain, he caws.

Danger, danger, danger.

We're back in the bog, and my uncle appears, waves the living cards away. *Time to let go, Viktoria. Time to let go*, he says. That's what Autumn means. Letting go.

I can't, I scream, but no words come out. Instead, I'm grinding my teeth. My jaw aches with the tension, the pressure. The bog is sucking me in again. Cold mud creeps up my calves, my thighs, my waist. *Wake up*, I think. *Wake up, wake up. You're dreaming.*

When I do wake up, it's with a gasp.

Liis is standing just inside the door, her hand still on the knob where she has closed it behind her.

Liis.

The relief is warm sunshine and cool breezes, vodka socks and garlic bread. I knew the body wasn't her. I knew it. *I knew it.*

I struggle to my feet, sway from the still-present exhaustion that's carved into me like roots in soft ground. And that's when I notice.

This is not the time for relief. It's not a promise that everything will be all right. It's not sunshine through treetops or butterflies alighting on the first flower of spring.

Liis stands frozen, ghostly, her skin red from crying, her eyes spider-webbed with red. Her normal humor has bled dry. Her expression tells me before she ever opens her mouth.

Anna is dead.

XXIX
AUTUMN

Anna is dead.

I know it before she says it. Perhaps I always knew it. Knew how this would end.

She killed her sister.

I wish I could climb into bed and Liis would join me, curl herself around my back. I wish for sympathy from the girl I called a liar, a curse. I don't deserve a second of it, and she doesn't offer it—just stands there, a beacon of pain.

"What happened?" I ask, my throat as raw as my heart.

"She got worse. They took her to the hospital. But the hospital didn't know what was wrong. They rushed her into surgery, but she never came back out."

"Where's Mama?" I ask, simultaneously longing to see her and dreading the moment she walks through the door to see her failure of a daughter. Alive when it's my fault my sister's dead.

"At the hospital. I think they'll be back in a couple of hours." Liis turns and slips into the kitchen, like she can't get away from me fast enough.

It's strange, how I feel now—all the tension drained out of me, all the tightness in my chest gone, all the fire of panic erased from under my skin. Where I should feel everything, instead I feel nothing. Like I've vacated my own body. Anna's leaving has hollowed me out like a tree struck by lightning. Charred and empty, but still here somehow.

Liis comes back from the kitchen with brown bread and butter and a cup of the cold birch juice her and her mama coax from the trees. I force myself to eat, drink. Nothing tastes like anything. Everything sticks in my throat like the last words I wish I'd said to Anna.

I love you. I'm sorry.

I barely remember peeling off my mud-soaked clothes, scrubbing my face until it's raw and pink, falling into Liis's bed, which still smells like Anna's feverish sweat. I close my eyes and sink back into the nightmares, half-aware, half asleep.

When Mama finally walks through the door and into Liis's room, she's the one who's clear-eyed and I'm the one who's floating away.

XXX
SUNRISE

I stay in bed for two days, and Mama does everything for me—rubs my back and twists her fingers through my hair and brings me soup and watches as I sip the tea Riina has prescribed. She sends Uncle Silver away when he comes to check on us; I hear her tell him I need to rest. She doesn't go to work. She doesn't hide away inside herself. She hasn't been like this since Da left, not even close since Anna disappeared.

She's different now, and not just because she's sad. For years she's been floating with nothing to connect her to the earth, but somehow this week she's found her anchor, her center, some strength she was missing before. Her wings, even. She hums to me as I fall asleep, and her hands in my hair are strong and sure, even as her cheeks are wet with tears.

The numbness recedes and I want to cry—not just because of Anna, but because I've needed Mama for so long. Now she's here, *really here*, in exactly the way I need. Like when she kissed me the night I left. I feel so grateful, then so guilty. Because how can I feel grateful when my sister is dead? How can I feel grateful when I never got the answers, when an unknown danger still hangs over us all?

At night, Mama curls herself around my back the way I imagined Liis might. She presses her face into my hair and kisses my head. "I love you, my wild one," she whispers. "I love you like the river loves the ocean. It broke me that you left. Stay with me, stay with me."

She hasn't called me her wild one in years. Not since I lost Anna. It was the one thing I had that connected me to both parents. Da left when I was so little; I have so few memories. But this I remember: a soft, masculine voice whispering, *Hold on now, wild one*. It was Mama who always preceded it with *my*. Not just wild one, but *my* wild one.

It's lunchtime on the third day when I find my words, press all the heaviness, gratitude, and hope into three inadequate syllables: "I'm sorry."

"Sorry for what, my wild one?" Her eyes are clear, and she's settled herself on the end of the bed, cross-legged and facing me.

I mimic her position but drop my eyes, wrap my hands together in my lap, try not to shake. "For Anna. I know it's my fault, and I'm so sorry. I wanted to save her. I tried, I really tried."

My voice is small, but Mama's isn't when she answers. She reaches across the gap and takes both my hands in hers. "It's not your fault, Viktoria. It wasn't your fault."

"It is. You don't have to say it isn't. I—" I pause. Am I going to tell her what I heard? I realize I am. There's no point in hiding it anymore. "I heard you...the day she disappeared. I heard you tell Riina I killed her."

I watch her hands as they tighten around mine. Even though I can't bear to look at her face, I hear the catch in her words, and I know she's crying again.

"Oh no. I didn't mean that, Vik. I never meant that. I was scared, that's all. I was so scared."

I risk a glance at her face. Her cheeks are shiny with tears, but her eyes are clear, and she's not looking away.

"It's not your fault," she says. "It was never your fault. I never should have said that, even in fear, even without you in the room. Please, forgive me."

These are the words that crack me open, fill that hollowed-out space inside me. Now I'm crying, and Mama is leaning forward to wrap her arms around me. I press my face into her neck and throw my arms desperately over her shoulders.

It's not your fault.

I don't know if I believe her, not fully, but something about her saying it brings every fear attached to those words to the surface. It's like being in the bog again—pulling each foot from the mud, every sticky inch releasing me slowly, surely.

I'm dangerous. Or maybe not. *I'm unlovable.* Or maybe not. *I killed my sister.* No. *I'm a monster.* No. All the uncharitable thoughts I've had about myself—the ones I could never quite look straight at for fear that they were true—rise to the surface, unstuck from the mud in my boggy heart. Maybe they're wrong. Maybe they're all wrong.

I sob and sob until my whole body feels dried out. Riina slips into the room with two cups of tea and then slips back out again. Kaos follows her in and refuses to leave, climbing into the bed and forcing herself in between Mama and me to curl in my lap.

"Can you forgive me for saying such a hurtful thing?" Mama's voice is a gentle whisper as she pushes the tears from my eyes with a touch so light it's like butterfly wings.

"I was never mad at you." I shake my head.

"But I hurt you. You believed the words." It's a question and a statement all at once.

I nod.

"Then I'm more sorry than you'll ever know. I didn't realize I was hurting you so much."

"It's okay," I whisper.

"It's not okay," she answers. "I should have noticed. I should have asked."

"What changed?" I ask her. And I mean *Why are you back now? Why can you stay clear-eyed now and not before?*

"Riina." She says the name like she's really saying *goddess* or *lifeline*. Like how I feel when I say *Liis*. "Riina helped me understand what I was doing, taught me how to bring myself back. It's not perfect. She says it'll take a long time. But I know how to remind myself where I am now."

I think of Liis in the annex, telling me how to calm my fear attack, and I wonder if it's like that. If maybe Mama and I were feeling the same things, and we just didn't know it.

She presses a cup of tea between my hands, and I sip, the

warmth soothing my sob-raw throat. "Vik, what would you say if I told you Riina and I want to live together?"

"Like, we'd live here permanently?"

Liis would be my roommate. Kaos could sleep on my pillow. For the span of a single heartbeat, my heart feels light at the thought, my body expansive. Then those feelings are swallowed by the guilt, the sharp-edged knowledge that living with Liis means living with the person I hurt most. The one I called a curse. The one who probably can't ever forgive me.

I'm surprised to find so many emotions can coexist. I can miss Anna so deeply that it pulses through my veins, and I can feel the loss of Liis like a full-body bruise even as she's still here, and I can still feel the hopeless, breathless desire to gather every living person I love and keep them with me always.

"Yes." Mama searches my face, deciding something. When I don't answer, she goes on. "She's the love of my life—Riina."

My eyebrows fly skyward, and I can feel my mouth pop slightly open. Mama laughs, the sound so bright it reminds me of sunshine. The first time she's laughed in so long.

"We were in love when we were your age, but of course it was illegal. So we hid ourselves, our true selves. But it was the best time of my life, Vik. We did everything together. She made me braver, happier, more myself."

My mind scrambles for the truth that was there all along. I see her and Riina tangled up in the bed, Riina's lips brushing her forehead. I see the tender way Riina always touched her. I see all the care Riina took with me for years—perhaps not only because I was Liis's friend but also because I was Mama's daughter.

"But…what happened?" I ask, thinking of Da, thinking of how distant she and Riina seemed before Anna came back.

"There were rumors. We thought it was safer if we stopped. I mean, *I* thought it was safer; she never wanted to. Then I met your da."

"But why did you marry him when you loved Liis's mama?"

"I loved him too. It was different, but it was still love." She holds my hand in hers again. "When he didn't come back, I was devastated. I thought I'd lost two great loves. And I didn't dare hope she'd come back to me."

She lowers her eyes. "It's terrible *how* she came back to me. It's terrible that I didn't ask for her help all those years—that I wouldn't let her help when she tried so many times. But she's here now, and I can't let her go again. I can't lose someone else I love."

Her eyes are asking if I understand, and I think I do. I can't lose someone else I love either. The truth sinks into me like the coins we used to toss into pools for the spirits: I have to do everything in my power to get Liis back.

"We'll have to be careful," she goes on. "You'll have to be careful. You can't tell anyone what we really are. If you think you can do that, we could be together now. Friends to everyone else, family between us who live in the house."

Be careful. The words hurt, because why is love a secret? How would Mama's life have been different if it didn't have to be? I don't have the answers, just another pinch of hurt in my heart. Another reminder of what Liis said in the annex: *I don't want us to change; I want the world to.*

I realize Mama's asking for my blessing, and the answer is easy. "Yes, of course, yes."

I want her to be happy. I want her to feel safe. I want us to be a family. And of course I want to live with Liis. Even if she never forgives me for what I said. I want to show up and show up and show up again. To follow her into her proverbial bogs and be brave for her like she's been brave for me.

I think of Anna and hope that if her spirit can see me, she knows I'm not trying to replace her—that I never could. That this idea of family is an expansive one, not something where a gap appears and you shove another person into it. Liis and Riina have always been my family, our family. *Anna, I love you. I miss you.* I feel guilty that she's gone, guiltier that so many good things could happen without her. I wish she could be here to see Mama come back to herself, to find out our family was doubling in size.

And I hope her spirit doesn't hate me for being happy while I miss her.

Mama pauses a moment, then adds, "When I say 'anyone,' I mean *anyone.* You can't tell your uncle or Margit either."

Her saying that makes me want to cry. Not because I ever thought I could tell either of them secrets. Because of course Uncle Silver wouldn't understand. Of course Margit can't keep a secret. But suddenly those truths—things I've just accepted about them for so long, bent my life around—feel like the heavy loss they are. Mama can't tell her closest relative who she really is. We will forever be holding our tongues, even in spaces where we should be safe.

I glance at the mural on Liis's wall and realization jolts me back into the moment.

"Liis's mama drew the cards. My oracle cards. She's the artist." I say the words with wonder. I should have known all along. The most mystical person in the village was always the artist.

"Yes," Mama agrees. "You know that some of the cards are us?"

"You?" I laugh, and it all clicks into place. "The Lovers! I always thought that card looked like you."

She nods vigorously. "And the girls with the wands. They're meant to be us too. I even drew one of the cards."

"Winter!" I'm almost shouting. It's the only card in the deck in a different style.

Her nose crinkles with humor. "How'd you know?"

"It's pretty obvious that one is not like the others."

"Thank you, Vik." Mama's voice is like the overflowing well, but this time happy instead of ominous. Joy too deep to contain. Joy hard fought for with so much loss lapping at the edges.

We sit quietly as I thumb through my cards, each infused with new meaning. These are Riina's dreams, thoughts, the lens through which she sees the world. I feel like I know her so much more than I actually do. Like I've been given a piece of her soul. Like she's always been my family, even before I knew.

"Will you do a reading for me, my wild love?" Mama reaches out to touch the cards lightly with a fingertip.

She hasn't asked for a reading in five years, and it takes my breath away to be asked now. My smile is wobbly as I start to shuffle. *Thwack, thwack.* The cards are featherlight to the touch, as familiar and mysterious as ever. The sound is a comfort, the shuffling motion a balm.

Anna is gone, and a part of me left with her. But Mama is back. Anna isn't suffering anymore. And I hold on to those things because they are the only lifeline I have.

"What do you want to ask?" My voice is calmer now, my eyes drying.

"Can I ask it in my heart and tell you after?"

"Sure."

I fan the cards, and she slips long fingers along the edges, selecting one from the middle.

"The Sunrise," I announce in a soft voice.

The art is a grove of trees with five beams of light piercing through the leaves, crossed in solidarity. It's a card of reconciliation, connection, healing.

"What did you ask?" I whisper.

"I asked the cards if the daughter I love more than my own life could forgive me for not seeing how hurt she was."

She reaches out to push the hair from my face. Kaos decides that's an act of war and hisses. It breaks the solemn spell, and we both laugh.

"I love you, Mama." The relief of the words is the first sip of hot tea on a frigid winter day.

We hug, and Kaos decides this is all too much and slinks away to eye us warily.

"We should talk about Anna," she says, pulling away.

I pause, then: "What happened to her?"

"The doctor said it was organ failure. They don't know why."

"I don't understand." My voice is a whisper.

"Neither do I."

We're both silent for a long time, because what else is there to say? There are no answers. Anna is gone. This time forever. Perhaps it wasn't my fault, but that doesn't bring her back. Like the bones in the woods, the tank in the pool, there is something within us now that we didn't invite and cannot banish.

"What do we do now?" I ask finally. It's a question I can't imagine an answer to. Because after this, what is there left for me? Just a well of unanswered questions, a bog-deep pool of fears.

"I don't know, my wild one. But I know we're in it together." Her hands are warm around mine, strong and steady despite the sadness etched in every line on her face. After a long pause, Mama goes on. "Liis told me what she could about your trip into the bog. Will you tell me the rest?"

Like Agnesia's well, I overflow. The question unlocks a torrent of words, and I tell her everything. The moose, Liis, Aunt Margit's asylum records, the tank, the teddy bear, the shoe, my fall into the bog, and—well, *almost* everything.

249

I can't tell her if we could have saved Anna, because I don't know.

And when I tell her about the body, I don't tell her it had Liis's face. It feels like the kind of thing I have to tell Liis first. Her secret, not mine. And the pact is that we don't tell each other's secrets. I forgot that for five years; I won't forget again.

Mama's breath catches when I tell her about escaping from the bog. "I'm so glad Riina told you how to get out. I'm so glad you remembered."

"Me too."

"Vik"—her hands are tight around mine—"promise you won't run off again. I wouldn't have survived losing you."

I nod, though I already know my promise is as brittle as the first layer of ice on a pond. Somewhere in my gut, I still want answers.

"When did you decide to come home?" Mama's voice breaks through my thoughts. "From the bog."

"I didn't," I answer. "Uncle Silver found me and brought me back."

Now Mama's eyebrows fly skyward. "He what?"

"He brought me back." I tilt my head. What about this is confusing?

"Why was he in the bog?" Her voice is breathless.

"What do you mean? He was looking for me, wasn't he?"

"How did he know you were there?"

"He said you sent him. At least...I thought that's what he

said?" Was that what he said? I sort through the memories. "He told me you called him."

She shakes her head, and we both stare.

Uncle Silver lied to me. The realization is the creep of unseen spider legs across bare skin. The hair-raising static of lightning to come.

"Are you sure that's what he said?"

I think for a moment. I was exhausted and sick—I'd just seen Soovana and crawled out of a bog—so I guess I could be misremembering. I guess I could have misunderstood.

I shake my head. "Maybe I'm wrong. We should ask Riina. She told us about plants that cause hallucinations. Maybe that's what happened. Maybe a lot of what I saw or heard wasn't real."

Even as I say it, I know that's not what I believe. I'm giving Uncle Silver the benefit of the doubt. The only thing that feels surreal about my last day in the bog is Soovana. The body was real. Liis's face on it was real. And my conversation with Uncle Silver was real.

"Maybe he meant that someone else called him? Maybe someone saw you go into the forest—like last time?" Mama's voice is uncertain, even as she suggests it.

"Maybe," I offer weakly. Then, catching up with what she said: "Wait, what do you mean 'like last time'?"

"He brought you back last time too, when you went too far in after Anna."

"I know. But I thought you sent him. I thought he was part of your search party."

"No, there was no search party. No one in the village would dare go near the bog to search for your sister. Riina and I scoured the parts of the forest she knows, but no one else came. I never found your uncle. Never told him. And I never asked how he knew. I just thought someone must have seen you go in."

Tension hums through me, a song with the wrong notes. Something is off about all this. About the lies. About him always knowing where I am. It's not enough to put a finger on, not enough to make an accusation, but it's enough to flip my stomach over with alarm. Enough to know that the pieces of the puzzle we have right now don't fit together—and the reason has something to do with Uncle Silver.

For days, I agonized over whether Anna was herself, whether we were safe. But it was the wrong question. We were always safe with Anna.

Are we safe with Uncle Silver?

He'd never hurt Anna, my heart screams. He always thinks he knows what's right, sure. He loves the party that tore our da away from us, sure. We can't tell him our secrets, sure. He's opinionated and patronizing, and he would happily put a hundred tanks in a hundred bog pools for the Soviets. But he loves us. We're his family.

And he's a liar, my heart reminds me. A liar with the answers.

XXXI
THE MINK

I need to know what Uncle Silver knows.

It won't bring Anna back. I can't save her now. Can't change things. But I have the unshakable sense there's something more I should do. Honor her, I guess. Find the truth even if it's too late. Force my uncle to reveal what he knows.

Because maybe the truth can't save Anna anymore, but could it save us? The rest of the dissenters with our secret loves and hates and desires to fly away.

I suppose it's a way to hold that slender thread between me and Anna just a little longer, across the space of life and death like we held it across the bog for so many years.

So I take the flashlight again, tuck it into my waistband. I pause as I pass the couch, counting Mama's breaths as she sleeps stretched out there—*in, one-two-three, out, one-two-three.* Then I glide across the living room like a ghost, barefoot since the only pair of shoes Liis has left after I lost hers in the bog are heavy winter boots, and both they and Liis are nowhere to be found.

This time, as I close the door behind me with only the faintest click, I turn *away* from the bog instead of toward it. Away from the asylum. Away from the bunker. Away from every place I believed might hold the answers.

This time, I turn toward Uncle Silver's house.

Liar, liar, Uncle Silver. But *why* is he lying? What does he know? It can't be anything that would have saved Anna. He's no killer, no kidnapper—right? But he's something. Something unsettling.

I need to know what.

It's late, but Uncle Silver works late. The house will be empty except for a sleeping Margit, easy to evade. There's a strange comfort in the idea of her being there, anyway, asleep in the other room. Because going to Uncle Silver's house alone scares me for reasons I can't quite put my finger on.

In under ten minutes, I'm there. Staring down the dark windows, the quiet, clean façade that might be hiding an answer. It's such a simple house. Like ours before the fire, but better kept. Less lived in. The couch not wearing thin in spots. The paint not chipped. The yard bearing no evidence that any weed has ever dared take up residence.

I slip the spare key from under the windowsill where it always is. I've never had to use it before but always knew that in case of emergency—if the Americans attack—this is where I was instructed to come. Distantly, I wonder if Uncle Silver knows about the bunker and if he would have led us there. If that's what this emergency plan really was.

Inside, the quiet is like a blanket. When I shut the door behind me, nothing else stirs. You can't hear the wind whispering through a crack like it did in our kitchen. Even shrouded in dark with the world shut out, the quiet leaves me feeling exposed. Like someone is listening, watching as my shadow moves through the dark.

I want to leave, I realize. I want to run out the door and never come back. Am I afraid that I'm finally on the verge of answers? Am I afraid of what those answers are? Or is it simply that this village is no safer than the bog, that I feel no less watched? That I can easily imagine Soovana appearing at the window, gnarled and treelike and moose-like all at once—his eyes a blinding light?

I force myself to move. I came here for those answers. Whatever they might be, I'm going to look them in the eyes. My heart beats out a frantic, disagreeing rhythm, but I ignore it.

In the living room, I find nothing. A tchotchke-less shelf of books that the hardest-line party member would approve of. Furniture perfectly dustless. Floor laid with a plush rug—the kind most people could never afford.

Margit's door is closed, and I slip quietly past her room to get to my aunt and uncle's. Like the living room, it's simple, clean, and minimal. The bed is immaculately made. The top of the dresser is home to only a single family photo and a stack of unused notepads with three pencils lined up neatly beside them. In the closet, clothes are organized by shades of black and gray. In the dressers, linens are folded with their corners precise.

At the very bottom of the very back of the last drawer, I find a stack of papers. Careful not to rearrange them, I methodically work through the pile. Like in the annex, there are medical charts with annotations I don't understand—blood tests, notes about an illness that must have been sweeping through the asylum. Neat, unemotional handwriting records that this was the "third heart failure" or "sixth death." I wonder who those people were, who they left behind. When someone you love goes into the asylum, do you simply never hear from them again? Are their relatives in Tallinn or Tartu wondering about them even now?

Do you even know if they die?

The questions are thick enough to choke on, but I force myself deeper into the pile. The medical records are followed by letters praising my uncle's work and dedication to the party, all signed by high-ranking people. The only thing unexpected about those is that they are all old. There are dozens from a few years ago, but there's nothing more recent than 1985.

I wonder if they stopped praising him, he stopped saving the letters, or he keeps the more recent ones somewhere else—his office, hung up on a wall.

What does any of it have to do with Anna, with us, with why Uncle Silver would lie to me, to Mama? Despair creeps up my spine. I've broken into my uncle's house, and I'm going through his things, and there is nothing here that answers any of my questions. *I'm sorry, Anna. I'm failing you again.*

There is only one more thing in the stack: a little brown envelope so light that it couldn't hold more than a few more pieces of paper. No hope flutters in my chest, but I open it. If I'm already violating my uncle's privacy for nothing, might as well make sure I violate it thoroughly.

As I tip the envelope, it's not more papers that slip out, though. Not medical records or meticulous notes or a letter from President Gorbachev himself.

It's a single photo. Out of focus. Worn at the edges.

In it, a hard-eyed teenage girl stands in front of a nondescript white wall, her mouth a downturned half-moon.

My heart stops, breath stuck in my throat. I flash back to the bog pool, the body bobbing to the surface, the mud-covered tree branch becoming the limbs not of a tree but of a girl. One of the people I love most.

Liis.

The photograph is Liis.

Just like the body in the bog was Liis. Just like Liis is also safe and sound and somewhere out there in her rubber boots.

The photograph—like the body in the bog—is a Liis slightly different from my Liis. She has two hands. No little arm.

Liar, liar, Uncle Silver. Liar with the answers.

But maybe not the answers I expected.

I'm ice and I'm fire, and I don't know the name of the dread that creeps silently across my skin—raising every hair, every follicle.

I don't know what this photo means. But I do know one more thing now than I knew an hour ago.

Uncle Silver's secret may not be about Anna at all.

But it's definitely about Liis.

XXXII
SUNDEW

What if Uncle Silver comes back? The thought slams into me in the vulnerable dark of his bedroom as I stare at the photograph. The possibility is an angry, churning thing. A violent fear that fights and screams and roils and devours. The sea during a shark feeding frenzy. A half dead beetle besieged by ants.

I need to get out of here.

But is it better to take the photo with me or leave everything as it is? Hide that I've been here. Hide that I know. My fingers tighten on the edge of the photo. I want to *show* Liis, not just tell her. So I pocket it with my cards and put everything else back into its tidy pile. I can only hope he doesn't pull this stack out often, that he won't notice the photo is gone.

I'm clumsy, shaking, and I'm making noise now. I hope Margit is sound asleep. Because I can't help the way the drawer bangs shut and the photo on top of the dresser falls onto its face. I replace it before I sneak from the room.

Don't wake up, Margit. Don't wake up. I chant the words in my head.

But as I pass her door, I know she is awake.

Because I can hear her crying.

I stop almost involuntarily. Margit is *crying*?

I don't think I've ever seen her cry. Even when the kids on the bus beat her up, she put on a brave face. Even when her mama started leaving for months at a time and I could tell it bothered her. And a new thought hits me now, with what I know about her mama. Was Aunt Margit sent away to other asylums? Doctors? Did Margit know? Was she holding so much in all this time? And now—is she crying about Anna? Or has something else devastating happened while my back was turned?

It's almost involuntary when I reach out my hand and open her door.

She doesn't notice at first, sitting on her bed and facing the window. Her hair is pale in the moonlight, her face in her hands, shoulders rounded as sobs shudder through her like the crashing rhythm of a storm.

"Margit?" I whisper as I step into the room.

She jumps to her feet, her face red with tears and etched with terror.

"Margit, what's wrong?"

"Nothing. *Fakk*, Vik, you scared me." Like her father, the word *fakk* in her mouth sounds ridiculous and wrong. She swipes at her face, and an expression of calm drops into place like a magic trick. Now you see the grief, now you don't. "Why are you in my house?"

"You're crying," I say, reaching a hand tentatively toward her shoulder.

She shifts away, and I drop my arm. "Oh, that. I didn't get

the internship in Tallinn, that's all. Foolish, really. Nothing to cry over."

She's talking too fast, lying—I know from the way her eye twitches, same as it did when we were kids and we'd ask for her help spying on her parents—but I don't understand why.

"So, you weren't crying about Anna?"

"What?"

"Anna. This isn't about Anna?"

"Oh! Yes! It's about Anna. That's why I'm crying."

The shifting lie makes me feel queasy. Every person in my life has turned out to have a secret. What is Margit holding back? "Margit, what's going on? You're acting weird."

She laughs, but there's no joy in it. "Look, I don't know why you're here. It's late. You should go."

"Tell me what's really wrong."

She brushes her clothes off, swipes a hand across her face again, and shakes her head. "See you later, Vik."

I reach out again, but she dodges my outstretched fingers and forcefully ushers me out her door, through the living room, and into the night.

I ask twice more what's really wrong, but she doesn't answer. Only rubs vigorously at her nose and shuts the door in my face.

I stand there for a long moment. Should I stay and try to make Margit answer the door again? Should I go find Liis and show her the photo, tell her about the body in the bog?

The latter thought makes the hair on my neck stand at attention. The photo isn't of me, but it makes me feel watched. Like someone—no, not just someone: my uncle—is tracking our every move.

Liis deserves to see this new piece of her puzzle. And she deserves the thing that has been tugging at my heart since I emerged from the bog: an apology. Even if she never forgives me. She deserves to know that she's a blessing, not a curse. She deserves to know everything I found out since we separated.

Even if I don't know what any of it means.

And so, still barefoot, I turn myself again toward the bog, somehow convinced that is where she'll be. She was found in the bog, feels a connection to it still. She'll be hovering at its edges, asking it for answers.

I realize, after a moment, that I'm moving toward the place where Anna returned, and my heart throbs like a fresh bruise. *Anna, I'm sorry. I'm sorry. I'm sorry.* The words are mantras, pressed into me like footprints in fresh snow. I trace them over and over.

When I finally find her, Liis is sitting on a stump at the edge of the forest, staring into the trees as the light fades. She glances over her shoulder and tilts her head at me.

"Liis."

"Vik." Her voice is cooler than mine, and I know I deserve it.

"I have something to tell you."

Her voice is a closed door. "Tell me some other time."

"It's important."

"I'm thinking. I need time to think."

I hate myself for imposing myself on her, but I'd hate myself even more for walking away when I have some of her answers. So I try another way in. "Think about what?"

She darts a glance at me that says, *Really, Vik? You already know.* Then, out loud, she says, "Nothing important."

Those two words are everything that's been wrong with our relationship for years. Every door I closed on every conversation Liis tried to start, but now with roles reversed.

"I want you to tell me." The directness of my statement sends a thrill across my skin as I step in front of her, hold her gaze. "I also understand if you don't trust me."

Her eyes widen in surprise, but she says nothing.

I take the silence as my cue to go on. "I'm sorry. I didn't mean what I said. You aren't a curse. You've never been a curse. You came into the bog with me, and at the first opportunity, I drove you away. I'm so sorry."

She presses her lips together and faces the trees, picking at the stump she's sitting on and tossing wood chips into the forest. And I wait. Horribly, unbearably, my heart aching and my stomach following suit.

"You can't talk to me like that," she says finally.

At first, I think she means my apology, and I scour the words for what I could have said wrong. But then it hits me: She means the original words. When I called her a liar, a curse.

"I know. You're right. I was so wrong."

"Do you know, though? Did you know that's what Marko called me when I tried to hold his hand in second year? That that's why Mama didn't tell me that she found me in the forest? Because people here believe anything, anyone, different is a curse. I thought you—of all people—would understand."

Heat wicks across my face. "No, I didn't know."

"So you're ignorant, not malicious. Noted." She laughs without humor, and my face grows hotter still.

Fakk. I hurt her even worse than I thought. Panic builds in my chest. She isn't going to forgive me. I've lost her. Really, fully, forever lost her.

I reach for her, and even though her body is tight with anger, she doesn't shy away as I rest a hand on her shoulder and kiss her temple. Even if she doesn't forgive me, she deserves a real apology—not just words, but something more. She deserves for me to reach across the gap I tore between us, no matter whether she reaches back.

"I'm so sorry, Liis. I'm sorry, and I love you. No matter how upset I was, I should never have called you a curse."

"And?" she prompts.

"And what?"

"And for breaking our pact, for pushing me away, Vik! You said something mean in the forest, but this is about more than that. You missed my birthdays! You didn't show up for berry picking. I invited you and you ignored me—over and over. This isn't just about you saying I'm a curse. It's about you treating me like I am!"

She's right. She's right. She's so right. I wasn't doing it to hurt her, but I did.

I realize just how big the hurt must be, how many moments I've missed, how alone I've left her. I think of the times I cried and screamed to get Mama's attention and still she floated along in a daze. Liis never cried or screamed at me, but it must feel the same—to do everything you can to get someone's attention and have them look right through you. It feels like it's about you, even if it isn't.

"I'm so sorry." The words are too small, but they're all I have. I press all my meaning into them and hope she hears it. But it's not enough. I know it's not enough. Then my face crumples in on itself, and tears wash hot down my cheeks. "I understand if you can't forgive me."

My hand is still on her shoulder, but she shakes me off and stands. She's going to tell me it's too late. I know it in my bones. And I don't blame her. I deserve it. I deserve to lose my best friend.

Instead, she hugs me—kisses my temple fast, like a bird pecking into the dirt—then sighs long and loud.

"I'm still mad at you, you dope," she murmurs into my hair, but the *you dope* part diffuses the *mad* part. "But you didn't do it on purpose, right? And you're back now?"

I nod against her shoulder as she whispers, "I need you to be back—for real this time. You can't go away again. You can't talk to me like that again."

We stand like that a long time, tears turning to hiccups turning to silence.

Liis sighs again, and I can still feel the tightness in her shoulders and neck as she pulls away. "I wasn't just thinking about you, you know. I was thinking about me—where I came from. I wish I knew who had the answers."

Uncle Silver. I pull back, keeping my hands on her shoulders. My real purpose in coming here remembered. "We should sit down. I have to tell you…I found something after you left."

Liis brushes her hair from her face with her little arm and wipes away tears with the other. Then she sinks to the ground, cross-legged on a dark bed of pine needles and dried moss, her back against the stump.

I sit beside her and tell her about the body. She bites her lip, pushes her hair back with her little arm again, and I wait while she thinks, blinking fast, breathing faster.

Finally, she speaks. "What do you think it means?"

"I don't know. I thought…could you have had a twin? Or maybe that was your birth mother? It's also possible I was hallucinating…" Even as I say it, I know I don't believe it. I'm saying it to make her feel better, and I'll stick with it if she wants, but I don't believe it. Not in my heart. That body was real, and it had her face. I breathe deep and say it aloud. "No, I wasn't hallucinating. She looked like you."

A beat, a breath. "There's something else." I reach into my pocket and produce the photo.

Liis takes it, and I watch every muscle in her face twitch and shift in a thousand tiny movements. Surprise. Confusion. Frustration. Fear.

The muscles land on fear.

"What does it mean?" This time the question isn't for me. It's a thing that hangs in the air between us, a confession that this creates more questions than it answers. Adds itself to the mountain of questions I'm trying to balance in my own heart. "Why would your uncle have it?"

"I don't know," I answer anyway.

"I think it must be my mother," she whispers.

It makes sense. A photo that looks so much like Liis, and a body that was the same. Liis as a baby left in the bog.

"What do you want to do?"

She pauses for a long time and then, fear melting into determination on her face, says, "We need to go back to the asylum. If your uncle was the one with the photo, he's the one who knows who this is, *who I am*. She must have been a patient. It's what makes sense. *She must have been.*"

When I don't answer right away, she goes on. "Remember when I asked you if an inmate at the asylum might have a baby? I couldn't get the idea out of my head. What if someone there had a baby and she got away long enough to leave me in the bog? Now I'm thinking maybe she was ill and escaped into the bog but lost me and fell into the pool. Maybe that was her—the body. Maybe that was my birth mother."

It doesn't explain anything else. Not Soovana. Not the tank or the teddy bear. Not Anna. Maybe Liis and Anna aren't connected at all. Maybe Anna's mystery can't be solved. But maybe the one good thing that could come out of this would be solving Liis's.

Or maybe they are connected, some part of me whispers. Maybe the answers for every mystery in our village are all stored in a rusty old file cabinet in an asylum office.

I realize that even though she hasn't asked it directly, she's asking me a question now. Will I break into the asylum with her? Will I help her figure out who she is?

If Liis drew a card right now, I have no doubt it'd be the Mink—the shrewd little weasel choosing a path in the forest with the glint of realization in its eyes, the card that means a plan is emerging.

I realize a plan is forming in the back of my mind too. A plan to help Liis, yes, but also a plan to read every file in every cabinet until I unravel Uncle Silver's lies, find answers for Anna. She may be gone, but she still deserves answers. *I won't forget you, Anna.* I still want to save her, even though I can't save her.

As I hug Liis again, the light dims further, casting a calm blue color over everything. It's been a long time since I thought the bog was beautiful, but now, I realize I do. It's the same place I played as a child. Dangerous, but stunning too. *It's not the bog's fault.* For the first time in so many years, I believe that. Really believe it, in the way I did before. The bog was my friend. My safe place. My world.

Until it took Anna.

But now I don't believe that it did.

These mysteries—the ones that have shredded us all to pieces—are something else. Something to do with soldiers and tanks and liar uncles, not sinkholes and wizard-shaped trees and overflowing wells.

I'm ready to go back in. Ready to touch the birch bark with wonder and tip my hat to the trees and trace the mirror paths back through the sacred grove to the place where the real danger lives: the asylum.

"When do we go?" I answer Liis's unasked question, and the glint in her eye turns to steel.

"No time like right now."

XXXIII
THE STARS

This time, walking into the forest doesn't stop me in my tracks. My breathing is fast, my body tight, but I don't freeze. I don't feel the familiar fear that I'm about to shatter into a thousand pieces.

Something about my bare feet against the cold earth and the familiarity of our route grounds me. I pass the boulders and touch them lightly with my fingertips. I acknowledge the birches with a tip of my imaginary hat. I reach up to tap the comb pointing the way to the oak grove, then tap it again, then a third time.

It doesn't take as long to tap out the rhythm and pass the comb.

We pass through the oak grove, pausing in the center for a moment of silence. I draw the trees a card because it feels like the right thing to do.

The Stars.

Now that I know Riina drew the cards when she and Mama were first in love, I see this one differently. It's a nighttime scene at the edge of a pool. A woman who might be modeled after Mama kneels beside it with her eyes closed. In one hand, she holds a cup to her lips, stars reflected in the liquid it holds. In the other, she holds the other cup out to an unseen person. Her love, presumably. Riina.

The card means hope, faith, the renewal of purpose, and those are my exact emotions as Liis takes my hand and squeezes before leading me toward the annex. Toward answers. Some hint that her mother was there once. Some indication of her name, who she was, what happened to her. And by extension, what happened to Liis.

The asylum comes into view through the trees—cold and tall and heartless—and my heart stutters. It's a fortress, a prison. Designed to smother, unmake, erase. If Liis's mother was here, there's a cruelty in that I didn't realize before. In the sharp angles of a fence to keep you in, the taunting of birdsong just out of reach. The cold, gray concrete like a tomb surrounding you for the rest of your days. Until you become a file folder with an intake form and a medical chart and a death certificate.

It's another cut in my too-tender heart. Because there's no way the woman who brought Liis into the world deserved that. There's no way anyone does.

And, I realize, it's another reason not to trust my uncle. It's more than the secrets. The photo of Liis's mother. The lies to my face. It's the fact that he can run this place. That he trusts the party on who they say is dangerous, and he helps them lock those people away.

I suppose some part of me always knew. Kept parts of myself from him. My cards, my folktales—certainly the parts of me that felt different, strange. The parts kids at school called *crazy*.

Liis and I emerge from the forest and follow the same route as before—through the vent and into the annex; removing screws; sliding through dark ducts; dropping to the cold concrete floor. I stow Liis's screwdriver in my pocket. She stops to brush the spiderwebs from her hair, and I cross the floor and reach for the file cabinet. *Answers, here are the answers.* My body hums with the certainty of it. We're going to solve Liis's mystery. Perhaps Anna's too.

But as I reach for the drawer to tug out a file, a noise stops me cold. I assumed the dust-covered annex was no longer in use. We stayed here safely just a few nights ago. No one came by; no one came in. And somehow I thought that meant no one *ever* came by.

It's clear I'm wrong, though, because in the other room, the front door *pffts* open and smacks closed behind someone. Footsteps echo across the floor, steady and purposeful.

Fakk. We can't get across the room to the vent without passing the open doorway, and on this side of the room, there's nowhere to hide—just a line of file cabinets flush against the wall. Our only hope is to press ourselves to the cabinets and hope whoever it is needs something from the main room, not from in here.

Liis flattens herself against a cabinet, and I follow suit, reaching a hand into my pocket to thumb along the edges of my cards, staving off the fear with their soft flower-petal feel.

The footsteps pound to the back of the main room, and then a door opens and closes. There's only one other door in the place: the bathroom. Someone's gone into the bathroom.

Possibilities crowd my mind. If they're just using the bathroom, they'll leave, and we should stay here. If they're here for files, we should run now before they come out. I glance at Liis to ask her thoughts, but she's already made up her mind and is pulling me through the main room to the front door of the annex.

The toilet flushes, and panic spikes through me, hot and sharp. But Liis has used the noise as cover to open the door and pull me through, pushing it closed behind us.

"Come on," she whispers urgently, glancing wildly around before moving toward the main asylum building.

Everywhere else is moonlit lawn, not a hiding place in sight. But if we can get around the corner of the building, we can stay in the shadows against it, and maybe we won't be seen.

I follow, wincing as I stumble over sharp, unseen pine cones and stub my toe on a rock, but we make it around the corner just as we hear the door swing open at the annex behind us. *Thank heavens*, I think, sliding deeper into shadow.

Liis crouches on the ground against the asylum wall, and I fold down to make myself small beside her. *Please don't come around the corner*, I urge the person from the annex—probably the security guard—silently. *Please go the other way.*

Liis is beside a small basement window—rectangular and barred—and the lights inside flicker on. We both suck in our breath, but the light doesn't reach us, and the guard doesn't come around the corner.

I'm frozen by the sudden unreasonable fear that the guard will come around to see why light is pouring from a basement window. I shrink into the wall and count my own breaths, trying to slow my racing heart. Liis isn't frozen, though. Instead, she's curious. She peers into the little window. I want to tell her to stop. What if someone sees her? But my mouth is dry, and I can't find the words.

The harsh fluorescent light makes her look like a ghost. Like the asylum is really the place that vanishes us, turns us into spirits, a mirror image of the bog.

In the light of the window, Liis's face morphs from curiosity to shock. She gasps and jerks back, her hand against her mouth, eyes wide.

"Vik —" She speaks between her fingers. "It's…I think it's…"

She can't get the words out, and she's motioning for me to look, so I squeeze myself around her — security guard forgotten, heart still smashing against my rib cage as if it could escape — and peer into the asylum's basement.

It takes too long for my brain to process what my eyes are telling me, and I know why Liis couldn't find the words.

Because I'm looking at something that can't be true.

I'm looking at something that changes everything.

I'm looking at my dead sister.

Anna is alive.

XXXIV
WOLF PACK

This Anna is what Anna should be: ten years old, still herself but grown a little, changed a little.

Her hair is cut short and lopsided. Her body taller and thinner, like a reed sticking out of a marsh. She's wearing a flimsy hospital gown and a pair of slippers, playing checkers at a table with a young girl. A door at the edge of my vision opens, and another girl enters the room—stealing what little breath I had.

Margit. Anna and a stranger and Margit are all in the room.

If they look up, they'll see me, but I can't bring myself to move. Rightness and wrongness collide inside me. If this is Anna, who died two days ago? Who walked out of the bog? And how? If this is Anna, has she been here the whole time? If this is Anna, why would Uncle Silver keep her from us? Why would he make us suffer all these years?

I'm struggling to form all the questions, they're coming so fast. But it doesn't matter. Because Liis and I are too distracted, too frozen, too panicked by what we've seen. We forgot that we were hiding. And when a hand comes down on my shoulder, I know forgetting was the most foolish thing we could do.

The guard has a handful of my shirt in one fist and a handful of Liis's in the other. His thick fist and sharp knuckles dig into my neck as he hauls us to our feet and marches us around the building.

He grunts into an intercom at the door, and my fear—normally a knot in my chest, a stabbing in my gut, a catch in my throat—is now electric, tiny bolts of lightning arcing through me. It's the panic of a rabbit uncovered by a fox. The panic of a moth slamming itself against a window.

Gold is the color of sunsets, not monsters. Yet, when my uncle throws open the side door and fluorescent light blazes all around him, it's all I can think: *Monster*. He's not the Ivy card. He's the Wolf Pack—flying through the night, teeth glinting. Ambition. Drive. Self-confidence that doesn't care what ambition costs.

This is the monster who has Anna.

Then the crescendo of my panic fills my body, because I realize now he has Liis too.

Uncle Silver meets my gaze, but his flicker of surprise is a tiny thing. The hint of a flame easily extinguished. His eyebrows settle into a hard line. Resignation. He will choose the USSR over me too. Over us all. He has been all along.

I've been marching compliantly with the security guard this whole time, but now I kick out as hard as I can, connecting with his shin with a satisfying thud—the electric panic under my skin a weapon.

"RUN!" I shout, and my next kick strikes his kneecap with a crunch.

Liis is hitting him too, lashing out with fist and little arm and twisting like a storm, but still the guard holds on to us. Still she cannot run.

My panic turns to fury, and I laugh—a sound of rage and release all at once—as I kick again, my heel slamming against his ankle.

Uncle Silver starts forward as if he's going to help his now-howling security guard, but I throw out a leg, and he trips onto the lawn instead. My body jolts with fear. *I've just attacked my uncle!* But then the fury swallows it whole. I've attacked a monster.

His eyes spark with anger and that familiar deep disappointment. I have become the thing he warned me against. I have refused to let go. Now we are here: monster and dissenter, face-to-face at last.

Mama calls me her wild thing, and that's what I am now. I'm kicking and scratching, throwing out limbs in every direction. A tornado. A windstorm. Soovana luring men into the bog and drowning them in the mud. If I've thought myself a monster for five years, I'll be one now. A powerful, capable monster who didn't destroy Anna—but will make the men who did destroy us pay.

"RUN!" This time Liis screams the command as she kicks the security guard behind his knee.

He doesn't let go, no matter how we twist and scream and

kick. We are a storm, but his grip is a vise, a bunker, an asylum. No matter how the wind howls, it cannot topple concrete.

By the time the security guard wrestles us into the building, Uncle Silver has seized my shoulders. The security guard restrains Liis with both hands now, pushing her ahead of us down the too-bright corridor. We both struggle less. Because what's the point when the door locked so audibly behind us?

"Secure her. I'll take care of...my niece." Uncle Silver frowns.

Secure. Is that what Anna is, monster?

The guard manhandles Liis into a small room up and to the left as I strain ineffectively against my uncle, my panic and wildness giving way to pain and exhaustion in a dozen different places. And as the rage drops from boil to simmer, somewhere at the edges of my fear, a truth shines bright:

Anna is alive.

Anna is *here*.

I am in the same building with my little sister for the first time in five years. And maybe that means I can get to her.

"What's going on?" I demand. "Let Liis go! Let me see Anna! What did you do to her?"

Uncle Silver doesn't answer, just wrestles me into another room on the opposite side of the hall from where Liis disappeared and locks the door behind us. The room is an office almost as sterile as the hall. Desk, chairs, bookshelf, filing cabinet. Everything is pristine. Papers are stacked on the desk, their edges in perfect alignment. He steers me into the chair across from the desk, then grabs two pens off the surface and locks them in a cabinet.

What does he think—that I'd stab him with a pen? The thought makes me queasy. He always said the inmates were dangerous, but is this what he meant? Not that they were dangerous, but that he was afraid. Because he knew if they grabbed a pen from his desk and stuck it in his neck, that might feel like justice.

"Viktoria." His voice is as authoritative as ever when he crosses to the other side of the desk and settles into his chair. "If you calm down and stop acting like a child, I'll explain the situation."

Acting like a child? I almost laugh. I feel more like an adult than I ever have.

"What's going on?" I ask again, forcing my voice to stay even.

"Are you going to behave?"

Are you? I bite back the words. Antagonizing him won't help when I need to find a way to get the key he just tucked into his pocket. When I need to find a way to get Liis and Anna and myself out of here. When I need *answers*.

"Yes."

"Yes, what?"

"Yes, I'll behave," I lie through clenched teeth.

"I never wanted you to see this. Your mother doesn't deserve to lose both daughters."

It's a confirmation of what my heart already knew: I won't be leaving this asylum. Uncle Silver will always choose his secrets over our family. He'll watch my mother retreat into herself for good this time, having lost Da, then Anna, then me. He'll pretend there's nothing he can do. He'll let her be destroyed.

And he'll do all that to someone he claims to love. His twin.

No wonder he can do all this to people who *aren't* his family.

He presses his palms to his desk and sighs. The skin under his eyes is shadowy blue, his face stretched, and I know he means it. He didn't mean for this to happen, and yet somehow he caused it.

I keep my mouth closed and stare, willing him to go on.

"Where do I start?" He runs his fingers through his hair.

"Anna," I say. "Start with Anna."

"She's fine. She's safe," he says, reaching across the desk to take my hand.

I pull it away.

"Viktoria, you need to understand. Nothing bad happened to Anna. Your anger is unjustified."

My unjustified anger rises up, heating my skin, but I bite my tongue. Uncle Silver responds to obedience, not threats. *Tell me, monster, tell me what you did.* I scream it in my heart.

"Then what is this place?" My words are biting, but Uncle Silver ignores the tone this time. Talking about his work is more important than demanding respect, I guess.

"It's one of the most important labs in the Soviet Union." His lecture voice is gone, and another familiar tone has taken its place: pride. Pride in his work. Pride in his country. Even if that work, that country, has torn his family to pieces.

"We're working on a military operation. The Americans could

attack at any moment. This is where we prepare—by building an army."

An army? Of what? Five-year-old girls? My confusion must be visible on my face because Uncle Silver chuckles and goes on.

"An army of *clones*, Viktoria. Just imagine. We could double, triple, even *quadruple* our forces. We could choose the strongest, the smartest, the best fighters. And when we lost someone, we wouldn't really lose them! Boys could go home to their mothers. Their clones could stand on the front lines! No one would ever lose anyone again."

Clones. My brain rejects the idea. Cloning isn't real, is it?

But then, it does explain things. Why Anna is here and a younger version of Anna is dead. Why children disappear year after year. Why I've never seen an inmate on the so-called asylum grounds. It's *not* an asylum at all.

Uncle Silver keeps talking as I try to force my brain to accept his explanation. "So, you see, I take people who have nothing to contribute to the fight and *I make them matter*. I make them *immortal*. Everyone will remember Anna forever because of what I've done. And don't worry, I won't let anything happen to you either. This is a nice place to live. We get shipments of Western teddy bears. Anna gets an orange every single week. Anything to keep our subjects happy."

Subjects. The word is sour, distant, clinical. Anna is a *person*, not a *subject*. Does he hear what he's saying? Talking about people, about *children*, like they're expendable.

I stutter out my next question: "How? How is it possible to clone a person?"

"The science would bore you, but suffice to say that this started as a small experiment when we first took over the asylum. We tried on the inmates. We tried on ourselves. The first breakthrough was with a seventeen-year-old girl we had here, and we realized it was easier with children. Our first viable clone came from that original girl, so we—ehm—*recruited* more like her. We used to have twenty or thirty at a time, but funding is trickier with the new government." He says *new government* like he's actually saying *wet garbage*.

My throat is dry and my thoughts spin. *Recruited* means *kidnapped*. He's been stealing kids from the bog—and if he had twenty or thirty at once, probably stealing them from other places too.

"What about all the adults who disappear in the bog?"

He sighs, frowns at me. "Well, Viktoria, you understand we can't have people knowing what we're doing. Most people are fools. They can't comprehend the importance of science. They wouldn't understand that their sons and daughters are ensuring nobody has to lose a son or daughter ever again. Ensuring that we can defeat the Americans and keep our people alive."

"So, what—you kill them?" My heart speeds up. *Say no, Uncle Silver. Don't be that much of a monster.*

"Not me, dear Lenin, no." I don't even have time to feel relieved before he continues, and his meaning becomes clear. "We always have a small contingent of soldiers patrolling. If anyone sees the kids or figures out what we're doing here, they take care of it."

So yes, then, they kill them. My stomach churns. The few times we've found people who wandered into the bog, everyone thought it was suicide. A whole village wrong about the way their own kept dying.

I already know the answer to the next question, but I need to hear him say it. "So, the girl who died at the hospital—Anna—she was a clone?"

He sighs again. "I was so hopeful with that one! Something's wrong with them. They don't make it past five or six. But—progress! They used to die as infants. We've come so far."

Horror crawls through me like a thousand spiders. How many babies have died here? I think about the Anna who lived with us this past week. She wasn't my sister, but she was a person. A scared kid who stumbled through a terrifying bog all alone to try and...what? Get away? No, not just get away. She was there to tell me. But she didn't think she could—so she tried to show me. Tried to march me back through the bog to the truth.

To Uncle Silver.

It was *Silver* who was watching, not Soovana. She was too afraid to answer because he was there and Margit was there. And the eyes she was searching for must have been cameras or listening devices.

I was so scared of the bog, so scared of losing her, that I didn't understand. She wasn't a bog thing, changeling, spirit, ghost. She was a scared child searching for a loophole in the rules of the world she knew: a world where Uncle Silver saw all and controlled all and—for all she knew—would steal her back the moment she voiced the truth out loud.

Uncle Silver made her knowing she would die, knowing she would suffer.

You get sick and then you die. That's what she said. That was her *truth*. At the time, an unsettling strangeness. Now, clearly her terrifying reality.

He decided she was nothing. A throwaway person—not even a person. A shadow. Because she didn't have a mother or a father or a sister, she didn't matter.

But he's wrong. Even when I asked myself questions about who she was, what she was, she was always a person. A scared kid. A hero, even.

She *mattered*. Being someone's sister isn't what makes you matter—being alive is.

"Why didn't you want her to go to the hospital? Why did you tell Mama she couldn't take her?" I force the questions through the suffocating reality of my uncle's indifference.

He sniffs loudly. "The story needed to stay contained! The more people who knew something—*ahem*—unusual was going on here, the harder it would be to contain it. As soon as it got sick, that clone was going to die. We bring in top doctors here to treat them, and they still die. There's nothing a hospital could have done, Viktoria."

A headache builds behind my right eye as I think about that

Anna again, about the gap in my heart when I found out she was gone, days spent in bed grieving. I picture Mama's face, her loss, her desperation. How many one-year-old, two-year-old, five-year-old Annas have laughed and played and taken their first steps and then *died*—for no reason but Uncle Silver's fantasy army? And how many other families in our village are floating off into their loss, feeling it eat away at their sanity day by day?

The Soviets have always treated our people as expendable. Sent tens of thousands of us to Siberia to work and die. Forced neighbor to report neighbor. Tried to instill us with patriotism that would kill us for their endless wars.

I'm suddenly so proud of Liis's protests that I could cry. I hope that even if I never escape, she does. That she makes it to the one she mentioned—the chain across three countries, the thousands upon thousands of people saying enough. *Enough. We do not belong to you. We belong to each other*.

I imagine myself back at school, joining the Young Pioneers at nine. I was proud of the distinctive kerchief, proud of being old enough to join the club. We were sworn in the same way at every meeting. "Are you ready?" "Always ready!" Ready for what?

The answer is clear now. To serve our country. To die for it. Cannon fodder, clone-army experiment. It doesn't matter. That's all we are to them.

My throat burns and closes.

"Why Anna?"

"What do you mean?"

"I mean she's your niece. Why did you take her? I thought you loved Mama, you loved us. Why us?"

"Oh, that." His tone is apologetic. "Policy, I'm afraid. I wasn't alone when I saw you two in the bog. We needed another child, and you were there. I convinced my colleague we only needed one. I thought at least one of you could go back to your mother. So, really, it's not that I took Anna. I saved *you*."

Saved me? I search his face, and I know he means every word, know he thinks I should be *grateful*. How could I not have seen how deep his commitment to the USSR goes? How could I have believed he cared more about his sister than his achievements? These answers are so much worse than anything I imagined. Spirits and monsters are one thing. A man doing this to his only family is so much more wicked.

He goes on. "That's why they left the bog alone. They were going to drain it, but when this project got approval, it made more sense to leave it there. A bog is the perfect place to keep secrets." He laughs, the sound high and sharp and wrong.

So it wasn't the bog that fought back against the Soviets. It was their own plans. Evil versus evil. A bog spared; a village ruined. A thousand trees alive; a hundred people dead.

He's got a new look in his eye now, and one corner of his mouth tugs upward. "Of course, now we have the breakthrough we've been waiting for—so thank you for that."

What? I'm so lost. Does he mean he's going to try and clone me?

"When I saw your friend, I realized who she was. I didn't recognize her when she was little, when you two used to play all the time. But now—she looks just like her! And sixteen! She's been living sixteen years! It changes everything. A clone living on its own in the village for sixteen years…"

My body turns to ice, fear crawling over my skin like a thousand spiders.

Liis.

No, oh no. He's talking about *Liis.*

A baby abandoned in the bog. An experiment. A girl who wants desperately to know who she is.

The photo. The bog body. It all locks into place. Time speeds up and slows down all at once as I realize what I should have the moment the word *clone* came out of Uncle Silver's mouth.

Liis is a clone. My best friend is a clone. She's in more danger than ever.

And I'm the one who brought her here.

XXXV
ANCIENT FOREST

The Ancient Forest card is a prison: a woman pulling at thick branches, trying to break through. You can feel her tension through the card, see how much she wants out in her inky eyes. Yet I wish I were her. Branches crack easier than concrete, and my own prison is a sickly yellow building where my uncle now marches me through the hall, his hand clutching my shirt again.

They have Liis. They have Anna. And I'm more trapped than I've ever been. There's no way out. I knew it in my gut, but now I know it with my hands, my eyes, my fingernails. The endless white walls around me, the total lack of windows to the outside. It wasn't the bog waiting to devour me all this time; it was this place. This prison. Coffin. Bunker with no exit. Home of a thousand dead babies, a thousand ruined lives.

He marches me down the sterile, fluorescent-lit hallway, passing door after identical door. Heavy and metal with little windows you can peer through. All dark, unoccupied.

The rest of our conversation blurs together as I process it. He knew I went into the forest because Margit saw me. He sent the soldiers after me, not Anna. He took me home because he didn't think I knew anything worth knowing. He didn't recognize Liis before because "Viktoria, do you really think I have time to go looking at every child in this village?"

Dark thoughts prick at me like needles. *I was the one who brought Liis here. I was the one who lost Anna. Every time I try to help, I make things worse.*

Dangerous.

Monster.

The familiar words surface in my mind, but something is different this time. They don't burrow into me like they used to.

I keep hearing Mama's voice—and Liis's. *It's not your fault.*

Not. Your. Fault.

I didn't know whose fault it was back then, but this time my heart keeps whispering, *Now we do.* Uncle Silver. It's Uncle Silver. He's the one dismantling the world around me, one person at a time. Him and the party he loves, the Soviets he sold his soul to.

The wild anger of an hour ago beats hot in my chest again, flames in my cheeks. For Anna—both of them. For Mama. For Riina and Liis. For me. And every other person my uncle has crushed under the weight of his ambition.

I ball my hands into fists, and for the second time tonight, I attack the monster that is my uncle. I whip to face him as I scream and shove as hard as I can. He keeps hold of my shirt, and I go down with him, a tangle of flailing, scratching, punching limbs. My knee is in his stomach; his knuckles meet my forehead. He releases me just long enough for me to shove my hand in his pocket and grab the keys—but before I can push away and make a run for it, he grabs my shirt again.

"Viktoria! This is pointless! Stop right this instant!"

I hold his gaze, both of us on our knees.

"No." I say the word with the force of every hurt inside me. Every hurt he created. Every hurt he ignored. Every hurt he told me to get over, even as he knew he could have healed them in a second.

Every hurt that's now a fire driving me on.

I am going to get away. I am going to save Liis. I am going to save Anna.

Because for the first time since this nightmare started, *I know that I can*. I know where they are. I know what happened. I know who we need to get away from.

I lash out with the keys in my fist, catching him on the right cheek. He howls as I draw blood but manages to keep hold of my shirt.

Too bad for him he can't hold me.

I duck out of the shirt, leaving it flapping uselessly in his hand as I scramble to my feet in my bralette. He falls backward from the loss of a counterbalance, and I fly down the hallway faster than I have ever run in my life. Faster even than when I chased Soovana into the bog, clinging to the thread of hope that I would find the answers there.

Before he's up and after me, I've unlocked the door, slammed it, and locked it behind me. He won't have a spare key on him. At least I don't think so. It'll buy me the minutes I need to get across the lawn, through the annex, through the grate.

Through the annex, through the grate.

No.

That's not how I'll save Anna, not how I'll save Liis. The fear that lives so deep in my belly, my bones, my skin and teeth and fingernails, halts me in my tracks. What if I leave and they disappear? What if I leave and I lose them both? Like counting breaths while Mama sleeps, I cannot bear to pull myself away.

I reach into my pocket instead, find Liis's screwdriver there, and turn back to face the asylum. I won't leave Anna or Liis—not even to go get help.

I am help.

I spent so long thinking I was dangerous. But I am only as dangerous as the bog is. I am the assassin plant and the twisted root and the pool that might be six inches deep or ten miles. And I am the soft press of birch bark on your face, the kiss of breeze through trees, the wonder of a cluster of sharp-tasting berries defying the odds to grow sweet in this inhospitable place.

I slip around the corner of the asylum, away from sight of the door where I can now hear faint yelling. As I hoped, there's a vent that matches the one from the annex.

Screwdriver in hand, I head to the last place Uncle Silver would expect:

Back inside.

I thought the asylum was a prison, but the vent is worse. Hot and tight and dark and sterile. I smell bleach through the slats that open into the ceilings and walls of dark, empty rooms. Every time I move, the vent makes loud metallic noises, and I flinch. My progress is a slow crawl, and I don't know where I'm going. Don't know which ceiling conceals Anna, which one hides Liis, which one leads directly back into my uncle's arms.

I'm going to be caught before I can find them. No longer dangerous, but ineffective. My jaw is tight with the fear of it.

I try to remind myself of what I felt in the bog: it doesn't matter where you start, just *that* you start. The asylum is only so big. Eventually, I will find one of them.

So I move. I contort myself. I drag my body through the vents. I peer through slats, hold my breath when I hear footsteps. Then, after an eternity of waiting, a clear, high voice shatters the silence—echoing sweet and strong and unwavering.

Liis.

Strong, brave, rebellious Liis. Protestor outside this place and protestor within it.

She is singing our secret, forbidden national anthem. "*Mu Isamaa On Minu Arm*"—"My Fatherland Is My Love." The same song that echoed across the bunker. The same one that beat from hundreds of thousands of throats at that Ivo Linna concert. The one the Soviets hate because it tells them that we have not forgotten. We will not forget. We know who we are, and they cannot take ourselves from us.

It is Liis's little rebellion in this prison. Just like the Soviets can't take her from herself, neither can my uncle. Neither can this place. I know what she means by singing it, and I love her even more for it. It is her battle cry. Her declaration of herself.

And though she doesn't know it yet, it's my way back to her.

For years I've pushed Liis away, left her behind, broken our pact over and over again because I thought it would save her. Now she's here. My distance *didn't* save her. And this time I won't break the pact. I won't leave her behind. I'll be there to save her—or we'll go down together.

I follow the sound—clear and bold as she calls Estonia her happiness, her fatherland.

When I reach the next fork in the vent, a voice joins Liis's down the hall. Then another. Fresh, young—the voices of children, the other inmates of this secret prison.

Fatherland, they sing. *Our land.*

Then a final voice joins in, and my heart stutters over the beautiful improbability of it.

Anna. My Anna. I'd know her voice anywhere.

"Flowers will bloom from my ashes…"

I hesitate at the turn. Liis's voice comes from one side, Anna's the other. I need to find them both. I need to be able to get back to this juncture. I pull my uncle's keys from my pocket and—with a terrible screech of metal on metal—carve an arrow into the vent.

The arrow points toward Liis, and I point myself toward Anna.

XXXVI
KNIVES, INVERTED

When I reach the vent opening in Anna's wall, every muscle in my body freezes.

Anna—my Anna—has pulled the single rickety chair in the boxlike white room to its center and stands on top of it, singing at the top of her lungs. This is Anna as expected: ten years old, changed by the act of growing up. Taller, thinner, her eyes still so bright. Not broken by this place, thank heavens. In fact, she's the opposite: singing patriotic songs, finding ways to be so herself, so Estonian, even in this place.

"Anna," I whisper the word, press my fingers to the vent.

She startles at the sound of her name, eyes wide as she scans the wall.

"I'm in the vent," I say, removing the screwdriver from my pocket and sliding it through the slats because Anna needs to unscrew the vent from her side.

She pulls the chair to the wall and hoists herself onto it, taking the screwdriver and clutching it in white-knuckled wonder.

"Vik?" It's the first word she breathes, and like when the other Anna said it, I feel something deep and tight and forever coiled loosen in my chest.

She speaks again, and it's in *Estonian*, and tears jump to my eyes. "Is it really you, Vik?"

"It's me."

After that, she can't undo the screws fast enough. She drops the screwdriver three times. Then the cover is off, and I spill into the room, awkward and bruised and not caring one bit. Then I'm up and across the tiny space between us, throwing my arms around her. She smells like industrial soap and sauerkraut and the strange, chemical tang of the building around her, but she's my Anna. *Alive.*

My stomach turns at the thought, because she is alive, but the other Anna isn't. And wasn't she my sister too? Didn't she deserve better? The thoughts taste bitter at the back of my throat. I feel too many things at once. Relief. Grief. Joy. Doom.

"I'm so sorry, Anna. I'm so sorry I took you into the woods. I'm so sorry I lost you," I murmur into her hair.

"You didn't lose me," she insists, pulling away to look me in the eyes, her own shining. "You found me!"

"I took you into the forest—"

"Yes, and Uncle Silver told me we were playing a game, hiding from you. That's not you losing me!"

I'm speechless, but my words aren't needed. Anna's overflowing with them. "I knew you'd come for me—I knew it! I used to pretend to *be* you when I needed to be brave." She slips a hand into her pocket, draws out Fire—the card she tucked into her dress so many years ago—and passes it to me.

I don't know how to feel. Honored. Unworthy. Shaken by her simple faith in me. Me, her sister who lost her. Me, her sister who took five whole years to come for her.

She's still whispering, breathless. "Did Anastasia find you? We boosted her over the fence. It was my idea. I told her everything so she'd recognize you. We're not allowed to go outside anymore because of that, but I knew it would be worth it. I knew she'd find you."

Anastasia. My mind snags on the name. The other Anna. She must have been the other Anna. That's how she knew my name. It's why she acted scared of Uncle Silver.

"Is Anastasia the…younger you? Your clone." Saying the word *clone* out loud feels like admitting I'm insane. I believe Uncle Silver about what he's been doing. I've seen Anna's clone with my own eyes. But it still sounds like a lie, a story, something from another world.

"Yes!" Anna smacks my arm several times in excitement, her body all jittery energy like a puppy. "She made it, then. She made it. I knew she'd make it!"

I lick my lips, my throat powder-dry, as more mysteries slide into place. Anastasia knew my name. It was the first thing she said when she came out of the bog. She knew me, like she didn't know anyone else. The gaps in her memory weren't gaps at all. Her memory was only what Anna told her, which wouldn't have included the layout of our house or what her old teddy bear looked like.

With a pang, I realize she knew my name, and I never knew hers. Not while she was alive. Uncle Silver stole even that—my ability to call her by her real name.

"Is Anastasia with Mama?" Anna's voice brightens with hope.

My stomach sinks. I can't tell her what happened, can I? That Anastasia made it to us, yes, but that she's gone.

In the background, the song goes on. Liis loops the lyrics, and the other voices harmonize: an unexpected children's choir bouncing between locked rooms. The sound brings me back to myself.

Anastasia is gone. Anna is here. *But she's not the only one.* Not the only one here and not the only one who deserves to go home to the people who love her.

"Anna," I whisper, "how many other kids are here?"

Anna frowns, hope dampening. But she doesn't ask about Anastasia again. Maybe has known enough loss to hear what I'm not saying. She only bites her lips and answers my question. "Right now? Two. Two real ones. Maybe more babies—I don't know. They never let us see them until they're a year or two old."

Real ones. Goose bumps rise on my arms and legs. How could a living person be not real? Anna—my Anna—is talking like Uncle Silver. Thinking of kids as real or fake, important or expendable, tidy categories that decide who matters. How else has he brainwashed her? And me—has something sinister crept from his worldview into mine in all the years he's been lecturing me?

I run my fingers through Anna's hair, press my palm to her warm, soft cheek. Then I push the chair back against the wall and climb onto it. We can't stay here any longer. Every minute talking is another minute Uncle Silver could find me here. Every minute is another minute he might move Liis or find a way to block our exit.

The urgency bites at my heels, sharp-toothed.

"Anna, it's time to run."

XXXVII
ASPEN GROVE

As we struggle through the vents, I keep Anna talking. Both because I have too many questions and because I can't see her and I need to know she's still behind me in the dark. Still herself. Still here. Still savable.

She tells me about the asylum. We're on the ground floor with three floors of labs and rooms above us. The doctors check her constantly—vital signs, blood work. Sometimes they take her into surgery, but she doesn't know why.

"Those are the bad days," she says, her voice gone shaky behind me.

Every word is another pain, the experiments growing realer in my mind as Anna's stories sidestep them. I picture her strapped to a table—helpless, asleep—and I want to scream, to smash another kneecap with that satisfying, permanent-sounding crunch.

"And Margit?" I can't get her off my mind. She was here. She knows. She's known the whole time and never told me.

Anna's whisper brightens. "I told Margit you'd come. She said you wouldn't. She said I needed to make peace with my life, but I knew she was wrong. You were always going to come."

298

Make peace. Let go. The same things Uncle Silver tried to get me and Mama to do.

"Margit's helping them keep you prisoner. To think I felt sorry for her, crying a few hours ago...I thought she was crying about you—"

"She was crying?" Anna interrupts.

"Yeah, and she lied to me about why."

"Probably Signe." Anna's voice goes even softer.

"Who?"

"Something happened to her—they won't tell us what. She's been gone for months. Margit keeps asking, and her da yelled at her about it yesterday. Said it's none of her business. Told her she'd have to toughen up if she wanted to make her mark on the world. But Signe's gone, and here that usually means *dead*." She says *dead* so quietly I can barely hear it, like saying the word will summon the thing itself.

Alarm sparks hot on my skin. Another girl dead. The truth of it sinks into me like teeth, like bog mud trapping my leg. Viselike and relentless and dangerous. Another. Girl. Dead.

No more, my heart cries. *No more dead girls.*

I came back for Anna. I'm going back for Liis. But that's not enough, I realize.

Not enough.

I can't leave *anyone* behind—not here, not knowing what I know. There are too many dead kids already. Babies abandoned in the forest. Bodies in the bog. He'd call them failed experiments, but they were people. *Real.* All of them real. All of them mattering, one as much as the other.

And that's not the only reason, I realize. There's something else welling up in me too—a drop of blood beading under a pinprick, the crack in the sky just before the hail comes pelting down.

Anger. It's anger. The thing let loose when I saw Uncle Silver silhouetted in the fluorescent lights.

I've been afraid for so long. Afraid of the bog. Afraid of myself. Afraid that I was dangerous, monstrous, broken. Afraid that I'd feel that way forever. Afraid that no one would ever love me through my fear, my brokeness.

And it's Uncle Silver's fault.

The injustice of it builds like a scream. He's ruined us, ruined us all. Mama, me, Anna, the kids down the hall. Even Margit, sobbing on her bed, heartbroken because he disappeared another friend of hers.

He's one of them. He's always been one of them: the Soviets who steal from us and shut us up and intimidate us into silence. He's worse than a thief. Stealing years and cells and blood and bone from my sister. And me, how do I wrap words around the feelings like broken glass cutting me every time I breathe? He stole *me*—the girl I was, the girl I could be now.

He stole Mama's tether to this world, five years of friendship Liis and I could have had. He stole Liis's past, her answers, her sense of who she is in this world.

We reach the arrow that points toward Liis. She's stopped

singing—and so have the others—but I press my thumb to the jagged mark and push forward. I'm starting to understand the vents. The way they branched toward Anna's room is a mirror image of the way they branch along this other side of the hall. Liis will be in a mirror room, another pale white box full of fluorescent light with a single cot and a single chair and air that smells of bleach and dust.

I press my face to every vent cover along the way. Each room is empty, quiet—until I find her. She's standing in front of her door, face angled toward the little window. And if I know Liis, she's calculating. Watching for a chance, the barest wisp of hope, a way out.

I almost smile. Because this time I'm the one following her into the dark. I'm the one with the way out. I am the Aspen card, touching one tree across the grove, connected to Liis even when she can't see me.

"Thank god you started singing. I might never have found you or Anna otherwise," I whisper through the vent cover, because the first things I want her to know are these: that I am here, that I came back, and that, by singing her tiny rebellion, she also saved herself.

Liis is all relief and fury, eyes shining with unshed tears, pulse beating visibly in her neck. So breathtakingly, brilliantly alive and here and herself. I led her here, but I did not lose her.

I did not lose her.

I will not lose her.

I am not dangerous.

"You came back." She smiles.

"I did."

"He's coming back here in an hour. He said he'd be back to get me," she whispers urgently.

I slide the screwdriver through the vent. "Then let's move fast."

Liis attacks the screws with vigor.

"I wish you were on this side," she huffs as she works. "This would be easier with two hands."

"Once we get you out of here, I'll do all future unscrewing," I offer. And I hope she knows it isn't just a promise to help when she needs help; it's a promise not to go away again.

As she works, I turn my attention to Anna. "Anna—" My whisper is urgent. "Do you know where the other kids' rooms are?"

"I think so. Karl is three or four doors back from here. Kristel is next to him. My room is across from hers. I don't know why they put Liis so far away."

"Can you lead us there?"

"I think I can."

Then the vent cover is off—Liis more masterful than I am at removing them—and Anna and I scoot back, turning our bodies at the nearest junction. Liis boosts herself up behind us and follows, reaching forward to wrap a hand around my ankle and squeeze. It's affectionate and powerful and grounding, and I feel something unknot in my center.

"Let's go," I whisper.

Anna's in the front now, and my heart hums with relief that she's visible ahead of me, as if by seeing her I am tethering her to the world. To myself. To our escape.

She leads us to the other rooms and speaks softly through the vents to Kristel and Karl, coaxing them up. I realize it is lucky she ended up in front. They know her. They trust her. They were all part of the plan to boost Anastasia over the fence and send her for help.

When we have everyone, we shimmy past the arrow leading to Liis and follow the third juncture back toward the vent outside—the one that led me here.

When I spill into the yard, it is with a sharp, furious triumph. The scent of bleach replaced by thick, earthy forest just yards away. The still, sterile air replaced with a dancing breeze. In the distance, a flicker of light. But this time I don't wonder if it's Soovana. It doesn't matter, because he never wished me ill. He never took Anna. And so if I see a flicker, I don't have to chase it through the night. I can tip my hat to the mystery of him and leave him to his wildness.

Now I incline my head to the bog. Perhaps the place I believed it was as a child. Full of danger and mystery—but the kind that demands wonder, not fear. The kind that takes your breath away, not your children.

The kind that I hope will save us now.

Hide us from Uncle Silver, lead us back home under the cover of trees instead of the exposed, vulnerable path along the village edge.

XXXVIII
PINE

Thirty tiny minutes. Three thousand heartbeats. Three hundred breaths.

Uncle Silver told Liis he'd be back for her in an hour, and now it must be half that. Or less. As I help the others from the vent, I wonder how much less. How long is our head start? How long until he knows what I have done?

Until he realizes that he isn't the only one who can disappear people.

I picture Uncle Silver's face when he finds the rooms empty. Each experiment—each person he denied their personhood— vanished under his nose. I hope his body floods with hot panic when he finds us all gone. I hope he knows he's failed.

Somehow, even as I wonder, even as the seconds tick forward, I'm not afraid. I *should* be afraid. I've always been afraid before. Afraid of so many things I realize now were irrelevant. But now I can't find the fear, the stomachache, the tightness in my chest. Somehow, there's no space for them.

As Liis and Anna help the other two from the vent, I reach into my pocket and slip the top card from my deck. I press the reassuring paper between my fingers.

The Pine is the courage card—the survivor card—a test of faith, a step into the darkness. Riina's art on this one is a barefoot woman with her eyes closed and her arms raised to the sky. A position as powerful as she is delicate. Around her, a cluster of pine trees stands with her, protective.

It's like Liis's mama is sending me strength, and tears jump to my eyes when I realize she's sort of my mama too. The most magical adult I've ever known is family now. The thought fills me with wonder. It's been the hardest week I've had in five years, yet now I have twice as many people who love me. Who maybe always loved me, even when I wasn't paying attention. And it's this love, this family, that I'm leading Anna back to. Anna, *alive*, after five years, is so close to coming home.

I slip Pine back into my pocket and take in the newcomers. The boy, Karl, is taller, older, lankier than I'd pictured him. The girl, Kristel, is just the opposite: short and young—maybe six or seven—and round like a cherub. She's the one I saw playing with Anna when I first peered through the window, a moment that feels so long ago now. They're miracles, both of them. Someone else's Anna, someone else's very heart. Almost back in the arms of the people who lost them.

"Here." Karl removes his shirt and holds it out to me, revealing a thin undershirt.

I almost forgot I was in a bralette this whole time. There was too much else to focus on. My face flushes as I slip into the shirt and fumble with the buttons, covering my suddenly cold midriff.

I press a finger to my lips and motion for them to follow me toward the corner of the asylum. Toward the annex. I have Uncle Silver's keys, but the front of the asylum—the way to the gate—is too exposed. I'll lead us out the back, through the bog, choosing a path I hope Uncle Silver won't expect.

That's the safest way out.

Liis seems to intuit my plan and slips ahead, letting me fall back beside Anna, my hand slipping into my sister's.

But as Liis rounds the corner, she freezes, then backs into us in her haste to get away from whatever's there. My heart sinks, and I motion for everyone to press flat against the wall. Then I peek around the corner.

The annex is closer than I remember, but there's no way we'll make it. Because just outside the door stands Uncle Silver, sour-faced as he listens to a woman with her back to us. I'm only halfway through thinking, *Who is that?* when I realize I know. When I realize how much it makes sense.

It's Margit's mama. The woman whose records we found in the annex. The woman with a top-secret government job that takes her away from my cousin for months at a time.

What was it Uncle Silver said? *We tried on ourselves first.* That's why Aunt Margit has a paper trail here. The first cloning subjects were Aunt Margit and Uncle Silver. But more than the first subjects: the leaders of the effort.

The thought takes my breath away. Aunt Margit wasn't an inmate. She's part of this.

My family has more than its fair share of monsters.

Aunt Margit gesticulates angrily, and her voice carries across the distance. "No, you listen to me. You know the protocols. We destroy the records if there's a chance of discovery. They'll want to move the facility. There's already unrest. The protests against the state keep getting bigger. Imagine the violence if they knew there were kids in here."

The security guard stands to the side, looking awkward, as if he doesn't know if he's supposed to go or stay. He opens his mouth to speak but then closes it.

"We'll find her." Uncle Silver's voice is desperate. "We'll contain it!"

"Contain it? She's been gone for an hour. She's told ten people by now. Your only hope is that she fell into a bog like Signe."

Signe. Signe who Anastasia mistook Liis for. Signe who disappeared. Liis's clone, her origin story. Signe got away into the bog, but she didn't make it. She's the bog body, the one I unearthed.

A piece slides free from the puzzle coming together in my mind. *Margit knew Signe.* She cried over Signe. She knows Liis. She would have seen the resemblance. And she clearly knows what her parents are up to, since she plays with Anna every day. Why didn't she tell them one of their clones was walking around the village? Why didn't Uncle Silver already know who Liis was?

Has Margit been keeping Liis's secret? Why?

"We have to go." Liis's breath is hot in my ear, her whisper urgent. "We'll have to go out the front gate while they're fighting back here."

I nod and follow her lead, but my mind is stuck on Margit. *Margit, whose side are you on? What do you know and not know?* She didn't tell us about Anna, but she also didn't tell her da about Liis. What does that mean?

We flee across the well-lit asylum lawn, and all my usual fear rushes back. Anyone can see us. All it would take is an end to their argument and one of the three sliding around the building into sight.

We make it to the gate, and Liis rattles it. A heavy lock dangles from an even heavier chain. She pulls out her screwdriver and starts trying to jimmy the lock.

"No, wait." I fumble in my pocket for Uncle Silver's keys. Desperately, I hope this one is included on the chain…

Everyone watches Liis and me, collectively holding their breath. We're too frantic to notice the footsteps behind us, the smell of good soap, the feel of another body joining the group.

We don't notice anything until she speaks—the missing piece of my puzzle.

Margit.

"What's going on here?"

XXXIX
MOOSE

The moment of reckoning, the Moose card, the sinking-gut feeling of knowing you're caught—it's all upon us now. It's a dead end, a folktale climax, the held breath where you either guess Ruupentiltsen's name or lose your child, outsmart the witch in her gingerbread house or lose your life.

"Margit!" Anna doesn't seem to understand the gravity of the situation. The rest of us are frozen—faces shaped by surprise or dread—but Anna throws herself into Margit's arms. And, to my surprise, Margit kisses the top of my sister's head.

"Margit." When Anna says it, the name is like a song.

When I repeat it, it's a funeral dirge. "Margit, please."

I mean, *Please don't turn us in. Please help us.* But also, *Please explain. Please tell me your role in all this.*

She doesn't say anything, though. Instead, she reaches into the carefully kept plastic shopping bag she uses as a purse and hands me a key. *The key.* The key to the gate. There must be a matching one on Uncle Silver's key ring, but it would have taken me too much time to test them all.

I thought my capacity for shock was exhausted, but here it is again—shock like a plunge into ice-cold water. Shock like falling through the peat into the bog.

Margit isn't here to catch us; she's here to save us.

The puzzle pieces that are my cousin shift in my mind and reassemble. What do you do when your parents are monsters? Perhaps you keep some of their secrets, but not all of them. Perhaps you cry alone in your bedroom because you're too afraid to tell. Perhaps you see someone trying to escape and you whisper Ruupentiltsen's name in their ear. Choose to do the right thing in the end.

I'm stone-still, but Liis springs into motion. She grabs the key from my hand and unlocks the gate.

"Margit," I say again. This time her name is the start of a question. "Come with us?"

What do you do when your parents are monsters? You save Liis with your silence. You try to keep the monsters happy. And when you get the chance, you *run*. This is how I want Margit's story to go—toward a happier ending.

Anna bobs up and down with excitement and nerves, shakes Margit's hand in a way that means, *Yes, come!*

The door is open, and Liis tears toward the trees. The boy—Karl, I remember fleetingly—sweeps Kristel into his arms and follows.

"Go, Anna," I say, and she glances at Margit. "We're right behind you."

She releases Margit's hand and sprints after the disappearing figures.

Margit is crying, her face folding in on itself. Her body is tight, hesitant. She darts a glance back at the buildings, then faces the ground.

"I knew and didn't tell you." Her voice breaks on the words.

And while the hurt of that truth spider-webs through me, so does a certainty: Margit doesn't deserve to be left behind with the monsters either. She didn't choose them—not in the end.

I reach for her, but she doesn't take my hand. Not yet.

"I don't know if I'm real," she whispers, and I realize *this* is the secret she's been carrying. Not someone else's secret but her own. Her tears aren't all for Signe. They're for herself too. She knows her mama was one of the first experiments. She knows they look alike. But she doesn't know the outcome, doesn't know who—what—she is. Is she herself or her mama? And does either answer make her a monster too?

I thought I was asking her to come, but I know now that I'm telling her. Telling her she's forgiven. Telling her we all had secrets. Telling her she's not a monster.

"You are. *Real.*"

I take her hand and kiss the palm, then lead her, first at a walk, then a jog, then a run, toward the woods. Ahead, the forest—so dark for so long—grows lighter, the earliest rays of sun finding their way through canopy to light the path. Like stars guiding us home. The dewdrops on the flytraps aren't poison; they're dewdrops. The trees aren't sentries, soldiers; they're my oldest friends. The bog isn't Soviet territory. It is—it has always been—ours.

Behind us, the real danger booms now, his voice clear as a bell.

"Viktoria, stop right there!"

Margit freezes, but I push her on. "Go. GO. GO!"

She listens, disappearing into the trees. But I don't follow.

Instead, I turn away from the bog, away from the village, away from escape—toward the monster that is my uncle.

XL
IVY

In the soft light of morning, the fence casts a complicated shadow that distorts my uncle's face as he strides toward the trees. He is Uncle Silver, and he is not, all at once. He is the Wolf Pack in my deck, all teeth and claws. And he is what I thought he was before: Ivy. Ambition working its way through the cracks to take over your life.

"How could you?" My words are knives, not a question but a weapon. To stop him here. To let the others run. And to shame him—if he can still feel shame.

The parental look on his face, like I'm the disappointment, like I need more discipline, tells me he can't—and makes me shake with outrage. He's only steps away from me now, his arm already reaching forward for my shoulder or wrist or the collar of Karl's shirt.

I let the anger bleed through me, conjuring the acid of assassin plants—turning my words into something that'll dissolve you if you come too close. "If you take one more step, I'll tear your eyes out."

He stops, startled. I can almost hear his thoughts. *How is poor, sad, quiet Vik talking back like this? Whatever happened to "Yes, Uncle Silver; no, Uncle Silver"?* The thought makes me so mad that

I smack my closed fist against my other palm for emphasis. It's satisfying when he jumps back. I hope he still aches from when I kicked him in the hall, still feels the sting of my fists and knee and heel.

"Viktoria! What's gotten into you? I explained that Anna is fine—and you can see for yourself. This behavior is unwarranted. Everyone is fine. Or at least everyone *was* fine until you—"

"Unwarranted? Uncle Silver, you were keeping us prisoner!"

He inches forward again, and I inch back. Step by crunching step over fallen leaves. The forest shivers, the breeze trembling like a thing alive.

His anger turns his face a mottled red. "*For. Your. Own. Good.* What—do you think my superiors would just let you go home? Do you think they wouldn't treat you a thousand times worse? *I* am the only thing keeping you and your sister from a real asylum or a bullet in the head. Ever think about that?"

"So, it's better to keep us prisoner than let someone else keep us prisoner?"

"Yes!"

I picture Anna and Margit, Kristel and Karl flying through the woods behind Liis—over spongy paths, through the sacred grove, past the comb that marks the way. I wonder how far they've made it, how much more time I can buy them. He keeps inching forward, but his pace is slow, and I keep it slow, taking small, deliberate steps backward—deeper into the shadows of trees, the birdsong-drenched spaces away from the asylum. Though now the birds are silent, the bugs too.

Listening.

"Tell me what happened to Signe." My voice is calmer but still sharp.

I already know the answer. They kidnapped her, did experiments on her, cloned Liis from her, and one day she broke free. She fell into the bog, like Aunt Margit said. My own personal nightmare. The body that rose up beside me while I fought for my life. But I need to hear him say it. And I need to distract him just a little longer. Every second he follows me into the bog is another they have to get to safety. To tell Mama and Riina. To get Karl and Kristel home.

To run.

To hide.

"How do you know that name?" His nostrils flare.

"Anastasia said it." I realize again that I never was able to call her by her real name while she was alive, and another dose of anger floods my body. "And so did Anna."

"She ran off. We've had trouble with everyone *breaking the rules* lately." His voice is pointed.

"Liar."

Uncle Silver manages to look incredulous. "Viktoria, this kind of back talk isn't like you."

Condescending prick. I don't usually use words like that, but it feels so right, so just, one of the most correct thoughts I've ever had in my life.

"Stop talking to me like that and tell me the truth!" I'm shouting now, and there's a wild freedom in it.

He hesitates, then: "Signe was too old. That's all. The best results are with children. So we sent her away. She's *fine*."

Another half-truth. *Signe's too old.* True. *She's fine.* No.

Liar, liar, devil, monster. This time, when I slam my fist into my palm, I make a noise I didn't know I had in me—frustration so deep it has no words. It reminds me of Kaos standing over the other Anna, asserting her intentions with something between hiss and scream. The sound is jagged-edged rage, bog-deep despair, a storm of loss and heartbreak and lies being ripped from my soul.

Uncle Silver jumps back as if afraid I'm about to attack him.

Instead, I turn, and with nothing else to say to him, I run. Away from the cold concrete blocks that have held my family hostage in a thousand different ways—into the bog that never meant me harm.

I expect him to go back. If he's going to stop all of us—Liis, Anna, Kyle, Kristal, even Margit, and me—he'll need backup. Soldiers. Security guards. Aunt Margit. Someone, anyone.

And when I look back, at first I think I'm right. He's turning away from me, pointing feet and face and cold, shriveled heart toward the prison he's been warden of for so long. The seat of his power. The phone that, no doubt, leads to whatever backup he needs.

But beyond him, something is wrong.

I trip over a root or a stick or perhaps nothing more than the uncertainty of what I'm seeing. Five minutes ago, the trees at the edge of the forest seemed sparse, the asylum visible beyond them.

Now they cluster together, a wall blocking out the light— blocking out the way.

I think of the lakes that disappear when their drinkers aren't grateful enough, the forests that pick up and leave in the night. Is this what the stories mean? Am I seeing what I'm seeing? Or have I just gone farther in, where the trees cluster closer, run faster, backed deeper than I thought I had?

I almost stop, but Uncle Silver is turning again. Back toward me, back toward the bog. The lines on his face are a map of uncertainty and anger and fear. And I don't wait to see where that leads us. I right myself and turn my face away from the sentry trees, the blockaded asylum.

Again, I run.

Behind me, his footsteps pound against rock and earth. And is it my imagination, or is something else rumbling? A growling deep in the earth's throat. The noise of trees ripping roots from packed earth, branches closing the gaps between them. The sound of boulders shaking their fists, weeds reaching out to wrap tendrils around fleeing ankles.

The bog that swallowed the tank fighting back.

Am I delirious with fear, or was I right as a child that there is magic in this bog? Magic that my younger self knew in her bones and her skin and her sun-soaked heart was not her enemy?

I glance over my shoulder, trying to look, trying to understand, but all I see is a flash of my uncle's face—pale, all fear now—and the briefest shimmer of light at the corner of my eye as the forest rumbles, shivers under my feet. Spark, flare. Lightning bug or lantern eyes.

Soovana?

Always there and never there. Just a flicker at the edge of my vision.

Perhaps only in my mind.

Or—

Perhaps on our side.

Perhaps real.

They say he's shy. That he prefers his own company. Don't go too close, stare too deeply, linger too long. Let him be. Let him be. *Let him be.*

Don't make him angry.

Never make him angry.

I manage a burst of speed, force myself not to look back again. Even when a crack breaks the morning in half, silencing the wildlife, sending a murder of crows into the sky like debris in an explosion. Even when the trees shift again on the edge of my vision. Even when Uncle Silver makes a noise I've never heard before—a scream and a shout and a sudden silence all mashed together.

The noise of an ending.

I don't see anything, but an impression presses itself into my mind as I flee. A shape tall and thin and hunchbacked, hair the color of stars, beard the lace of lichen cakes on tree branches. Bare feet one with the rich, black earth. A pine-root staff holding him up.

Keeper of bogs. Protector of the wild things, the wild places. The throat that swallowed the tank, the heart that never wanted to keep their secrets.

When my heart feels as though it will beat through my chest, and my breath is acid in my lungs, and I have passed the grove and passed the comb and passed the skulls outside the bunker—now scattered and broken and pressed into earth—I finally slow and glance behind me.

The forest is as it ever was. Golden in the growing morning light, branches tangled above, moss springy underfoot, assassin plants tucked into hidden corners awaiting their moment of glory.

My uncle is nowhere to be seen.

Soovana never was.

I turn and stumble on toward Liis's house.

XLI
IVY, INVERTED

I think about the comb—and I force away the urge to return, to go back and tap, tap, tap it again. Instead, I tap the ground with my feet—trace the path back to Liis's house. *Save us, save us, save us*, the rhythm of my jogging sings through my mind.

Something inside me is certain that Uncle Silver is gone, that whatever just happened behind me means his ending. But Aunt Margit isn't gone. The soldiers aren't. Whatever happened to my uncle—or didn't—in the forest, we aren't out of danger yet. I don't know if we ever will be. The soldiers will come for us as soon as they can. All we can do now is run.

I finally burst through the trees, Liis's house getting bigger with every step. I stumble through the back door and almost knock Margit over. The room is in chaos.

Riina is sobbing with her arms around Liis, kissing her head over and over as Kaos runs, screaming as only a fox can, around their legs. Karl is catching his breath, hands on his knees. Kristel shies into a corner.

Anna is laughing in Mama's arms, and Mama's face lives a dozen lives in the span of a minute, staring at her and then at me. Shock. Joy. A collapse into tears.

"How, how, how?" she sobs.

I'm a storm of emotions—joy and relief watching my sister and Mama hug, stomach-dropping guilt that Anastasia isn't here with us too. I want to throw myself into their hug, but Margit straightens beside me, and she looks so alone that I take her hand instead. It's strange to feel protective of Margit, but I do.

I know what it's like to wonder if you're a monster.

The others have started to explain, but I fill in the gaps for Mama and Riina. Uncle Silver and Aunt Margit. The clones. The Soviet soldiers who will come for us any moment. We're their dirty secret, even more expendable than we were yesterday.

I don't tell them what happened in the forest. I don't know what happened in the forest, myself.

When I finish, Mama and Riina move as one—rushing around the house, throwing food into bags, ordering kids to fill canteens and sling them over shoulders. Kaos tails Mama from room to room, clicking something in fox language in a way that would be comical if the tension of the moment weren't so heavy across our shoulders.

It takes almost no time for us to be out the door, Riina in the lead. But the moment we are, everyone freezes.

Stretched across the lawn—an ominous mirror image from the night our house burned down—is half the village: fingers twisted around kitchen knives, eyes bloodshot with the aftereffects of homemade vodka, faces contorted in the kind of anger that can only mean this is the end of our story. That in my rush to get away from Aunt Margit and the Soviet soldiers, I forgot another danger just outside our door.

I can almost smell the smoke to come. I wonder if this time it's us who will burn.

XLII
THE SUN

W e're leaving," Riina says. "Just let us go."

She expects the worst again. We all do.

Margit clutches my hand like I'm her last connection to life, and I reach out for Liis's little arm with my other hand. Mama holds on to Anna like they're fused together. Kristel ducks behind Karl's legs. Kaos guards Riina, baring her teeth to the roiling, hostile crowd.

I brace myself to run, but instead a sound somewhere between a gasp and a scream issues from a woman in the crowd. It's Ulli—the woman who led the mob last time. She's shoving her comrades, flailing madly to get to the front, where she falls to her knees with a shaking hand over her mouth. She releases her tree-branch club, and it falls harmlessly into the dirt beside her.

"Karl."

I turn toward the gangly boy. His mouth hinges open, and in two strides he's in the dirt with Ulli—his mama—holding her.

"What?"

"How?"

"Witchcraft!"

"Miracle!"

A chorus of murmurs, questions, uncertainties flickers through the crowd. Hope flames to life in people's eyes, and they examine us, brows drawn. Then another person screams—a young man with short-cropped blond hair and blotchy pink skin.

Kristel's da.

"What happened? Where are the rest of them?" Ulli stands, grasping Karl's hand like a lifeline, the same way I held Anastasia when she first emerged from the forest. Her voice is soft enough to break. Hope has sanded down her jagged edges.

Riina opens her mouth to speak, but instead my sister's voice rises above the crowd. "The asylum. The Soviets took us all."

The silence is so complete it's like we've all stuffed cotton in our ears.

Then Anna tells them everything, and something swells in my chest. Pride, I think. Wonder. The realization that I've done it. I've saved my sister. My body didn't have time to take it in before, but now it can—my skin humming with the wonder of it.

Change rolls through the crowd with Anna's every word. Surprise, horror, fear, anger. My own journey reflected back at me.

"Go," Ulli says, finally, pulling Kristel's da to his feet. "Get Kristel out of here. They'll be coming for them again. The tanks will roll in any minute."

And she's right. We need to go.

Kristel and her da don't need to be told twice. They run toward the village. Riina starts to go as well, motioning for us to follow.

Ulli holds up a hand to stop her. "I'm sorry. I'm so sorry. We didn't understand."

"We were all afraid," Riina offers generously.

Ulli burned my house down, so I can't say I agree with this easy forgiveness. All I want her to do is let us run.

First, she turns to the crowd, Karl's hand still clutched in hers. "Block the road through town. Make it harder for anyone to come after these children. And then"—she says, her eyes burning, voice rising—"we take the asylum."

The thought warms me. If there's anyone we missed, Ulli will find them. If my aunt or uncle are still there, they'll have to face what they've done. These people are no longer a danger to us, but they *are* a danger. To the Soviets and anyone who stands with them.

We're running, but we're not leaving that loose end unraveled behind us.

She turns to us and makes a shooing motion with her hands, like we're a cat that's wandered into the pantry. "What are you waiting for? *Run.*"

I don't know why we were still waiting for her permission, but those words unfreeze us, and we go, following Liis and Riina into the forest and away from the asylum. *Away, away, away.* I count my footsteps like they're breaths. *Step, one, two, three. Stomp, one, two, three.*

As we move, I imagine the village. Ulli and her comrades joining arms, crowding across the road—a human blockade, a quiet defiance, their own human chain, their own protest. Screaming inside their hearts, *You cannot have any more of our children. You cannot have any more of our blood.*

My cards thump against me in my pocket, and I think of the Sun—the card full of flowers turning their faces up toward that bright orb. The card means harmony. Warmth. Positivity.

Hope. Perhaps it also means hope.

<hr />

Where are we going?" Mama asks, echoing the question that's been banging around my heart.

We've been walking for hours when we finally stop for lunch in a cluster of trees behind a small farm. We pass around brown bread, canteens full of water, handfuls of berries.

I expect Riina to answer, but Liis does. "The Baltic Way. The human chain across three countries. That's where everyone who wants freedom will be today. That's where we'll find help."

As we all fall quiet, chewing, drinking, resting, Margit wanders away from the group to stare into the trees. I follow.

"Why did you keep her secret?" I ask when I'm close enough.

I know she might want privacy, a moment to process. Because what must it be like to leave your parents behind? Your dreams? Your whole life? My cousin's life is so much more complicated than I ever imagined. And my feelings about her are more complicated now too. I feel sick thinking about what it must mean to have parents like that. Sicker when I remember her questions about being real—about whether she is her own mother, copied, remade, capable of the same things.

But there's anger here too, smoldering in my gut, burning at my skin. It has been pushing past my nerves more and more the farther we get from the immediate danger of being caught. She may have spared Liis, but she didn't spare Anna. And I need to understand why. I need to understand what's going on in her head.

So I don't give her the privacy she might crave. Instead, I take the first opportunity that presents itself to get her alone, to ask the questions buzzing hot along my skin.

Why did you keep her secret? My question still hangs in the air, unanswered.

"Which secret?" She doesn't look at me, her eyes resolutely on the ground. And she's right. There are so many secrets. Every person in this clearing, every person in our village, had secrets. Who knows how many of them Margit's been hoarding?

"Liis. You knew who she was. You must have. But you didn't tell your da. Why?"

She waits so long that I think she might not answer. But eventually she turns to face me. "I just…felt wrong about it."

"What do you mean?"

"I mean…after they took Anna, I didn't really feel okay about it anymore. That made it—made everything they were doing—real. Then they took Signe from me, and I couldn't stop thinking it was wrong. It was all wrong." She breaks off, takes a deep breath before going on. "I didn't realize who Liis was until a couple of years ago, when I got to know Signe. Before that, I only talked to Anna when I was at the asylum."

She darts a glance at me, tears beading in her eyes now, and presses on: "Signe hated it there. I couldn't hurt her more than they already were. And telling Da about Liis felt like it would hurt her, I guess. Since she sort of is her."

Liis makes her way across the clearing and slips quietly beside me, listening.

My next question has sharper edges. "You knew about Anna the whole time. If you felt so wrong about everything, why didn't you tell us?"

"And what would you have done? She was already there. He wouldn't have given her back." Her sharpness matches my own.

"We would have gotten her out. Left. Run. Something! We could have done *something*. Something other than letting people experiment on her for five years." I can't tell if I'm still angry or just devastated now, thinking about all that time where Anna was a prisoner, a lab rat, alone. My body feels heavy, thick with those five years lost.

Margit's gaze drops again. "I didn't know what to do. I never knew what to do. I just…wanted them to love me. It's different—keeping a secret about Liis. They would never have known that I knew, even if they found her someday. But if I told you about Anna, they would know it was me."

She's afraid of her parents, I realize. And I should have realized it before. Not just afraid of what she is but afraid of them. Should I tell her that her da is gone? Would that make it easier—or make it worse? Or would the magical quality of his demise earn me another judgment from my cousin?

"What would they do to you if they found out?" Liis asks in a whisper.

Margit bites her lip. "I don't know. I can't explain it. I just... couldn't disappoint them. I couldn't give them a reason not to love me. I know it sounds foolish. *I know*. But there's no other way to explain. That's just how I felt."

A reason not to love her. I suppose it's like the years I spent believing Mama thought I was a killer, the years I spent drowning in the impossibility of proving her wrong. I guess Margit knew her parents' love for her was fragile—one wrong move and it would come crashing down. And then what would she have?

I know what it's like to feel unlovable. And the bleakness of it tamps down my anger again. All Margit had were bad choices, so how could she have made any good ones? It's a miracle she kept Liis's secret.

Another truth slides into place for me. "That's why you were around so much more lately...Uncle Silver sent you to watch Anna."

To watch all of us.

I always knew Margit was no secret keeper, but now the truth sinks deeper. She was a secret collector. A spy. Part of the threat.

Her anger comes as a surprise. She spits her words like they've been stuck in her throat for years. "I hated it. I hated it so much."

She balls a fist, presses it against her leg. "I never wanted to be involved. I just wanted to go away to the city, to leave all this shit behind. But if they were watching you, they were also watching *me*. Which means I've never been allowed to be anything except perfect."

The word *perfect* lingers between us in the silence. The same thing Uncle Silver asked of me but I never delivered. The thing Margit felt she had no option but to deliver. Because it made her real. Or lovable. Or safe.

Except she was never safe. And she knew that too. Which is why she's so angry. And that anger, I realize now, was always there. Masked as hostility or superiority or bossiness. An outward display of control when her inner world felt so without it.

Will she feel safer or less safe when she knows Uncle Silver is gone? I decide this is the moment to find out.

"Margit, something happened to your da in the forest. I'm pretty sure he's dead."

Dead. The first time I've said it aloud.

It's impossible to name every complicated emotion that battles it out on my cousin's face. Grief. Fear, I think. Loneliness. But I glimpse a flash of relief there too. He was her father—and he was the warden of her personal prison. Always watching. Always demanding. Never answering the question tucked at the bottom of her heart: *Who am I?*

I wonder, then, if that was another reason she avoided Liis, avoided Anastasia. Avoided our house. Because it was a reminder of who she might be, of how unsafe she really was. How could she be near the clones and not wonder if she was one of them?

How could she be near us, her family—imperfect failures that we are in her parents' eyes—without the constant reminder that proximity to her da couldn't save anyone from being watched, being used, being stolen away?

A reminder that this world was designed to eat us all.

She doesn't say whatever it is she's feeling about her da. She doesn't ask me how he died. She doesn't ask me how I know. Instead, she closes her eyes, and the two words I never expected to hear from Margit are so soft I almost think I imagined them.

"I'm sorry." A pause. She opens her eyes, lets her breath out, long and shaky. "I really didn't know what else to do."

My cousin is only a few months younger than me, but right now she looks like she's years behind us. Small and growing smaller: hunching her shoulders, tucking her chin to her chest, wrapping thin white arms around herself. Anger burned down to reveal a scared little girl.

It's Liis who reacts first, and that's no real surprise. Liis is courage and generosity personified. The Raven, the Earth. Determination, grit, and love. She leans over and presses her cheek to the top of Margit's head, wrapping her right arm around her. It's the only time I've ever seen Margit not shy away from Liis, and I realize now that was a kindness; getting close to Liis would have brought Liis closer to Uncle Silver. Perhaps Margit stayed away for Liis's sake as much as her own.

I step toward them but pause, trying to untangle my feelings. Margit the spy. Margit complicit. Margit who hurt me. Margit who saved us. Margit this scared, small version of herself who needs us.

Kaos spies Liis and skitters away from the rest of the group to dogpile onto a now-disgruntled-looking Margit. Anna follows, flinging herself into Margit and knocking all of them over, even as Kaos hisses at her to back off.

If Anna and Liis and even Kaos can forgive Margit, I can't be the one holding back. Not when she left everything behind. Not when she chose us over them in the end.

I drop to my knees, reach across the tangled mess of a group hug in the grass, and kiss her on the temple.

XLIII
EARTH

Our legs are tired from the running, our hearts tired from the tears. But we make it to a bus before anyone catches up to us. No sign of Soviet soldiers. Just a ragged group of survivors on plastic seats watching fields and trees rushing past the windows in a blur of green and brown. The bus takes us toward the main road where Liis's protesters should be. Where she hopes safety will be.

There's no one else on board, which makes me nervous. *Will Liis's protestors be there? Will there be anyone to help us?* Liis seems so sure, but my nerves still spark with worry.

Most of our group sits at the front, just behind the driver, who still looks not entirely thrilled to have a fox on board, despite begrudgingly agreeing to it minutes ago. Now he mutters to himself as he drives, second-guessing his decision. Anna and Mama share secret laughter behind his back.

After the fox negotiations, Liis slipped away from the group and tucked herself into the back row, and I followed. Kaos curls up on her feet, as if she's comforting her. And there's something in Liis's posture that makes me want to do the same. I tuck away my worries about where we're going and what we'll find there, slip my hand into hers, and squeeze.

"Liis," I breathe into the silence. "Are you okay?"

She's quiet for a long time, and when she speaks, her voice is heavy. "So, I'm a clone."

My stomach flips. We've been running, running, running—moving every second since the asylum—and I haven't had a chance to tell her. But apparently she's overheard enough to piece it together herself.

"Signe, the body in the bog—she was me. I'm her."

I nod, take her hand in mine, and wait for her to go on.

She faces me now, her expression tight, like every part of her face is trying to squeeze into the middle. "I was the imperfect clone. They left me behind because I was different. That was the answer to my mystery this whole time. I wasn't lost. I don't have a mother out there somewhere looking for me. They threw me away, like I was nothing."

Something fierce and protective rises in me, carrying with it all the terrible heaviness of so many years spent feeling like nothing myself. "You," I say, squeezing her hand and staring into her eyes, "*are perfect.* You are the most perfect girl. The one who survived. The one who grew up."

Then, after a breath: "No, that's not it. It's no one's fault that they didn't survive, didn't grow up. But you are perfect because you are *you*. Liis, we saved them. You saved them. You saved Anna. If you hadn't been brave enough to tell me your secret, lead us back to the asylum when we found that photo…they'd still be experimenting on kids. You *matter*. You changed things. You changed *me*."

I don't know if it's enough. The truth behind Liis's secret is all questions and no answers. She was someone's experiment. She's something new. I'm sure—more sure than I've been of anything in my life—that Liis is still Liis. She matters just as much as ever. But I don't know if she feels the same. I don't know if my certainty is enough.

"It feels like the world is made of paper," she says after another long silence. "Like any moment I might step too hard and fall through. Everything I knew was wrong." Tears fill her eyes, and she presses her lips together. "Do you think I'm not real?"

She says the last two words in a way that tells me they're her greatest fear. I think of Anna's casual comment a few hours ago. *Real ones.* As if the kidnapped children were real and the clones were not. The kind of not real that made Uncle Silver and Aunt Margit leave babies in the woods to die, watch them die again and again in a lab, mourning them as lost opportunities, not people. I realize that Liis will probably have to keep this secret her whole life. There are too many others like Uncle Silver who would think she's expendable.

It's not that different from being Estonian, I suppose. Not Russian, not fully Soviet. With our language without gendered pronouns and our endless singing and our sacred oak groves full of gifts for the trees. This is what the protests are about—the fact hits me in a new way now. The protests are about being treated like an acceptable loss, something other, something less than real. They're about declaring ourselves human too.

With a pang, I realize it wasn't only Uncle Silver and Aunt Margit who cut these questions into Liis's heart. It was me too. When I told her I wasn't sure Anna was Anna, I was saying so much more than I knew. If Anna wasn't Anna, Liis might not be Liis.

Do you think I'm not real?

I feel the truth of my answer in my gut, my bones, my very soul. Anna is Anna and Anastasia is Anastasia and Liis is Liis, and every single one of them matters.

Every single one of *us* matters.

I hold her gaze. "You're the most real person I know. It doesn't matter how you got here. It matters who you are."

"No wonder I've always been such a weirdo." She says it like a joke, but I know her heart isn't joking.

A memory from a few days ago wraps its arms around me, and I kiss her on the temple. Echoing the words she used to comfort me, I ask, "Who ever said I wanted you to be like everybody else?"

She smiles in a way that doesn't quite reach her eyes, and I feel like I'm talking to both of us when I go on. Because Liis is the best person I know, so if we both have our doubts, maybe that just makes us…human. Because I'm a girl who's spent five years feeling irreparably wrong. But I—we—are also the girls who saved my sister in the end. We're the girls who reunited those kids with their parents. We're the girls who unearthed the secret that's been hurting our village for twenty years, a protest perhaps just as powerful as the ones Liis loves so much.

There's something firm and clear and awestruck rising up, filling my chest. *Pride*, I think, or admiration—for myself, for Liis, for us. For what we've done. If the world thinks we're imperfect girls, well, imperfect girls sure get things done.

I throw myself around Liis, hugging her with all the conviction coursing through my body, and I whisper, "I don't think you're imperfect. But if you are, so am I. And if we are, maybe imperfect isn't bad. Maybe it's just normal. Human. *Real.* Maybe it's like you said in the annex: It's not us who need to change. It's the world."

XLIV
SACRED GROVE

If I had a feather for every lie we've been living with, I'd turn us all into birds and we'd fly away to see the world. Finland with its Levi's jeans and bright green greens and meat so red it might be plastic. Italy with its style and sunshine. Perhaps even America, where the cowboys live.

Instead, we're here, fighting for our feathers. Fighting for our freedom. Not in some far-off place. Here. *Estonia.*

We disembark the bus along a country road. From the rusty bench that is the bus stop, we can see the protest—the road overflowing with people, megaphones, laughter, music, the fields around us full of cars.

The sound of our secret national anthem rings out clear and perfect in the afternoon air—a thousand voices harmonizing.

We join in before we even arrive.

People welcome us when we reach the chain, smiling, laughing, clapping us on the backs. It's the most I've been touched by strangers in my whole life. It's jarring and intoxicating all at once, the energy of each moment electric.

Everyone is here. Punks with mohawks and Repeal the Deal T-shirts and safety-pinned jackets sing at the top of their lungs.

Traditionally dressed grandmamas—all flowing skirts and poufed, embroidered sleeves—take their hands and sing along. Families swing small children between them, and I think of Da. I wonder if he and Mama ever swung me like that, ever laughed like we were free. Workmen raise their fists in triumph with women in hand-embroidered headscarves.

Throughout the crowd, Estonian flags wave madly through the air—illegal, brazen, and gorgeous with their thick stripes of black, white, and blue. Two little girls run screeching along the line with arms full of flowers, playing some game no one else needs to understand.

Someone's using a rolled-up newspaper as a megaphone in the distance, but I can't hear them above the nearby singing.

"There are so many people," Liis says in wonder, her cheeks wet with tears. "There are enough for three human chains."

And she's right. There were three hundred thousand people at the rally last September, and this line stretches farther than we can see. Toward Tallinn—our capital—in the north and toward Riga, Latvia, to the south. Could this be as huge as the rally before it? Bigger even? Hundreds of thousands of people singing and shouting and dancing to say, *We are real. We matter.*

"The chain is supposed to go from Tallinn to Riga to Vilnius in Lithuania. Three countries who want to be free." Liis's voice is alive with awe. "I don't think anyone believed it'd actually be a chain, that we'd have enough people. But this…If every road is like this, it must be the largest protest in our history."

With that, we join the chain ourselves. Liis slips beside me to my right, and I take her little arm in my hand, soft and yielding, and intertwine my other hand with Anna's. Margit is beside her, crying, Mama on Margit's other side, rubbing Margit's back.

We stand and sing and let a thousand voices lift our hearts, soothe our aching feet and arms and souls. We're part of something much bigger than our own fight. We're part—quite literally—of dismantling the secret and not-so-secret evils the Soviets have been committing.

I can see the asylum in my mind's eye: Aunt Margit forced to flee, villagers rescuing anyone left behind, and fire—I'm certain there's fire—licking through windows; racing through files; turning that evil, those secrets, to ash.

Where will we go? The question tugs at me, but it has no power here. Not with thousands of voices raised in song. Thousands of Estonians hand in hand, saying, *We have had enough.* Thousands of broken people, our edges cutting through the Soviet lies.

XLV
FIRE, INVERTED

They call them tickets to Siberia, these flimsy pieces of paper we all hold. It's a joke as dark as the Estonian winter, when the sun rises at eleven and goes down by three. Because what they really are are registrations—for Estonian citizenship. Not USSR citizenship. *Estonian.*

In other words, *rebellion.*

These flimsy pieces of paper are a rebellion.

Like singing our patriotic songs, thousands of us hand in hand. Like Mama and Riina's stolen kisses when we walk through the forest, the way they giggle over shared secrets like they're teenagers again. Like Liis's very life outside a research facility.

And like joining hands across three countries—all two million of us. Because that's how many there were in the end, according to Radio Free Europe and Finnish TV. Our protest reached from country to country, joined the three capitals—two million voices strong—and news of our plight spread around the world.

The Soviets punished our grandparents for thinking the wrong thoughts, so we know these pieces of paper might be tickets to the labor camps. That's where the joke comes from. Still, we have them. Still, they remind us. We are Estonian. We are human. We belong to ourselves. We are *real*.

For six months after we fled the asylum, we lived in spare rooms and crowded apartments with friends of friends of friends, but now we're home. Back in our village, back in the witch's cottage. No sign of Uncle Silver or Aunt Margit. The asylum is a hollow, blackened thing where teens go to drink and tell ghost stories. The clones are already myth and rumor. If there were any babies in the facility when Ulli and her friends raided it, they've been secreted away to grow up without whispers dogging their heels. The Soviet soldiers have retreated to more important places.

Now it's just the village, the factory, the forest, and the bog. And us.

We stand at the edge of the trees where a tower of stones marks our memorial to the other Anna—Anastasia. It was Anna's idea to show her our citizenship papers, Anna who knew her best. It's Anna who comes out here most often to say hi to her, like Anastasia can still hear Anna's bright-eyed stories, her patriotic songs.

And who knows? In this bog, maybe she can. I've started tipping my hat to the trees, thanking the bog pools for their service just in case. Today, my pockets are full of cranberries—an offering to Anastasia or Soovana, I'm not sure which. Either way: a thank-you.

"What should we say?" Liis asks, staring at the pile of stones.

Anna turns to me. "Do a reading for her. She always wanted a reading when I'd tell her about them at the asylum."

I squeeze Anna's shoulder, pull the cards from my pocket, and shuffle.

"You choose," I tell Anna, fanning them toward her.

She reaches her left hand and waves it theatrically over the cards, selecting one from the middle like the day she disappeared so many years ago. She flips it with a flourish, reveals it to us all.

It's Fire, inverted. I almost laugh. Of course Anna would pick Fire for Anastasia. For all of us, perhaps. The card that invokes transformation. The art a girl nearly in flight.

Anastasia has already flown away, gone to wherever spirits go. And the rest of us are building our wings, one feather at a time, for the day the Soviets lift our cage. Then these flimsy pieces of paper will be Estonian passports, not Siberian tickets.

Anna hands me the card, and I slip it back into my deck.

"We miss you," I say, and even though I didn't really know her, even though I thought she was someone else, I mean it with all my heart.

It's not fair that she never had a family before us—that in her five short years, she had only a few days with a mother and sister, with anyone other than lab techs and a handful of other kids. But even though we didn't know exactly who she was at the time, she's ours now. Mama's daughter. My sister.

I hope if you can know things after you die, she knows that.

Knows that she belonged.

Knows that she was real.

HISTORICAL NOTE

In 1939, long before this story began, the Soviet army invaded Estonia and began an occupation that would span decades. More than a hundred thousand were killed. Tens of thousands more were sent off to Siberian slave labor camps where more than half would die from hunger, cold, and torture. Seventy thousand Estonians fled their country. And those left behind lived in constant terror.

In the 1980s (when our story begins), things were *finally* starting to change across the USSR.

In a movement called perestroika (which means *transformation* or *reform*), politics, the economy, and the rules of day-to-day life started to change. Where the Soviets once met protests with violence, now they sometimes looked the other way. Where once USSR citizens were afraid of being reported by their neighbors, now they could start to reconnect and heal and trust one another. Where once the wrong word could get you sent to a labor camp, now people began to speak their minds.

Perestroika was a complex movement, but the bottom line is that *things were less scary than before*. People started to speak out. They started to sing a little louder, assert themselves a little more, be a little bolder. Things were a little more hopeful than they'd been. So the Singing Revolution began—with songs and flags and community.

Of course, that doesn't mean fear was gone from the region. This was also the era of the Cold War (1947–1991)—when the US and the USSR were both terrified of being attacked by each other. Both had nuclear weapons. Each considered the other their greatest threat. In both countries, kids in schools ran nuclear drills—like a fire drill, but for what would happen if the so-called enemy dropped a nuclear weapon.

The US and USSR battled it out during those decades by funding wars in other countries and conducting psychological warfare. They spied, propagandized, and tried to out-technology each other with space programs, weapons, and (yes, really) even research on superhuman abilities such as psychic powers and invisibility.

The US funded secret military programs that it hoped would turn soldiers into people who could walk through walls, psychically view top-secret meetings, and render themselves invisible. The USSR, meanwhile, poured a billion dollars into trying to crack the code of mind control.

Which is why this was the perfect setting for a book about clones.

There's no documentation I've seen that suggests either side was trying to clone an army (unless you count the Soviet scientist who tried to create human-ape hybrids in the '30s). But with soldiers running full speed into walls to see if they could magically transport themselves through, it wouldn't be that surprising if both countries were also covertly racing to unlock the secrets of cloning.

Aside from the cloning, I've attempted to keep this story as historically accurate as possible. It's true, for example, that people had to steal and bargain for most of the things they needed because shops were often empty. It's true that men sometimes drank aftershave and gasoline to get drunk (as alcohol was illegal for long periods during the occupation). It's true that women weren't allowed to fly planes. And it's true that vodka socks were supposed to cure pretty much anything that might ail you.

It's also true that on August 23, 1989, *two million people* from Estonia and its neighboring countries of Latvia and Lithuania (together known as the Baltic States) formed the Baltic Chain of Freedom—a human chain stretching *over 400 miles* across all three countries.

The event, organized by the pro-independence movements, was a peaceful protest meant to tell the Soviets that the people of these occupied countries were united. United in a desire to reassert their statehood. United against the horrors of the oppressive USSR and its restrictions on movement, identity, even belief. United in their longing for independence and freedom.

This wasn't the first protest in the Baltics. But it *was* one of the first that wasn't met with Soviet violence. It was one of the largest. It was the one that drew some of the widest press coverage. And it was most definitely the first time that protesters stretched, hand in hand, across the three countries. More protests followed. People continued to gather in large groups to sing Estonian songs—telling the USSR with every note that they were no longer going to stay quiet, stay home, stay out of the way.

Soon after the Baltic Chain of Freedom, Estonian leaders started to register Estonian citizens, giving out those small, flimsy, precious slips of paper that confirmed a person was *Estonian*. Not defined by the USSR but by their original heritage, their language, their culture.

Registering as Estonian instead of Soviet was a revolutionary act. People joked that those slips of paper were "tickets to Siberia," the people who got them afraid that they'd be sent to labor camps like their grandparents. But no Soviet soldiers loaded trains to Siberia with these brand-new citizens. Instead, over 860,000 Estonians registered—nearly every adult in the country at the time—and a frustrated but weakened USSR tried (unsuccessfully) to reason them out of their desire for autonomy.

In 1990, those registered citizens voted for the first time, electing a non-Soviet governing body. They made Estonian the official language. They made it illegal to fly the Soviet flag. And then, on August 20, 1991, Estonia joined many other Soviet-occupied countries in their ultimate declarations of freedom as they ushered the Soviets out of power.

Several months later, the Soviet Union dissolved completely. Today, it is no more.

In the final standoff between the USSR and Estonia, the Soviets attempted to take back the TV tower in Tallinn to control the country's information sources. Estonians showed up in force, blocking the road and the area around the tower with their bodies to slow the tanks. This was the inspiration for the scene in this book where the villagers decide to block the road to facilitate Vik's family's escape.

If this history interests you, the documentary *The Singing Revolution* does a fantastic (and not-boring) job of explaining Estonia's bid for freedom and the brave people who stood up to the power that had been oppressing them for generations. It was one of many resources that informed the history contained in this book, in addition to personal interviews with those who lived in Estonia during the Singing Revolution; academic papers; books; articles; and personal visits to museums and historic landmarks in and around Tallinn, Tartu, and more.

I chose to set this book in Soviet-controlled Estonia for so many reasons, but mostly because it's ultimately a book about finding strength together, about connection, about healing, about trusting your neighbors even though they've hurt you in the past, about *coming together as one*. And that's exactly what the Baltics did to gain their freedom. They joined hands and sang and blocked roads to keep tanks away from what was precious to them.

Like Vik, like Liis, even like Margit, they found their way to one another and stood united against their oppressors. They refused to back down, and they refused to go it alone.

It's a story that inspires me, and I hope it inspires you too.

MENTAL HEALTH NOTE

Viktoria has obsessive-compulsive disorder (OCD) and complex post-traumatic stress disorder (CPTSD). For a number of reasons, I've chosen not to name her diagnoses in the book itself and to let her explore them without understanding them.

In part, I did this because there was a time in my life when *I* was Viktoria—a mentally ill girl trying to figure myself out without a diagnosis. She wouldn't know why she had to check her sister's breathing, why she had these bone-deep certainties that the worst was always about to happen, why she couldn't get rid of certain terrible thoughts even though they scared her witless.

When I see books and TV and movies talk about OCD, it's always kind of a joke. Haha, she has to turn the doorknob three times! Haha, he has to knock three times! Or, oh, she's so organized and type A!

The truth is that OCD takes whatever your deepest, darkest, sometimes most unreasonable fears are and slams them into you over and over again. You can't get them out of your head (the obsession), and something inside you decides that you have to do a ritual (the compulsion) in order to keep that fear from coming true. Some people have both obsessions and compulsions, while others have mostly or entirely obsessions (they call this pure-O OCD). Vik (and myself) have both.

For Vik, afraid of losing everything, she checks to make sure her loved ones are breathing. She struggles to leave the room or the house because she feels like her presence is keeping them alive. And sometimes she encounters random compulsions, like tapping the comb on the way to the oak grove. OCD can manifest in many ways, but these are Vik's particular rituals.

The most common treatment for OCD is exposure therapy, which means forcing yourself to tolerate the thing you're afraid of without doing the ritual that makes you feel better. If I'm afraid I'm going to throw myself off a bridge, exposure therapy might ask me to walk across the bridge over and over, to sit with the feeling and let it become less important instead of using a ritual to get rid of it. What Vik doesn't realize is that the intense situations throughout this book are forcing her to do just that: to face the things she's so afraid of, to leave her sister and go into the bog instead of counting breaths until Anna's last.

Now, in both myself and Vik, OCD is combined with CPTSD. CPTSD comes from repeated trauma, from feeling powerless in the face of life or death. In Vik's case, the disappearance of her da and then her sister—the constant sense that anyone could die or disappear at any moment—roots deeply within her and gives her a lifetime of trauma reactions.

The symptoms of her CPTSD are complicated. She has near-constant anxiety about losing people she loves. She's hypervigilant—always on edge, ready for fight or flight. She avoids people, places, and things that remind her of the disappearance and keeps everyone at arm's length. She can't shake the fear and shame of that day. And—importantly—she believes she's dangerous and blames herself.

Vik's Mama also has PTSD, though I have given her different symptoms to show how distinctly we all experience it. She has extreme trouble focusing and dissociates (disconnects from her body, self, and situations). She is detached from her own daughter. And she struggles to stay present in any given moment, especially if there's an additional stressor at play.

One of the most common treatments for CPTSD/PTSD is talk therapy, and another is what one therapist of mine called "grounding." When having a panic attack or flashback, grounding means focusing on the physical. In Vik's case, Liis recognizes her panic attack as what she calls a "fear attack" and helps Vik ground herself by focusing on the warmth of Kaos in her lap, the soft fur under her fingers. Vik also grounds herself by touching, shuffling, and counting her cards, though she doesn't realize what she's doing is grounding.

So, why am I explaining all this at the end of an adventure story? Because for much of history, mentally ill people like me have been invisible. We've gone unexplained. Unexplored. Unseen. *And I want you to see us.* I want you to know what it feels like, even if only for a moment.

And if you think you might be like Vik, I want you to be visible too. To the people around you. To yourself.

I see you. I wrote this book for you.

ACKNOWLEDGMENTS

This is the fourth time I've written acknowledgments for a novel and the first time I've *wept* over them. This is also the first book whose sale left me a sobbing mess in the middle of the living room floor.

Because every book I write matters to me, but this was the first book I wrote for my younger self—the girl I wanted to change the world for. Because this book took over two years and two agents to find its perfect editor. And because part of me believed that by exploring my mental illness on the page, I might have doomed this story to never see the light of day.

I was right that the battle was more difficult; finding this book's place in the world was hard-won. But *find its home it did*. With the exact editor it needed, the exact publishing team who would take this deeply personal project and help me build it some wings.

For all that, I have so many people to thank. Starting with my agent and editor: Paige Terlip and Kade Dishmon. Paige, I told you this book was my heart, and *you fought for it*. Thank you times one thousand. Kade, you once told me that you want to publish books where teens can put their hardest feelings. I knew at that moment that this book belonged with you.

To Veronica Park, who read this project as both book and script and told me what genre I was writing. To film agent Olivia

Burgher who heard a short pitch and agreed to join the little army fighting for this story even before the book deal.

To my book community, continued accomplices in book crime—every single one of you is precious to me. Specifically, to David De la Rosa and Daniela Petrova, whose brainstorms gave me courage and the story shape. To early readers Zoe Wallbrook, Elizabeth Brookbank, Sarah Mughal Rana, Natalia De la Rosa, Maria Linn, Tina Chan, A. Z. Louise, Gladys Qin, Emily, Clara, Iris, Elia, Zoë, Meghan, and Abby.

To the team at Holiday House including Mary Cash (Editor in Chief), Nicole Gureli and Kerry Martin (Design), Evangeline Gallagher (Cover), Raina Putter (Managing Editor), Jill Freshney (Copy Editor), Manu Velasco (Proofreader), Julia Gallagher (Legal), and Michelle Montague, Terry Borzumato-Greenberg, Alison Tarnofsky, Sara DiSalvo, and Kayla Phillips (Marketing and Publicity). It's been a pleasure, and I look forward to the rest of this book journey with you all.

To Lani Frank for cheering on my tiniest milestones. To Kristel for reading through an Estonian lens. To Meghan Walker and Emily Tisshaw for two incredibly thoughtful sensitivity reads (and the consult that came before). And to Margit, Signe, Angelika, and Eva for insights into what it meant to be a teen girl in Estonia in the '80s and '90s.

Additional gratitude to Andrei, who reminds me why I write and who I am. I adore you. To Ines, who held my hand in the scariest moment of my last year. To my Bal pals, who can put it

ba
w[l]